30 SHADES OF DEAD

A collection of mysteries to honor the 30th

anniversary of Sisters in Crime

Edited by N. L. Quatrano

WC Publishing

an On-Target Words company

ISBN: 978-0-9975986-7-4

Published by WC Publishing
An On-Target Words company
Hastings, FL USA
www.OnTargetWords.com/WCPublish

For information on bulk purchases, please contact
OnTargetWords@gmail.com

Printed in the United States of America

Dear Reader,

Sisters in Crime, Inc., is now a global organization with more than 3,600 members and 50 chapters worldwide, dedicated to promoting the ongoing advancement, recognition and professional development of women crime writers.

But 30 years ago, Sisters in Crime was founded by a handful of women mystery writers including BJ Rahn, Sara Paretsky, and Phyllis Whitney, who noted in 1986 that women mystery writers weren't being reviewed at a percentage equal to the successful books they were writing, nor were they being nominated for awards in the Mystery Writers of America organization.

During Edgars Week in 1987, women interested in changing the status quo were invited to Sandra Scoppettone's SoHo loft for a breakfast meeting. Nancy Pickard was their first president with Margaret Maron accepting the VP position. And there they created Sisters in Crime.

The authors in this collection are all Sisters in Crime members. You'll see both genders contributing, and we do so with great pride: in our work, our genre and our organization.

We invite you to join us in our celebration of the 30th anniversary of this versatile, encompassing and powerful organization. Every story includes some element of thirty or takes place thirty years ago.

Enjoy this short story collection in the way it was conceived: to entertain *you*, the mystery reader! There are psychological thrillers, cozies, romantic suspense, historical, and the P.I. and cop varieties. It is not by mistake that there are ***thirteen*** stories here.

Thanks for reading and please feel free to post reviews wherever you do that!

Nancy Quatrano, Editor

DEDICATION

This collection is dedicated to the many pioneers in the writing business that fought and continue to fight, valiantly for equal opportunities for women writers in this diverse genre.

To our fans, our librarians, our booksellers, and reviewers, we say a heartfelt "Thank you!"

Table of Contents

ESCAPE TO PARADISE

Karen Bostrom

Funny how when you finally give up searching for something missing you find it in a place you'd never dreamed of looking. That's what happened to me while my husband and I were celebrating our thirtieth anniversary in the Florida Keys.

It all started when I stopped at a small strip mall in Islamorada to get souvenirs for the folks back in Jersey. I'd already bought an overpriced bottle of champagne and back-up steaks for an intimate dinner at our rented condo in case my husband returned from the marina without catching any fish. Doug likes browsing in stores as much as I like baiting hooks and drinking beer, so we'd both been relieved and grateful that I'd volunteered to spend my morning shopping without him. I also hoped to find a unique anniversary present while he was happily off in his Jimmy Buffett wannabe Hawaiian shirt, trolling for another large fish and swapping stories with a bunch of strangers on a big boat.

My plan was to shop in less than an hour, snag a Key lime pie that the condo manager had recommended, and chat with any locals I met to get information for the travel column I write for my hometown newspaper. Then I'd be free to head back to the pool and enjoy a frozen margarita and the murder mystery I'd brought from home.

* * *

The moment I stepped out of the oppressive humidity into the Paradise Gift Shop, I sighed. Air-conditioned comfort and quality merchandise, not shelves full of gaudy plastic flamingos or rows of cheap magnets and keychains. I quickly selected some Key lime salt scrub, a set of palm tree coasters, and mango-based barbeque sauce for the girls at the newspaper. I placed them at the register along with a whole Key lime pie from the freezer and called out, "Anybody here?"

"Be with you in a minute," a Southern drawl answered from the back room. "Help yourself to some orange juice in the back corner while you wait."

"No, thanks," I said. "I'm not ready to check out. Still looking." I stopped at a display of angel items. "Oh, I love these angel earrings. May I try on a pair?"

"Of course, Sugar. One of my best sellers. My daughter and I make those and all profits go to the county women's shelter."

I paused to remove my earrings and try them on. "They're perfect!" I said and stared at the delicate angel wings, long and sleek, swinging back and forth. The last time I saw something like them, they were on the art teacher at the shelter where I used to volunteer years ago—but those were pewter. These were painted with the bold tropical colors of macaws. Thanking Doug, I decided to keep them on and treat myself to an anniversary gift.

Next, I glanced at the watercolors lining the walls. Most were full of palm trees and beach scenes, but a few, like one of a pink fishing boat, reminded me of the Jersey shore. Was that the famous old Miss Belmar charter boat? And the carousel on a boardwalk? It looked like the one from Asbury Park where I used to go as a kid.

As I studied the paintings, the woman's voice startled me. "Sorry to keep you waiting. Hard to get the paint off my hands."

Turning, I saw a petite woman with short spiky hair the shade of cherry Kool-Aid emerge from the back, wearing earrings identical to mine. She wiped her hands on a rag absent-mindedly, and asked, "Find everything you need, Sugar?"

"Not yet," I said as I approached the cash register. I looked into her Kelly-green eyes that were such a contrast to her shocking red hair. How old was she? Maybe fifty? The kind of flamboyant person you'd never forget, so why did she look so familiar? I frowned. "I swear, you remind me of someone back in Jersey, though nobody up there sounds like you and I've never seen eyes that green! What's your name?"

She broke her gaze and started twisting the paint rag before tossing it into the trashcan. "It's Ellie, Ma'am," she said. "Can I help you find anything else or shall I ring these things up?"

"Reba McIntyre! That's who you look like," I said.

She exhaled and nodded. "Yes, Ma'am. I get that a lot. The red hair and the Southern accent. Wish I could sing like her. Anything else?"

"I still need something for my husband. Something unique to remember our thirtieth anniversary in the Keys."

Ellie turned, and with a wave of her hand, gestured to a shelf of hand-painted stemware behind the counter. "How about a pair of special wine glasses to remember a romantic evening?" she asked. "I can personalize them with your name or any kind of drawing you like."

I leaned closer to examine the artwork - bright, whimsical and professional. "I love them, but we're only here a few more days at the Summer Isle condos and I want to surprise my husband tonight."

"No problem, Ma'am," the redhead replied. "I'll do the artwork this afternoon, and you can pick 'em up before we close at five."

"Great!" I pulled out a photo of my husband and his sailboat from my wallet and handed it to her. "Could you paint a picture of his boat on his glass? Maybe with some fish and the state of Florida? On mine, I'd like tropical fruits, the sun, beachy stuff." I pointed to one of the glasses on the shelf. "Oh, and a heart with each of our names and a '30' on it like that one."

The woman studied the picture and placed a blank order form on the counter. "Fill this out and check the pictures you want. Print your names exactly the way they should appear on each glass. Since they're custom, you must prepay. No refunds."

"Of course," I said. I completed the form and placed a credit card on the counter. Her hand trembled slightly as she examined them. "Doug and Melinda Walker?"

"Correct. Is something wrong?" I asked. "Too many letters or pictures?"

"No, no. Just want to make sure everything's spelled right. You wouldn't believe how hard it is to read other people's handwriting," Ellie said as she rang up the other items and wrapped them. She hurriedly returned my card and handed me my purchases. "Mrs. Walker, I'll bubble wrap the glasses and slide them into a tropical gift bag. No extra charge. In fact, I'll drop them off at the front desk of your condo around four so you won't even have to come back. You just take it easy and enjoy your anniversary!"

She walked quickly toward the door and held it open for me. I got the distinct feeling that I was being herded out of the store. "Well, that's very generous of you, Ellie. Thanks."

"We Floridians love our tourists," she said and smiled. As I stepped outside, the door slammed shut behind me, setting off the angel chimes. I was definitely not feeling the love!

I muttered, "Did I just get the bum's rush, Southern style? Humph! Strange. She'd seemed so friendly at first." As I backed out of my parking space, I noticed the "Open" sign had been switched to "Closed." Was it something I said?

I shook my head and drove off. If Doug had been with me, he would've sighed and said, "Maybe it's her lunchtime, honey. Or she had to use the bathroom. Or she wanted to get started on the artwork without being disturbed. Do you always have to make a story out of nothing?" In my experience, though, if you get a feeling that something's not right, there's usually a lot of something behind every nothing!

* * *

After lunch, I treated myself to a large piece of the Key lime pie. After all, I had to test it before serving it to Doug, didn't I? One taste and I knew I'd have to go back and get the name of the person who made them for Ellie. If I she was in a friendlier mood, maybe I'd get the recipe or the life story of the chef for my column. I smiled. Doug's a CPA. He'd like it if I could make buying a pie into a tax deduction for my part-time career.

At the pool, I settled on a chaise lounge and started reading my mystery. I'd only gotten to the first dead body, when the condo manager approached, carrying a bag. "Special delivery," Joan said and handed it to me. "Ellie from the Paradise Shop just dropped this off for you. Said to make sure you got it right away."

I glanced at the sun. "Is it four o'clock already?" I asked.

"Oh, no! Barely two. Ellie said this was a rush job and she had to close early today. Wanted to make sure you got this in time for your anniversary."

I slid the glasses out and examined them. "Beautiful! What an amazing job. And so reasonable. I swear she should sell these online. Between the Key lime pie and these, she could make a fortune."

Joan nodded. "I keep telling her the same thing. But she says she's happy keeping her business small. Less pressure. She loves the slower pace and laidback lifestyle of the Keys. We all do. It's much more peaceful than living up North. And no snow to shovel."

"Tell me about it!" I exclaimed. "After this past winter, and Hurricane Sandy a few years back, many of us Northerners are dreaming of escaping to Florida. Now that our daughter has moved to

Miami, Doug and I plan to do just that. But your Reba look-alike is a native, so I guess this area is all Ellie's ever known."

"Ellie does sound like a native with that Southern drawl. Lots of us escapees from the Northeast pick up that speech pattern after we've lived here as long as she has."

I frowned. "Really? I thought she was born and raised in the Keys."

"No, Ellie and her daughter moved down here a little after I did, maybe twenty-five years ago. Just before her husband retired. He was originally a Florida boy, then Louisiana I think, but after being in the Navy he settled up north. He was in law enforcement. Doesn't talk much about it. His daddy had a bungalow that Jack used to visit every year for the fishing and hunting. Good man! Always willing to give his neighbors a hand. Quiet and peaceful. Just like the Keys."

Intrigued, I patted the lounge next to mine and asked, "Want to join me for a margarita? I've got another plastic cup."

She shook her head. "Well, bless your heart. Tempting, but no thank you. I've got to man the front desk with a clear head till five. I only meant to deliver your package, not talk your ear off. You enjoy your anniversary. The bonfire will be out back on the beach tonight after sunset. I'll reserve two Adirondack chairs for you and your hubby."

"Thank you so much, Joan."

She winked and left. I returned to my novel but had trouble concentrating. Instead, I was replaying my conversation with Ellie in the gift shop, wondering why I couldn't stop thinking about her abrupt change in behavior. And why did she look so familiar?

* * *

When Doug came back from the marina, he was in a great mood, having caught a fish for dinner. I was, too, since he filleted it and fried it to perfection. He loved the glasses and suggested we take our champagne and dessert out by the water's edge and toast to another thirty wonderful years. As we watched the sun set over the Gulf, I told him the story about the gift shop owner who'd seemed so friendly at first but then practically shoved me out the door.

"Mel," he said as he clinked his glass to mine, "Happy Anniversary, honey. Let's make a deal. No shop talk. No making a mystery out of nothing. Tonight, we're only talking about us. And less talking, too," he added, leaning over to kiss my neck and slip the strap of my sundress off my shoulder. "This is the only kind of uncovering I want to do tonight!"

I laughed. "Deal!" I wrapped my arms around him and kissed him. Watching the bonfire and feeling the gentle breeze, I let go of all my nagging questions and enjoyed the best anniversary celebration ever. And I didn't even think about that shop owner's strange behavior until Doug brought it up again early the next morning.

* * *

After a lovely evening, Doug's alarm went off way too soon for me. "It's still dark," I mumbled.

He gave me a quick kiss and hug and whispered, "Go back to sleep, honey. I'll be out of here in five minutes. You can have the car for the day. I'm meeting another guy in the lobby to get to the marina by five. Have fun. And go easy on that lady in the store."

"What lady?"

"The one that painted our wine glasses. The one who stopped being friendly to you and rushed you out yesterday," he added as he slipped out of bed.

I groaned and covered my eyes just before he turned on the light and started getting dressed. "What makes you think I'm going shopping again? I'll be by the pool today. Relaxing. Alone. Abandoned."

Doug laughed. "I know you, Mel. With your curiosity, you'll be back there with some excuse to *fish* for information while I'm fishing for fish."

"Hey! You're supposed to be nice to me on our anniversary, especially since I'm not whining about you going out on a charter boat almost every day."

"Honey, we both love fishing. Just different kinds. Hope you find out what you want!" He gave me another quick kiss, switched off the light and left with his tackle box and pole.

As much as I tried to go back to sleep, the events of the previous day kept replaying in my head. Why couldn't I shake the feeling that I'd seen Ellie before and that she really didn't want to see me? When sunlight filled the room, I gave up and went for a nice long walk. Walking often clears my head.

Doug was right. I was dying to go back and talk to Ellie to satisfy my curiosity. I'd had quite a nose for a story when I'd majored in journalism at Rutgers, not that I needed it the first few years I'd worked on the police blotter, listing burglaries, thefts, and domestic violence complaints. Not exactly Woodward-and-Bernstein exciting. With my imagination, a few cases had seemed to have the possibility to become a gripping drama worthy of an episode of Law and Order – but somehow it never happened. Doug sometimes teases me in his best Rocky Balboa voice, "You coulda been a contender!" If only I'd sniffed out a big story maybe things would be different. But I guess it wasn't meant to be. At least not yet. Kind of like the big fish that got away or a dream shoved onto the back burner, on life support and dying slowly.

After my daughter was born, I'd been content with my part-time job and freelancing in an occasional food or travel magazine. I'm good at highlighting interesting characters or local events in my weekly op-ed human-interest weekly column. And I confess that even though I harbor every journalist's dream of someday scoring a big scoop or winning a prize for a hard-hitting expose, I feel warm-and-fuzzy when I write short pieces that touch a few hearts and make people reflect on life. I've always been a good listener and most people love telling me their stories and seeing their names in print. It's a "win-win" for everyone...everyone except for a few reluctant folks like Ellie.

I came up with two good reasons, not excuses, for heading to the Paradise Gift shop. Not only could I order a pair of those wonderful wine glasses for my in-laws' upcoming fiftieth wedding anniversary, but maybe I could convince Ellie to let me interview her, a successful local artist who ran a delightful gift store and sold amazing Key lime pie. If I could include the recipe in my column, that'd be even better. But when I arrived at the store, I was surprised to find the lights out and a sign on the door. "Closed for Vacation." Vacation? That didn't do me any good, not when we were leaving on Sunday. No chance to get her story or more gifts. And I wanted closure on both. Maybe I could catch her before she left town. I'm nothing if not determined.

I headed next door to the liquor store and placed a bottle of wine by the cash register. The clerk I'd chatted up yesterday smiled and said, "Good morning. How was your anniversary?"

"Perfect, thank you," I said. "We love the glasses that Ellie made for us, too. I came back to order a set for my in-laws, but her sign says she's closed for vacation. I'm so disappointed. Any idea when she'll be back?"

"Not exactly. She stopped in yesterday and told me she'd be gone until next week. Said everything was fine, but something has come up. Funny, they don't usually go away this time of year, not with her daughter home from medical school and tending bar for the summer."

I laughed. "Yeah, it's tricky getting time off from a summer job. Plus, I think her daughter helps do the artwork on those glasses."

"Yes, and I doubt if Andi would leave either job on the spur of the moment, not when she needs money for fall tuition. Why don't you stop by the Conch Bar and Grill and ask for her? They serve the best conch chowder there, and maybe she'd do those glasses for you before you leave."

"What's Andi's last name?" I asked as I paid.

"Jones."

I thanked him and filed that information. Jones. Such a common name. Ellie Jones. Didn't ring a bell, but people get divorced so often nowadays, who knows if mother and daughter shared the same name? Maybe I could find out more at the tourist bureau or the local paper.

The woman at the tourist bureau was willing to drone on about pirates and Spanish explorers, but not share information about locals. When I told her that the Paradise Gift shop was closed for vacation she furrowed her brow. "That's odd. Ellie usually lets me know when she's away so I don't refer tourists to visit her store while she's gone. I can suggest other places you might enjoy, though." I left with a bagful of brochures and the directions to the office of the local newspaper, the Islamorada Times.

Before heading there, I glanced through a sample copy she'd given me and jotted down a few questions to ask the publisher. It was mostly an advertising guide for tourists, but it had some articles describing local businesses. If we decide to move to the Keys, maybe he'd hire me as a freelance writer. Plus, it might make a great opening to get him talking about Ellie.

The Times was an even smaller operation than I'd envisioned. I introduced myself as a writer and potential future resident to the man in a tropical shirt sitting at one of the cluttered desks. He got up to shake my hand. "I'm Ted Mayer, owner, writer, publisher, and almost everything else." He laughed. "When you're ready to rent or buy, I can recommend a good realtor. And who knows? Once you're a neighbor, maybe you and I can work something out. We love tourists, but if you're a local, you become family. And family sticks together. Come see me when you really decide to move on down. Friendly folks fit right in."

"You mean like Ellie Jones at Paradise Gifts? She sure sounds like a real Southerner after all these years, doesn't she?"

The man narrowed his eyes. "You a friend of hers?"

I smiled. "Not a friend, just a satisfied customer. I met her yesterday and bought some of her stemware. Very talented lady. I was hoping to do an article about her art and her shop, but when I went back to get some more gifts today, the sign on the door said she's closed for the rest of the week."

Ted frowned. "I didn't know that, but I doubt she'd want an article focused on her. She keeps a low profile. Advertises her shop, not herself. I've tried to run a feature on her and she always refuses. If you like, I could recommend a few other shop owners that would love some free exposure."

"No, thank you. I just wanted to get another set of those personalized glasses before I leave the Keys. Is there any way I could reach her before I go home?"

"Well, Ellie's husband Jack has a charter boat business. Premier Fishing. If they're not out of town, he may be willing to connect you to Ellie." Ted passed me a business card and rose. "If you can persuade Ellie to let you write up something about her, attach it to an email and send it to me. Maybe you've got a better gift of gab than I do and can change her mind. If I use it, I'll send you a check. 1000 words. $25." He showed me to the door. "Good luck, little lady, and have a nice day."

Back in the car, I wondered why an artist like Ellie wouldn't want extra publicity. I searched for phone numbers of Ellie and Jack Jones on my iPhone but found no listings that matched. I then Googled Premier Fishing and swung by Robbie's Marina where Jack's boat, The Great Escape, was supposed to be docked. His slip was empty. When I asked a man working on a nearby boat if Captain Jack was away on vacation, he shook his head no. "Just out on a routine charter for the day, ma'am. Should be back soon. Check the schedule," he'd said and pointed to a box attached to Jack's sign.

I took a brochure and studied Jack Jones's picture. He didn't look familiar, though he did resemble Santa Claus wearing sunglasses and a Tommy Bahama shirt. Nice boat. The kind Doug loves to go fishing on.

To kill time while I waited for his return, I took pictures of tourists paying three dollars for a bucket of smelts to feed the huge tarpon leaping up along the crowded pier. Still hoping to see Captain Jack, I had a mahi-mahi sandwich at the tiki bar as I eyed his still-empty slip. I finally decided not to stay any longer, but at least I left with a plan. That night? Convince Doug to book a charter on Captain Jack's boat, guaranteeing him another guilt-free day of fishing with only one tiny string attached – to be an observer for me. I figured that would be easy. And dinner? Hopefully, he'd be willing to eat at the Conch Bar and Grill to satisfy my curiosity about Ellie's daughter.

* * *

As luck would have it, Doug had caught a lot of fish so he insisted on grilling at the condo, but he promised we'd go to the Conch Bar and Grill for drinks afterward. When I asked him if he'd book a place on Captain Jack Jones' charter boat the next day, he was thrilled to humor me and do it online. "Anything to make you happy, dear," he said with a grin. "It's a sacrifice, but I'll leave you alone while I go fishing again. I don't promise to interrogate the guy, but if he's a talker like you and some of these characters, I'll see what I can find out to solve your little mystery of his missing wife. Who knows? Maybe it will be your big scoop."

I smiled and gave him a hug. I tolerate his teasing about my dream of being an investigative reporter when he's willing to help me ferret out information. I've never uncovered anything worthy of Dateline News, 20/20, or the Forensic Files, but I always feel better when I can put a nagging hunch to rest. Trusting my gut and my intuition, I knew I'd uncover what it was about Ellie and her behavior that bothered me. Or at least give it my best shot.

When Doug and I finally arrived at the bar, I was disappointed that the only bartender on duty was male. We climbed onto the last two empty rattan barstools and Doug whispered in my ear, "Well, Sherlock, no lady bartender. Maybe we can just enjoy the evening and work on your case tomorrow. Can you take the night off from snooping?"

I smiled and nodded. "I'd like a pina colada if you can get that guy's attention."

"My pleasure," Doug said and waved the bartender over. "Two pina coladas, please," he ordered and then started singing the Garth Brooks song.

As the man in the Hawaiian shirt slapped down two napkins and started mixing our drinks I asked, "Is Andi Jones here tonight?"

"Yeah, she'll be in soon. She's working the wedding reception out back. You a friend of hers?"

"I met her mother yesterday. She's a very talented artist."

"Yeah. Andi's a great kid and a hard worker. Just like her mom. Good people."

By the time Doug was on his second island drink, I persuaded him to dance to one of my favorite Bob Marley songs playing in the background. Soon our drinks were gone and still, no female bartender had appeared.

"Time to go, Mel," Doug said. "I need to get to bed soon if I'm going to get up at four to go fishing...for your information," he reminded me with a grin.

I agreed and started to get up when someone tapped me lightly on the shoulder, "Ma'am? I'm Andi. I hear you were asking about me."

I turned and looked into a very familiar face. Ellie's face–a younger, mid-twenties version with long chestnut hair, high cheekbones, and big brown eyes. It was the face I'd known as Beth Russo so many years ago. But the face in my memory had been gaunt and scared, framed by stringy brown hair, fear in her eyes, glasses slipped down her nose, and sad eyes looking down at the bruises on her arms. Her thin frame had been hunched over, not confident and vibrant like this young woman who stood in front of me.

"I understand you know my mom," she added.

"Yes," I stammered. "Well, actually I just met her yesterday. I...I'm here because I want to buy another pair of the glasses you two decorate for special occasions, but your mom's store was closed today. I was hoping you weren't away on vacation with her so that I could get them before we go back to New Jersey in three days."

Andi's brows knitted together. "I couldn't get off work but she stayed home anyway. Said she needed a rest, but if she can't do the art for you, I will. I'm in my final year of med school and I could use the extra money." She grabbed a napkin and handed me a pen. "Here. Write down your cell number and exactly what you want on the glasses. I can bring them here tomorrow at four when my shift starts."

Before we left I scribbled the information with my name and number and handed it to her along with enough cash to cover the cost. "Thanks, Andi. I'll be here tomorrow at four."

When Doug and I hit the muggy air outside the restaurant, I took in a big gulp of air. He put his arm around me as we walked to the car, "You okay, Mel? You're awfully quiet. And you're rarely quiet. You look like you've seen a ghost."

"Yeah, I just did. The ghost of a woman I used to know. That girl, Andi? She looks just like Beth Russo. Remember the battered young woman with the cute little girl from our first apartment building in Asbury Park? I met Beth when I was covering the police blotter and working on that domestic violence article about twenty-five years ago."

He whistled. "She's the one who got beat up by her husband Sal all the time. That S.O.B. swore he'd kill her and get custody of the kid if she called the cops or tried to divorce him. You helped her get a restraining order and gave her fifty bucks to escape to the woman's shelter."

"Yeah. And now it turns out that Beth Russo isn't MIA or dead at all. She's living as Ellie Jones. Wow! What a story! Sal got killed in a shootout during a drug bust and Beth disappeared with Andrea without a trace. No one ever heard from her since. And now I've found her! After all this time." I shook my head. "I knew Ellie looked familiar, but with that shocking red hair and drawl, I didn't connect the dots. And those Kelly-green eyes must be from contact lenses. She used to have those huge wire rims."

I paused as Doug unlocked the car door and we both slid in, grateful to breathe in the blast of air conditioning when he started the engine. "Mel, she must have recognized you and it's obvious that she doesn't want to be found. And maybe the authorities don't want her found either. Didn't they squash your domestic violence story that was going to feature Beth?"

I nodded. "Yes. I tried to find out what happened to her for years, but nobody would give me any information. I think it was hushed up because of Interstate drug trafficking and connections to shady mob businesses. Beth was terrified of that bastard and all the thugs he hung out with. Someone must have ratted on him and his associates. Maybe it was Beth. Could be why she disappeared that night and never returned."

Doug nodded. "Mel, except for you, she had no friends or family in Jersey to contact or to risk coming back to visit. And she sure didn't want Sal's family to know where she was. Back then before the Internet, it was easier to disappear and create a new life without being traced than it would be now.

"He made her life a living hell. Beth was terrified of pressing charges when he beat her. And with his temper and abuse, Beth was lucky he didn't kill her and dump her body somewhere. Remember that goodbye message she stuck under our door? It was clear she left town to save her life and her child's. We figured the authorities stopped looking for her when you gave them that note."

"Yes, but maybe they knew where she was all along. I always thought she must have had someone else's help to get away. It took a lot of careful planning and more than my fifty bucks for her to vanish and start a new life."

My mind was racing. "You know, Doug, according to the lady at the tourist bureau, Ellie's husband Jack Jones was in law enforcement up north. A cop would be a great resource if you wanted to go underground, but an FBI guy would be even better. If I recall, John Jones was the name of the agent I spoke to back then. He was businesslike but kind. And furious that any man could abuse his wife like Sal did, especially a sweetheart like Beth. After she disappeared, he stopped by and asked me to let him know if I ever traced her or if she ever reached out to me, but she never did.

"I always thought it was weird that six months later when I tried to reach Agent Jones as a follow-up to my domestic violence story, I found out that he'd retired. Left the state. Another agent told me off the record that he'd gone back to live in Louisiana. But now I bet it was the Florida Keys. Maybe they were all throwing me off on purpose. What a story! It would make a great movie!"

Doug put his hand on mine. "Mel, I begged you to stay out of it back then, but you didn't listen. And you know? You were right at the time. Taking Beth to the police station probably saved her life. I'm sorry you lost your big story then, but now I'm thinking that you need to let this go. Stay out of it. It's not right to dredge up the past now."

"But Doug, finding Beth Russo alive and well in the Keys could be a lead story in the Press. Might even make national news. I could make it part of a new series on domestic violence or coauthor a book with Ellie. It might do a lot good for some people."

"Yeah, maybe. But what about Ellie and Jack? And her daughter? It could do a lot of harm to them. After all this time, do you think

Ellie wants the world to know she's been a fugitive? To have her private life exposed? And if there were a mob connection back then, maybe she still needs to stay hidden."

I fell silent for a moment. "Well, I'll keep it secret for now but I have to know the truth. You never know. Maybe she'll want to share her story and give some other battered woman hope."

* * *

The next morning, I promised Doug that I wasn't going to rush to reveal Ellie's story. Yes, I'd do more digging to unearth facts about the current Captain and Mrs. Jack Jones of Islamorada, Florida, as I'd originally intended. I already knew the truth of her identity. To me, her daughter's face was proof that Ellie was Beth Russo. Plus, the Jersey paintings. The angel wings. Her dedication to women's shelters. But what I should do with that information? I still didn't know.

One thing I know for sure is that sometimes when you can't figure something out, the best thing to do is nothing. Not even reflect on it. Just let it go and surrender to whatever you want to call your inner wisdom, your gut, your heart. So instead of trying to solve the problem of what to do with my discovery of a longtime-missing person found in the backroom of the Paradise Gift Shop in the Keys, I spent that morning walking, swimming, napping and reading my latest cozy mystery without agonizing about what to do. After lunch, I ate two slices of key lime pie without guilt and stretched out by the pool.

I must have started to doze off when I heard a soft angelic Southern voice say, "Melinda?"

I opened my eyes to see Ellie Jones standing next to my lounge chair, holding a gift bag in one hand and something clenched in her other hand. "Here are the glasses you ordered from Andi last night. Money back, my gift to you, and my thanks, long overdue, along with this," she said as she placed a small medallion on the palm of my hand. "It's the angel coin you gave me so many years ago before I left." Her voice cracked a little. "And I'm here to talk to you, to explain anything you want to know, and praying you'll keep my secrets."

I studied the worn medal in my palm and then looked back at her face. It really was her. Beth, after all these years. I rose and hugged her. "I can't believe it! It's you! And you're okay. I was so worried about you and Andrea. Andi. She's grown into such a lovely young lady."

"Thank you. She's so precious to me." Ellie broke away and took a deep breath. "Melinda, I know I can never truly repay you for your kindness in helping us get away from Sal. So many times, I wanted to contact you and tell you we were all right. But I was terrified of being found. Even after Sal was killed, I was told that those thugs from the drug underworld might somehow find out that I'd given evidence against them and Sal. They might track us down, kill us to get even, to make an example of us. They might have killed Jack, too. I knew when I entered the Witness Protection Program that I was going to have to cut all ties with my past. You were my one regret."

I motioned for her to sit down. "Jack was the one who helped you the most, wasn't he? As John Jones, FBI agent, he gave you the money and means to get down here and stay in his dad's old place, right?"

She nodded. "Melinda, I bless the day you took me to the police and they contacted the FBI. They'd been investigating the interstate drug ring Sal was part of, and they promised me if I testified against them, they'd help me and Andi get away. They gave us new identities and Jack was assigned to my case, He was a widower, near retirement, and after a few months, we fell in love and wanted to stay together. So when he retired, we moved here to his old family homestead. I was afraid of being recognized, but Jack told me to let go of that fear. To be bold. Dye my hair red and stop acting like a timid victim. Jack set me free. Free to relax and do artwork and raise Andi in this beautiful place. She forgot Sal and the violence. Jack and I got married and he even adopted Andi. We have a good life, Melinda. And I want to keep it this way. Please don't tell folks back in Jersey you found me. Beth Russo is dead. Ellie Jones is alive."

"But it's such a wonderful story," I said. "And telling it could inspire other battered women to escape, to realize that they can start a whole new life, too."

"Melinda, I've been helping other battered women ever since I moved down here. Been paying forward what you did for me. The original fifty bucks and a lot more." She touched the angel earrings and her heart pendant. "And I don't want you to ruin the life I've created here with my family by spilling my guts in the newspaper."

"I understand, but—"

"No, I don't think you *do* understand what it's like. When I saw you yesterday, I recognized you almost immediately." She smiled and touched her head. "You haven't dyed your hair fire-engine red like I did or started wearing bright green contacts. But seeing you made me panic. That old fear rushed back, the fear of being discovered. Of defending myself. I couldn't tell you who I was. I just wanted you to go away. I even tried to get Andi to go to Miami with me on a shopping trip so you couldn't bump into her. I know what a caring lady you are, but you're also a bulldog. I knew you'd keep digging until you figured out who I looked like, and we both know it isn't a country western singer named Reba. Once you saw Andi, you'd know my secret. But she doesn't. I've never told Andi the whole horrible truth about her biological father. And I don't want to. Not now. Maybe not ever."

"Don't you think she's entitled to know?"

"Maybe someday, but not now. Not when she's doing so well and almost through medical school. She wants to be a pediatrician and do good things."

I sighed. "It would be a really great story, Ellie. It's got everything, including a happy ending in a world that's full of bad news. It's so hard not to write it."

Ellie smiled. "Yeah, I know it's a big temptation to get credit for solving a mystery close to three decades old. But I hope you're still the kind of lady who wants to do the right thing, to help people, not exploit them. Please? Don't tell my secrets. Let me keep the wonderful life you helped me to start again. For Andi, and Jack, too. He's a good man. He risked his government position and pension to hide us down here. Because of him, I enjoy my life. I don't just survive or get through another lousy day. I love living my life now. Please, don't expose me to the world."

I looked into her eyes and sighed. "I have to write that article for myself, but I give you my word that I won't ever publish it without your permission." Ellie closed her eyes with relief, and I continued, "But I'd still love to write a little piece for your local paper about a talented artist who owns a charming gift shop in the Keys. You can read it before I submit it. I'll take your photo from a side angle or looking over your shoulder. Focus on your business, not on your personal life story."

She nodded and shook my hand. "Yes, we could do that. And Jack will be so relieved. You know he's an ex-agent. He already noticed your husband's name on his charter list for today's fishing expedition and planned on avoiding any conversation with Doug all day."

"Well, how about meeting at the Conch Bar later for drinks around seven with our husbands? They can talk fishing and we can talk about our daughters and future plans. And I promise to leave a certain part of the past where it belongs – in the past."

As she left, despite the disappointment of letting go of publishing what could be a breakthrough news story, I felt good, surprisingly good. Some secrets are meant to be exposed and shared. Others are best kept hidden between close friends, no matter how juicy they might be.

I looked down at the angel medallion and smiled. I knew that I'd just received the most valuable souvenir I could ever imagine, one I'd rediscovered in the most unlikely of places when I wasn't even looking for it. And I knew that Beth Russo had to remain dead so that Ellie Jones could live the life that Beth had only dreamed of.

# #

About the Author

Karen Bostrom is the author of several published short stories and DANGEROUS SANDS, a romantic suspense novel set at the Jersey Shore. A retired teacher, she's now pursuing other passions: being a Reiki Master and a B.E.S.T. (Bio-energetic Synchronization Technique) Practitioner, ballroom dancing, traveling, creating art, and writing nonfiction to facilitate living an amazing life! She believes NOW is the time to live happily ever after. Visit www.karenbostrom.com

AT THIRTY WEEKS

Christine Clemetson

Chet Montgomery knew one damn thing for sure: his best pal Darren deserved to die in peace.

And it had to be tonight.

Chet hit the gas and the Chevy Bel Air's tires crunched on the frozen grass. Overgrowth and branches scratched the underbelly as the car rumbled up the hill. The coned headlights lit the abandoned field.

The radio announcer's voice crackled from the dash.

...Ray "the Duke" Peterson here on KMAK radio... bringing in the night with your favorite tunes...

At the top of the hill, Chet shifted the gear to park. Darren's knuckles were whitened on the passenger-side handle. "We got until the night before the inauguration," Chet said. "Let's go over the drill again."

"Not sure about this," Darren said.

Chet clicked off the radio.

Here it comes.

"Not sure about what?" He fingered the polaroid of Dorie hanging from the rearview. He used to go ape over that white nurse's cap.

"I wanted t-to tell you...to t-tell you...Shit." Darren hopped out and flicked the empty pack of Lucky Strikes on the ground. "Maybe we shouldn't be doing this."

"You're telling me this two days before?"

"I've thought a lot about this...and...and it's just not right."

Chet trailed Darren up onto the overlook. A battered split-rail fence staked the perimeter of the property. Even a few miles away, the tall thin windows of the White House glowed brightly against the black sky. Houses and official looking buildings surrounded it like soldiers.

If he had binoculars, Chet could have almost spotted their target.

Didn't matter tonight, though.

"Would you look at that view Daddy-O?" Chet asked.

"Did you hear what I s-said?"

Chet pulled his attention from the lights, and onto Darren. Planning and figuring took two years solid, eight months alone to get the route down to a five-minute window. "You're leavin' me high and dry? Is that what you're saying?"

Darren dug a stone from the soil with his boot and skipped it along the frosty grass. "Just can't do it."

"Plan won't work?" Chet pressed. "Or you straight up won't help me?"

"I just got that job with the city, and...I want t-to get back to the way things were before."

"Jesus Christ. You told Agnes, didn't you?"

Darren lowered his head like a guilty dog. "She's my wife now. I had to tell her."

"You've become such a predictable husband. Doing as your wife says."

"No...no. You and me are friends. I'm looking out for us."

A tinge of guilt ripped through Chet's insides. No way. He'd come too far to let Darren control this.

"You swore that day on Hickam field you'd help me make good. I swear, I gave blood." He raised his hand. "Hell, I even gave one of my fingers to win against the Nazi's, and then I come home to find Dorie—"

"She didn't want to do you wrong." Darren stuffed his hands in the pockets of his bomber jacket. "She got keen on someone else. That's all."

Chet flinched. *Did he really believe that?*

"S-she said she was sorry," Darren added.

"In a letter?" Chet's boots stamped on the grass. "She needs to understand what she did."

"The police are swarming like ants. You can barely walk by that place, let alone get close." A siren shrieked somewhere from down the hill, punctuating his point.

"Boy, Agnes got those claws deep in you, huh? She told you to say all this?"

"I'd do anything to help you. You know I would." Of course, he would. They'd been friends since first grade. "But this just doesn't f-feel right," Darren added.

"What kind of garbage is that?"

Darren paced some and returned, his eyes cast downward. "I stole the blueprints for the president's place. I helped you stakeout the security. I did everything you asked."

"You did, and I couldn't have done it without you." Chet's gut clenched, but there was no other way. He'd went over it again and again. "You've always had my back."

Darren hunched, tapped his boot against a fence post. "If we get caught, they'll give us the chair."

"So you're the voice of God himself now?" Chet mocked.

A gust of air whipped between them.

Chet edged real close. "I sat quiet for too long. Too many years."

Sweat on Darren's forehead reflected in the headlights. "You do it by yourself then. I won't say nothin'."

Chet narrowed his eyes. "But you told Agnes already."

"She won't tell nobody either." Darren's voice whined.

"That so?" The beats in Chet's neck quickened. "Then we don't have a problem, do we?"

"I gotta get going."

Chet slapped his buddy's shoulder and squeezed hard. Just like he had when the kids at school taunted Darren for being shy. Or after they survived that first week at boot camp.

One last time.

He hauled in a breath and headed for the car. "Hop in then. We'll cruise down by the drive-in."

Darren waved. "Told Agnes's mother I'd pick up milk. Not too far to walk."

"You got it, Daddy-O," Chet said, swallowing hard. "You tell her I send my best. I'll come for pot roast this weekend."

Surprise morphed into relief on Darren's face. He nodded, started down the hill. His shoulders dropped a little and his step relaxed.

Darren must've felt safe. The way Chet wanted it to be all along.

His friend deserved that respect.

* * *

Even with her eyes closed and nestled in the four-poster bed, Doris felt it. Blair House, the president's guest quarters, had a grace about it. Some called it exquisite.

Past presidents had found their voices there, negotiating with other dignitaries, and making decisions that impacted millions. History radiated from the walls, and even from the marble floors— where Abraham Lincoln once stood.

She felt every ounce of its importance.

But man oh man, what she would have given to spend their last night before the inauguration in their George Street home. But

Tommy wanted to show the American people that the house was open and safe, especially after the attempt on Truman's life two years earlier. It was the right thing to do.

With all her heart, she believed it.

But sometimes a very pregnant and very uncomfortable woman just needed her own bed. Thirty weeks down, ten more to go before this little gal or guy prepared for a grand entrance. And hopefully not a minute later.

Doris rubbed her belly. Pangs and twinges rumbled inside. Probably gas. Or heartburn. Or the baby wanted a chocolate malt.

And so did she.

Too bad the malt shops were closed by now. Milk would have to do it.

Perspiration plastered the cotton nightgown to her chest as Doris eased herself over on the mattress. Over tea, President Truman's wife Bess had cautioned about the warmness on the bottom floor of Blair House, even in January.

Doris should have believed her.

"Tommy..." She stroked her arm across the empty, cool sheets. "Tommy—?"

"Here, honey." Tom Flynn stood at the tall, narrow window. A strip of moonlight put a shine on the rose-embroidered drapes.

"Why aren't you sleeping? You don't want bags under those Frank Sinatra eyes when the whole world is watching."

His footsteps padded across the wood floor. The bed coils creaked as he sat. "Tomorrow is a big day for all of us, First Lady-elect Doris Flynn."

Doris pushed herself up onto the pillow. She fingered the corner of his mouth with her thumb. How she still fell in love with that smile. "You'll be a fine president."

"When I put my hand on that bible, it means something much bigger than me. I want to make my country proud."

"You worked hard. You promised what was right."

"How can I unite the people? How can I get them to believe in *me*?"

She grazed her hand down his arm and locked her gaze on him. "You deserve this more than any man I know. You have heart, Tommy."

"I made promises, Dorie. With the Cold War, I just don't know. I don't want to let the country down."

She tugged on the collar of his navy-blue robe, the softness molding between her fingers. She had run right over to Klein's department store that very day he won the gubernatorial race in Maryland.

Every governor needs a distinctive robe, she had told him.

Then they made love in their apartment that entire night.

"You'll do everything you promised and more. The people believe in you." Doris brought his warm, sturdy fingers to her middle. "*We* believe in you."

Tom squeezed her hand and leaned in close. The woodsy scent of his soap ran over her body like a warm blanket. "At eight-years-old, I struck out at the baseball game, and I cried like a baby. Sitting in the dugout after all the other boys left, Mama told me if I worked hard on and off the field, I could be President of the United States one day."

"Even then she knew what kind of man you'd be. When you say that oath, she'll be up in Heaven drinking her scotch."

He held her cheeks in his hands and kissed her nose. "She also told me I better marry you."

"Smart, smart woman." Doris ruffled his hair. The love in his eyes made her warm inside. "Now, get some sleep, Sinatra."

"I think I'll take Molly in the backyard and walk off this energy. Bright moon tonight." He tightened the tie on his robe.

Doris eased herself to the other side of the bed. "Would you be a doll and get me a cup of milk? This baby is doing cartwheels."

"Be right back."

He returned within minutes. Milk wavered in the glass as he placed it on the nightstand. She touched his arm and kissed him on the lips.

"You're a good egg, Mr. President."

"President-Elect," he said.

"Only for a few more hours." Even in the dim light, she didn't miss his smile broaden.

"C'mon Molly." The basset hound crawled from the rug at the end of the bed and then trotted behind him.

Doris sat up to take a sip of milk and noticed the dog's collar shimmering on the floor near the door. How many times had that thing fallen off? Tommy wouldn't be able to get the leash on without it.

She scooped it up and grunted, and then waddled down the hall. Officer Michaels's wide shoulders filled the doorway.

"Can you give this to Tommy—I mean the President-elect?" Doris asked.

"Yes, ma'am." As he disappeared outside, cold air funneled in, raising goosebumps on Doris's legs. She hugged her arms closer and stepped back down the hall.

A crack sounded from outside. From a gun? The air in her throat hallowed out.

She twisted back and peered through the open door.

A figure lay sprawled in the yard. Officer Michaels jogged toward it.

"Tommy!" She cradled her stomach and barreled down the concrete steps. *Nooo. My God. Oh my God. Not Tommy.* Her bare toes squished in the icy grass.

Another shot and–

Officer Michaels toppled forward.

Every cell–every muscle–in her body stiffened.

"Help! Someone help!"

She dropped to her knees and clutched the collar of Tommy's robe, the blue material spongey with blood.

"Tommy, no." She huddled closer, touching his hair, his cool cheek. "Please, please. Can you hear me?"

"Run." Tommy's voice was garbled.

"I—I can't leave you—"

The baby jiggled and pushed at her insides. Where were the other officers? Where was the Secret Service?

"Save...our baby," he whispered.

"Hang on Tommy. You hear me?" She smoothed his hair back. She stifled the cry in her throat and forced the quiver from her voice. "Help is on the way."

Movement drew her gaze to the woods. A squall of snow blustered across the yard as if warning her, telling her to go back inside.

Doris stood, one muscle, one vertebra at a time, her sheer nightgown flapping in the wind. She tracked the dark spaces between the trees. Tick. Tick. Tick.

A shadow stepped out. Metal flashed in the moonlight.

Aimed at her.

Her knees buckled. *No. No.* This can't be happening.

The shadow stalked toward her, the dim moonlight uncovering his face.

Chet?

A shutter rose in her lungs.

The notes he left flashed in her head. The paper always smelled of car oil, the words scratched with a knife.

No one else can have you, Dorie.

Her fingers twitched on her cheek, on the skin where bruises once stained. He swore he'd never stop.

Shouts closed in, from somewhere near the house.

* * *

Not close enough.

A blast pierced her ears, propelling her to move. Chet would kill her. He'd said so.

Doris stumbled over uneven ground, her hand trembling on her stomach. *Sssh. Baby.* The patch of woods skirted the edge of the property. She had to get there, get cover.

The thicket wouldn't protect her long. *What now?*

Think, Doris.

What had that Secret Service agent said about the safe house built after the assassination attempt? A sob lurched to her throat. Why hadn't she listened, instead of re-decorating the oval office in her head?

The sound of branches crunching drove her forward. She ducked away from strips of moonlight and plunged deeper into the shadows. Vines bristled the pads on her feet.

Breathless, she pressed her back against an oak, gulping in the raw air. The baby twisted and turned inside. "It's ok, baby. It's okay."

Doris scraped her nails into the bark.

Think.

Hadn't the agent said there was a body of water north of the cherry trees? Wasn't that near the safe house?

"You can't hide!"

Chet's voice slithered over her skin like a snake.

Doris ran faster. Blackness stared back from between the trees. Her life depended on the memory being right.

Minutes later, the soft trickle of water filled her ears.

"C'mon, c'mon," she whispered.

A creek ebbed beneath a narrow footbridge. With each step, the rickety wood whined and swayed.

No sign of a shed or cabin.

Dread crawled up her throat. She cowered behind a bush. The glow of dawn reached upward, just beyond the trees.

Oh, my God. No.

How could she hide from Chet in the daylight?

* * *

"Ray 'the Duke' Peterson here with you on KMAK radio overnight. Bringing in the day with this hit tune *You Belong to Me* by Patti Page."

Duke clicked off the microphone and started the turntable. The silky voice filled the small radio station. He settled back in the metal chair, closed his eyes, and imagined Patti Page belonging to him.

Seconds later, the click-click-click of the teletype machine brought him upright.

Something flip-flopped in his stomach. No good news ever came at dawn. Duke forced his eyes to the machine and focused on the words filtering in.

Halfway down the page, he stopped reading.

Good God. No.

The words blurred on the paper.

Could he deliver this to the American people? No. No way. He couldn't do it.

He swallowed dryness and ripped the paper from the machine. He cut off Patti's crooning about being lonesome, his fingers shaking on the microphone.

"Hello KMAK listeners. We're breaking into your regular tunes to report an assassination attempt on President-elect Thomas Flynn at Blair House in Washington D.C. At four thirty a.m. Eastern Standard Time, an unidentified man shot President-elect Thomas Flynn in his stomach and his condition is grave at this time. The shooter is still at large." Duke stopped, the words clogged in his throat. "It is believed that First Lady-elect Doris Flynn has been kidnapped. Her whereabouts and condition are unknown at this time. White House police officer Ben Michaels has sustained a gunshot wound to his shoulder but is expected to recover. Stay tuned to KMAK for breaking details as we learn them."

He paused a beat. Then slammed the microphone button and added words not on the page.

"This just in. Police suspect Chet Montgomery to be the kidnapper. If you know his whereabouts, contact the authorities immediately."

He switched off the audio.

The door flung open. Mr. Chester shuffled in, his shirt buttons mismatched, his tie hung loosely around his neck. "Just heard."

"Sir, I need to leave."

Mr. Chester patted his shoulder. "We'll be here when you get back."

Duke grabbed his tweed jacket from the coat hook. "Thank you, sir."

"Everything will be alright, son. They'll find your sister and she'll make a fine first lady."

Duke nodded, his footsteps already pounding down the cement hall.

* * *

Doris trekked deeper into the woods and finally spotted a structure. An American flag twirled and fluttered from a wooden pole in front.

She clutched her middle and ran toward it. Could this dingy place be the safe house? The flag screamed *patriotic*, but otherwise, the place looked abandoned.

If it was empty, she could wait there for help.

The porch steps wobbled beneath her numb toes. Dust and grime spattered the single window.

As she pushed the creaky door open, a bath of yellow light emerged. The squeak of loose floorboards reached her ears. "Is anyone here?"

An old man in long john bottoms and a plaid shirt jumped from a cot, holding a rifle, its long barrel aimed at her center.

"Whatcha doing here, girl?" The old man's voice croaked like a frog.

"I—I—"

"Who's got your tongue? Say it, girl."

"Is this the safe house?"

"Safe what?"

"Please. I need someplace to hide."

He pointed to her stomach. "Whose blood is that?"

"Chet shot the President." A sob escaped her lips. "And now...now he's after me."

The crinkles around the old man's eyes tightened. "Slow down, girl. You say President Truman's been shot?"

"No, no. My husband, Tommy."

"Tommy?"

"Thomas Flynn, the president-elect. We're staying at Blair House."

He pushed past her and smudged the window with his fingertip. Slabs of daylight now sliced through the glass. "You say your husband is gonna be president?"

"Chet's after me. He wants me dead." A shiver crossed the back of her neck. "Please, we have to do something."

"What's your name?"

"Doris Flynn, but I—"

"When's your husband's birthday?"

What? Doris backed up a little. The man was crazy, but going outside again...images of what could happen rushed into her mind.

"We need to get help."

"You want me to help you? Tell me his birthday. Every president's birthday is branded in this old brain, including Thomas Flynn."

* * *

"July fifth."

In the concave of his eyes, confusion transitioned to respect. He lowered the rifle and lifted his shoulders. "Gotta be more than three miles. You ran all that way?"

"I need a phone or...or..."

"I'm Henry Lincoln Harroway, named after Abraham Lincoln himself. No first lady or her baby is gonna get hurt on my watch." He tossed her a mangled wool blanket from his bed. "Huddle up in that corner by the fireplace, Missus."

"I don't know... I don't..."

"I'm gettin' help. Isn't that what you want?"

She nodded quickly. Words lodged in her throat like stones.

"See that?" Henry gestured to a rusty chain hanging next to the door. "Bolt it after I leave."

He clomped down the front steps and disappeared into the woods.

With shaky fingers, Doris fumbled with the chain. She wrapped the scratchy wool around her shoulders and scooted into the corner he'd pointed out.

Staring at the lock, in her peripheral she noticed a framed portrait of George Washington and all the other presidents lining the room.

Minutes later, the little house shuttered.

"Open the door, Dorie." Chet's voice wormed inside.

Doris stood and scrambled back, stumbling over a crack in the floor.

"I followed you here. I know you're in there, Dorie."

Supporting the bottom of her abdomen with one hand, she snatched an ax from the corner next to the wood pile.

"Either open the door or I'll kill 'em right here on this stoop. And you know I will."

"Don't do it, Missus." Henry's voice rose above a whisper.

And then a thud.

"Henry? *Henry!*"

She scoured the back of the room for another way out, her eyes blurring with tears. No other windows or exit. "He's just an old man who didn't do anything."

"You're not listening, Dorie."

The ax dangled from her hand, her bicep trembling. "Please, Chet. Don't do this."

The door cracked on its hinges, the frame splitting. Chet pounded his foot at the ragged edges until space widened enough to fit through.

Doris clenched the wood handle tighter and lunged forward, swinging.

Chet ducked and swerved, yanking the ax from her and twisting her into a choke hold like a toy doll. She squeezed her eyes shut against his rancid breath.

"You still aren't making good decisions, Dorie."

The bag hanging from his shoulder thudded to the floor, and he ripped out a piece of rope. He pushed her onto the bed, his eyes sweeping over her like a piece of meat at the butcher.

"No!" Heaving in hard, she kicked at his thighs, fumbling to sit up. "Let me go. The police are looking for me."

He slammed her wrists together and wound the rope tight, the fibers burning into her skin. She snarled back, kicking harder, but he corralled her ankles together and secured them with more rope.

Chet sneered, eyeing her bunched up nightgown. "You came pretty far, even for your condition. It'll take some time for them to track you."

Beyond him, Doris caught sight of Henry's lifeless body on the porch.

"What do you want Chet? Why are you doing this?"

Chet knelt and closed in, his eyes opened wide. The crinkle of his leather jacket made her heart pump harder.

His gaze loomed on her stomach. "If you had just talked to me, maybe we wouldn't be in this here mess. I could've been better for you."

"You're right. I know that now." Her voice wobbled. If she argued, he'd come at her harder. Just like he had smashed in her back door because she forgot to tell him good night.

He pushed hair from her eyes, trailing his index finger to her chin. "You're conniving, Dorie. You told me you loved me. You made a *promise*."

She bit her lip until the iron taste of blood coated her teeth. "Please just let me go."

"What did I do? Why wasn't I good enough?"

The small bluish vein ticked at the base of his throat. She knew that vein like she knew the feel of his fist.

"I should've…been honest with you. This is all my fault."

Chet stood, smoothed the wave in his hair. He retrieved the revolver from his waistband. "You're saying that to save your skin. You think I'm stupid, too?"

A shift on the porch pulled her gaze to where Henry lay. Had he moved?

"I'm truly sorry."

"Nah. Don't believe you."

"Please, Chet. I have to take care of my baby."

"*His* baby." The words hissed from Chet's tongue like a frog rolling up a fly.

Doris punched her legs. "Help! Help—"

"No one's gonna have you, Dorie." Chet raised the gun. The delirium in his eyes told her he had already made up his mind. "Not even me."

* * *

Duke maneuvered through the throngs of spectators now gathering on the streets curtaining Blair House. An army of officers blocked the perimeter.

An ambulance blared in the distance.

He pushed deeper into the crowd, scoping for the guys in charge. Camera bulbs flashed.

He knew what was coming, but he didn't care. The truth had to get out.

An official-looking guy with a badge hanging from his lapel and dark-rimmed glasses grabbed onto Duke's arm and led him through the web of people.

Mill Sherman stood at the entrance to Blair House. He eyed Duke. "That stunt risked your sister's life."

"You weren't telling the truth."

"By broadcasting Chet Montgomery's name, you just screwed up the case. He'll bolt now, knowing we're onto him."

"You should've gotten him before this," Duke said. "How many times has Dorie told you he was crazy? Or *I* told you? Or any of her friends told you? You're the one who messed up."

Sherman's top lip curled in a sneer, as if not believing some radio announcer kid could tell him how to protect the first lady-elect. Even if he was Dorie's brother.

"You just better pray that we get who did this," Sherman said.

"It's Chet! I'll scream it to the world," Duke said. "Tell them how you never followed the leads. The signs were all there."

Sherman stalked closer, his breath smelling of stale cigarettes. Sweat beaded above his eyebrows. "Are you threatening me?"

"Even after Chet took those pills and went crazy, you still didn't arrest him. If something happens to her, it's on you."

For a second, guilt filled Sherman's eyes. Then he shook his head as if shaking out the notion. "You're crossing the line," he hissed.

* * *

"Because she wasn't in the White House yet? Is that why? Not important enough to follow up?"

Sherman waved to the officer. "Get him out of here."

"You can't keep me." Duke yanked his arm from the officer. "I have to find Dorie."

"Keep you?" Sherman's voice mimicked a teacher scolding a child. "This is for your own safety. I can't have you running around like a loose cannon risking this investigation."

"You are the one that put my sister in danger. You caused this."

Sherman gestured to some guy in a black suit, and they hauled Duke down the sidewalk to a waiting police car. Duke watched news reporters press in against Sherman, like vultures smelling an animal carcass.

Any leads on the shooter, Agent Sherman?

Is Mrs. Flynn still missing?

A moment later, Sherman's police car thrust into gear, its tires screeching. The smell of burning rubber loomed.

A sickness filled Duke's stomach. What the hell had Chet done?

* * *

The Pall Mall trembled between Agnes' lips, the crusted tip threatening to topple. She rocked back and forth, staring through the sheer curtains. Morning light crept between the apartment buildings across the street, hesitating to come in, as though not wanting to know the truth.

The skin on her bones hurt.

Blinking even hurt.

"Please sweetie." Pearl shuffled in, her bony fingers clutching a burnished silver tray. Steamy liquid sloshed over the porcelain cup's edges. "Put something in your stomach."

Eat?

Act normally?

Agnes shook her head, words paralyzed in her throat like flies in a spider's web. Stuck. Unable to go forward or backward.

Her mama meant well, but the foreboding in her stomach swelled. Something felt wrong. Terribly wrong.

Pearl plucked the cigarette from Agnes's mouth and smushed it in the glass ashtray. "You need to keep your strength up."

The radio played static, leaving only bits of the reporter's voice.

...doctors are still hopeful at this hour. President-elect Thomas Flynn is out of surgery with a good prognosis...First Lady-elect Doris Flynn is still missing. Police are asking...

Pearl crinkled her gray eyebrows together. "My goodness. Who would want to hurt our president?"

Footsteps thundered outside

"White House police," a man's voice barked.

Agnes knuckled her toes into the carpet. The rocker stopped. She had to stick to the plan. Tell them what they wanted to hear.

She yanked at the words from inside her throat, dug at them.

"They must've found something. "Pearl smoothed her stained lace apron. The flimsy oak door squeaked on its hinges.

"Agent Sherman here." Another officer followed close behind. "Mrs. Jones?"

"Is this about Darren?" Pearl asked.

"We're looking for Chet Montgomery."

"Darren's friend Chet? No...no." Pearl twisted a button on her dress. "No, he's not welcome here anymore. He didn't even have the decency to pay his respects to Agnes after they found her husband."

"Mind if we take a look around?"

Pearl stepped aside.

Sherman's suit jacket swung rhythmically as he strode to the kitchen, and then to the hall, and returned.

"Why aren't you looking for Darren's killer?" Mama asked.

They are, Mama.

"The local police will get you those answers, ma'am. But right now, we need to locate Chet Montgomery."

The other officer bypassed Sherman to the rear bedrooms. Drawers squealed open and shut.

Pearl let out a moan. "Someone shot my son-in-law dead. Some coward shot him in the back. Why aren't you looking for *him*?"

Agnes pulled at the words harder. But her tongue lay dormant, unwilling. She turned slightly, pinning her gaze on Sherman.

Just go to the stream.

Pearl rubbed her daughter's shoulder. "Agnes is all alone now."

"How would you describe Chet and Darren's friendship? Cold ones up at the hill on Friday nights?"

Horror filled Pearl's eyes, narrowed them into watery slits. "Those two boys served our country together. Like brothers."

Agnes coughed. Please. *Please.* Sweat circled her neck like a choker.

"We believe Chet is involved with the attempted assassination on the president-elect," Sherman stated.

"I told...Darren...not to do it," Agnes whispered.

Silence blanketed the room like a winter coat.

"What...what are you saying?" Pearl asked.

"Chet wanted Darren to drive the getaway car." Agnes slid a cigarette out from the pack, her fingers shaking on the lighter. "But I told him to tell Chet no. And now he's dead."

Pearl sat on the couch, clutching the crucifix around her neck. "Don't tell me those boys had something to do with all this?"

Agent Sherman directed his team outside. Muffled voices sounded from the yard. Seconds later, he returned alone and sat opposite Agnes on the ottoman.

"After the shooting at Blair House, what was their plan?"

"They didn't *plan* to shoot anybody if that's what you mean." Agnes ground the cigarette in the ashtray. "Chet wanted to scare Dorie, that's all."

"Mrs. Blake, the first lady-elect is missing. You need to tell me what you know."

Agnes stared at the curtain. "Darren came home from the war with this awful stutter, and slower in the head. He didn't understand what Chet wanted to do. I'd swear an oath to that."

"But *you* understood what was happening, didn't you Mrs. Blake?"

A sick feeling swirled in Agnes's center. She squeezed her eyes shut. "Chet was obsessed, mad that Dorie married Tommy."

Agent Sherman tapped his shiny shoe on the floor. "Where were they planning to take Mrs. Flynn?"

She looked up at Mama, hoping for encouragement, but instead, glassy eyes looked upon Agnes like she was a common rodent.

"There's an old stream a few miles west of a small house. Chet intended to take her there, before...."

"Before?" Sherman asked.

Agnes turned on her seat, stared him in the eyes, straight into that center-most point that would believe her.

"Killing her."

* * *

Chet rammed the revolver closer to Doris's temple.

"Don't do this." Doris jerked, thrusting her arms upward. The baby squirmed inside. "If you have any decency at all left, if you ever loved me, please let me go."

"A little late, don't you think?"

A sound from the open door made Chet turn, breaking the moment. *This was her chance.* She lurched up, but dizziness swarmed her head and she fell back onto the mattress.

Chet returned his attention to her. "Don't you try anything Dorie."

From where Doris could see, Henry's arm had changed position. The rifle rested at his feet.

Was he alive?

Blood thundered in her head. "Whatever you want, Chet. I'll help you out of this."

Chet cocked an eyebrow. "Help me out of shooting the president of the United States?"

"Just tell me what you want. Tell me how we can both get out of this alive."

"Only one of us is getting out alive, Dorie. That I know for sure."

Heat swelled inside her chest. To save herself and the baby, she had to keep talking, get him to believe her. "What if I tell Tommy I changed my mind?" She paused, swallowing hard. "I want us to be together."

Chet paced and leaned his shoulder on the wall, scuffing the floor with his boot. "How come I wasn't good enough for you? Did you ever even love me?"

* * *

Henry got to his knees, wobbling, and then to his feet. He turned to the door. Confusion filled his gaze.

"You know I loved you." She forced her body to stay still. Forced her eyes to stay on Chet. *Ssh little one. It'll be okay.*

"I did for our country. For us, Dorie. I worked hard every day to come home to *us*. What else could I do?"

She twisted her legs, the rope burning her ankles. "You deserve someone better," she lied.

"Someone better than the wife of the president?"

A motion yanked her attention past Chet. Henry hunched in the doorway, his eyes open wide and glassy. Blood trickled from his head down into his eyebrow.

Get the gun.

"You still love me, Chet." She put a fake lilt in her voice, the play talk he used to love. "I know you won't hurt us."

Chet raised the revolver and aimed it at her. Right at her baby.

"Too late, Dorie."

Her breath hitched. "Please, Chet…please… I'll give you money, whatever you want. You don't have to do this."

"But I do, Dorie. That's the problem, see? I can't let anyone else have you."

The gun cocked.

"Nooooooooo." Her wail mimicked a wounded animal.

She squirmed and rolled herself off the bed, thudding to the floor on her side. The roar of the shot made her cower in a fetal position.

Something pounded, and the floor shook. She kept her bound hands close to her middle.

Trembling coursed through her body, taking all other feeling with it. She squeezed her eyes shut. Had the bullet hit her?

Had it hit her baby?

Slowly, she peered up.

Chet was sprawled on his back, eyes stiff and staring at the ceiling. Around his head, blood spattered the floor like raindrops.

"You alright, Missus?" Henry lumbered in and grabbed the ax from the floor. He worked the blade through the rope on her hands and ankles.

"I'm f-fine."

He helped her to sit on the bed and snatched the blanket from the floor. He wrapped it around her shoulders. "And the babe?"

Doris clung to him, nodding, her teeth chattering. She breathed in the goodness of this stranger.

"Good to hear, Missus," he said, patting her shoulder.

She pulled away, examining the clunk on his forehead. "How bad is it? I'm a nurse."

He scoffed. "Clumsy is all. Nothing a shot of whiskey won't help."

Doris squeezed his arms. How did she begin to thank this selfless man? Wetness burned her eyes. "You saved our lives."

"Like I said, no first lady or her babe gets hurt on my watch."

She pressed her lips together, not trusting the words at first. Her throat clogged. "Tommy will want to thank you too when he—"

"He'll be all right, Missus." He tightened the blanket around her. "I've been around for a long time, and I know a strong President when I see one."

* * *

Agnes put the hairbrush down on the sink and stuck her head out of the bathroom to hear the radio.

...the Duke here of KMAK radio reporting that President Thomas Flynn was sworn into office this morning at Roosevelt Hospital. First Lady Doris Flynn is resting comfortably beside him. That little boy or girl had quite an ordeal but doctors are predicting a healthy delivery in the middle of March....

"Are you ready?" Pearl called from the living room. "I'm not sure how long the police will wait."

"Yes, Mama."

Agnes stared in the mirror. She closed her eyes halfway and pouted her cherry red lips, trying to appear innocent. She dabbed rouge on her cheeks.

"The questions could take most of the day," Pearl said.

Questions. Like it had been a normal event on a normal day. Her mama hadn't accused Agnes of wrongdoing since the police came. Too much to admit to neighbors, more likely as not.

"Be there in a second."

Agnes adjusted her wool hat, her fingers trembling on the hat pin. Agent Sherman was a sharp cookie. Would he buy it?

You messed things up, Chet. She sunk her head lower, fighting the whimper, the cry that wanted to come out. She patted the handkerchief to her mouth.

I sent the cops there to find Dorie dead. Not you.

Such a simple plan.

They'd use basket-case-Darren to do the grunt work, get rid of him, and then finally dispose of Dorie. And then she'd meet him later after things settled down.

Why'd you get yourself killed?

Chet had promised to make her life different. Happy. No more living with a dumb husband and old mother. They'd swim in the Caribbean, for Christ's sake.

She'd pledged herself to him, given her body to him in the backseat of the Bel Air.

Given her soul to him.

But that bitch Dorie killed him.

A warm tear plopped on Agnes's cheek. She primped the wave in her hair.

Chet had told her she was prettier than Grace Kelly and cooked pot roast and gravy better than his own mama.

She had to do this for him.

Agnes stared in the glass. *Right?*

Sherman would believe a widow in mourning, wouldn't he? If not at first, then she'd apologize over and over. Cry the tears men hated. Plead for mercy. Tell him that she should've gone to the police the minute Darren told her about the idea.

Explain that young women today didn't want to disappoint their husbands.

Maybe even say she'd considered taking her own life.

And after Agent Sherman believed her, she'd finish what Chet started.

# #

* * *

CHRISTINE CLEMETSON

About the Author

Growing up in a small Jersey shore town, Christine wouldn't have been caught on her beach towel without a good book. From this, she caught the fire of creativity and discovered she had her own stories to tell. She earned her degree in Literature, and went on to pen stories that send readers running for the covers! You can catch up with her at https://cclemetson.wordpress.com/ *and on Twitter:* @cdclemetson.

THE BROKEN HEART

Christine W. Kulikowski

"Lancelot, Laance-a-lot!"

I pulled the phone from my ear. My sister was screaming, and I knew why. Her ghosts were pestering her again.

"Come. Come right now! They're here."

"Emma, Emma, Emma . . . calm down. Don't I always come running when you need me, day or night? But yet again? I've stayed overnight. I've searched everywhere inside and outside the house. There were no spooky visions, no clanging chains, no dying wails; I didn't notice cold breezes. I looked for ghost goop. There are no ghosts in your house. There—are—no—ghosts—anywhere."

"But there are hauntings!"

"That makes no sense." Her logic always escaped me.

"I'm older. I know more than you do."

My sister was born three minutes before me and clubbed me with her superiority before she could speak. I looked at the galleys of my latest mob novel scattered on the dining room table and the rug and the chairs. They had to wait.

"I'll be right there. In no time." I shoved my phone into my pocket and jogged the two blocks to her house.

It was *modern Victorian* the Realtor had said. It was a bright and airy color, not quite yellow and not quite green. A cheerful house, I thought. *How could it be haunted?*

Emma opened the door before I could climb up the porch stairs.

"Don't just stand there, Lance. Get in here."

"I'm all yours, Boss Sister." Emma had named herself that as soon as she could talk.

"You made me buy this house."

I'd heard that too many times. Any guilt I felt had long evaporated. Emma was passionate for the truth. She had few shades of temperament. When she was unhappy she said she wanted to die. When she was happy she was jumping out of her skin. She felt other people in her heart. It made her vulnerable to charlatans, in a way. Emma would invest everything for a noble cause. Whenever she was guilty of a childish sin, she'd say, "Lancelot made me do it."

"I can't make you do anything. You're older. You just said so a little while ago."

"But you said it was a steal. Half the price you would normally pay. Why? It's haunted. That's why."

I looked into her dark blue eyes. "I know you wanted this house as soon as you saw it. I can't figure out why you turned against it."

I searched the house. It was daylight. Could ghosts appear before dark? I'd never heard that. But I started to look under furniture, in corners, in cupboards to show good faith.

My mother had left me as the trustee of our inheritance. She had worried that Emma was "too good to be real." Emma had a fine mind, however. Until last month she wrote op-ed pieces for the county daily. She knew how to investigate before forming an opinion.

The downstairs and basement rooms were open-concept. No places for ghosts to hide, I thought. You could look from the foyer to the deck and the woods beyond. The basement was five feet above grade and bow windows poured in light on three sides. The kitchen wasn't open to the great room, though. It was just for the cook.

"I'm going upstairs now. Do you want to come?"

"I'll wait, Lance. I know you're trying to soothe your loony sister."

I continued up the glass and chrome stairs. I guess they were the *modern* part of *modern Victorian*. At least nothing could hide under them.

I was guilty of one thing: I never told Emma that the surgeon who had owned the house had committed suicide in an upstairs bedroom. He stabbed himself in the heart. Three times. Maybe he wasn't a good surgeon. Before the knife was pulled from her husband's heart, the widow put up a For Sale sign. She sold the house cheap, like a foreclosure. Maybe she loved him so much she couldn't bear to stay in the house. Or she hated him and wanted to run away and forget this part of her life. She obviously didn't need the money.

I came back down. Emma was still standing by the stairs.

"You didn't find anything, as usual?"

"No, I didn't, Emma. You were so happy at first. Two acres of protected woods behind you. Open concept. Quartz kitchen counter. A restaurant stove. Three refrigerators—meat, dairy, and whatever."

"But since then I lost a job I loved. I had to give up my subsidized apartment to buy the house. Now you're paying the mortgage. I have the right to be miserable and angry. Not at you."

"We have the money from Mom. You'll feel better soon and you'll find a job again. Are you taking the pills the doctor gave you?"

"I am. But you forget I'm being haunted. The pills don't get rid of ghosts. Can we sell today?"

That gave me a double take. "I guess we could. Do you want to live in our old house again? I don't care about upgrading it or buying new furniture, but you would feel awful. It's not your style."

She started to cry hard and soon was gasping for air. Now what? She'd been normal till now, except for the ghosts she sees. The sudden bursts of tears came from an Emma I didn't know.

"Let's sit in the kitchen, sweetie. Don't cry. I'll think of something."

"You don't believe me, do you? At first, I couldn't either. But there are ghosts here and they scare me."

I took her by the hand and put her in a kitchen chair.

"Coffee?"

"No. Tea."

"You know that the English drink coffee these days?"

"So what? They should hold onto a tradition that encourages rest and conversation."

"What about charwomen? Did tea mean rest and talk to them?"

"Stop it, Lance. Why do you want to bicker over trivia? You're not funny."

I scooped some Earl Grey leaves into a dainty Ainsley teapot. It's an antique, a working teapot, the kind with a strainer molded behind the spout to capture tea leaves. I bowed and served it to her with warm cream in a tiny Royal Doulton cream pitcher. I poured cream and then tea into a delicate Ainsley teacup. I couldn't find an Ainsley creamer. Emma didn't complain about the mismatch. I grabbed a craft beer I never heard of and sat down opposite her.

"I'm trying to amuse you, not bicker. You're so miserable. What are your ghosts doing to you, Emma? Do they clang chains, scream, throw things? Can you see them clearly? Are they Ghostbuster ghosts?"

"Don't patronize me. I'm out of work and blackballed. It makes me miserable, not insane."

"I know, I know. That was totally unfair. Why don't you write it up for *The Daily Kos* or *First Amendment Journal*?"

Emma had worked her way up from reporter to the op-ed writer for *The Daily Board* in no time. The paper was sold in March, just when Emma bought the house. The new op-ed editor asked her to write an opinion piece on the latest cuts in Medicare and Medicaid emphasizing how well they matched the needs of the elderly and the poor in our county. Emma nearly blew her hard drive banging out scathing satire, irony, and indignation. She named names. Her editor didn't check her copy and it went to press as written. The new owners weren't pleased. They had backed all the cuts and seen their taxes cut by ten percent. Her new editor never worked at a paper that allowed opinion. Opinions were assigned. Emma's assignment was to prove that the lower reimbursements worked just as well as the higher.

The next morning all hell broke loose. She was ordered into the executive editor's office. He and the op-ed editor ranted at her. They accused her of sabotaging the newspaper. Emma was dumbfounded. She had never heard such vitriol spat at anyone. She hadn't realized that the last election brought out the coward in her colleagues. They clung to their jobs like burs. No one came to her defense.

Emma was dragged over the coals. She lost her job, her pension, and her health plan, as the Patriot Act permitted, for conspiring to destroy a legitimate business.

Emma had savings and cashed in her IRAs before anyone found them. After that, she climbed into her bed, covered her head with a quilt, and refused to get up. I had to pry her out to see a doctor

"Em, when did you have the doctor check your meds?"

"What's that supposed to mean? That depression is craziness? You jerk. The pills don't make me hallucinate."

I waited silently and studied the wrinkles on my knuckles. *What to do now?*

"I haven't been keeping appointments. I try to remember the pills. It's a farce anyway. They don't exorcise the ghosts." Tears poured again.

"What do the ghosts do to me? I'll tell you all of it. Yes, I hear clanking but not like chains. It's like stainless steel kitchen pots being thrown around. I know there's nothing happening in the kitchen. I've checked. I hear them anyway."

"So, it's kitchen pots clanging. What else?"

"I don't see shadowy shapes. I see mist out of the corner of my eye, but when I look it's gone."

"Gone?"

"Yes. But then I glimpse a mist in another place through the corner of my eye and it disappears, too."

"But what are you so scared of? Noise? Fog? You're losing too much sleep over this. Every day you look thinner. The circles under your eyes sag to your nose. Ask your doctor to prescribe sleep meds. Maybe two or three good nights of zzzs will exorcise the ghosts."

Emma started to sob, deep, wrenching sobs like she would vomit up her soul. I had to take her fears seriously. I'd never heard her cry like that.

"Stop it. Stop it. Believe me. Just once believe me without question."

I was very uncomfortable. Frivolous repartee tried to slip through my lips–that's my fallback when I see emotion in other people. I quashed the jokes. My sister was a nervous wreck, an old-fashioned disease I understood.

"Emmie, something else is terrifying you. It's not only flying saucepans and indoor fog."

Her sobs quieted, but her eyes kept sluicing. "Come closer, Lance. Closer. Closer."

When we were cheek-to-cheek she turned her lips to my ear. "It's the numbers. In dripping blood. They change every day."

I pulled away to stare into her eyes. They looked like shimmering cobalt silk. They unnerved me.

"What numbers?" I whispered. "Can we talk a little louder so I don't miss anything?"

She cleared her throat but her words were hoarse. "They appear everywhere."

"Always the same numbers each night?"

"They change every night."

"Did they come with the house? I mean, did they start as soon as you moved in?"

"No. Nothing happened in March, except that I bought this house and then I was fired. But on the first of April, I saw them. One-foot long and in bright red blood. At first, I thought you were punking me because it was April Fool's Day."

I bit my lip. Every time I had jogged to Emma's house I had searched for signs of her ghosts everywhere I could imagine. Not walls, though. Nothing caught my attention on the pale-yellow paint. Now, when she's hysterical, now, when I'm ready to lock her up, she springs bloody numbers on me.

"Emma, what the hell are you talking about? I'm sorry. I shouldn't swear at you."

She heard neither the "hell" nor the "sorry."

"It started with thirty days and there were words: 'to go for 30.' The next night it was '29 to go for 30.' The blood was darker and thicker every day. Last night it said '13 to go for 30.' That's when I will die."

Just like that. The numbers meant she would die.

"What? Are you crazy? Sorry. You're not. Hey! I get it. April 30 is your thirtieth birthday, sweetie. You have locks on your door and on the windows. You can choose if you want the joker to come in. Not Joker. A secret admirer?"

I sounded nuts myself. I was pretending to interpret bloody words I never saw. I was soothing her by letting her believe her hallucinations were real. Was this better than arguing?

"I'll build you a safe room!"

"Shhh." She put her finger to my lips. "Don't try so hard to believe me. Or cure me. They can unlock the locks, they can sneak under doors, they can glide through the glass. In thirteen days, I'll be gone."

"Where? You've given a lot of thought to this, haven't you? So thirty is D-day? Sorry. The day. I'll be here on the twenty-ninth. Very early. I'll lock you in a safe room and I'll defend you." I was trying to sound like a real knight but came off like a boastful fool. "Emma, you're so calm. You weren't when you called."

"I had a little hope then. I don't anymore. You can't fight the invisible foe, Lance. You don't have The Force in you. Build me a safe room. You won't feel guilty when I'm dead. Go ahead. Go!"

I went. I pulled all my savings. I still had the inheritance and fat royalties. I brought in cadaver dogs, rescue dogs, drug dogs—even Roscoe, the bedbug dog. I remembered that hunting dogs flush out birds and pests. I called them in, too. I got firefighters to check for signs of arson, past or yet to be. They checked between walls with a hair-thin camera scope attached to a computer. There were no strange objects, no cubbies, no shelves. No bodies, either.

I checked on Emma every day. With four days left I couldn't think of any more to do. I asked her if she could think of anything I hadn't.

"Psychic?" she suggested.

"You can't be serious. She'll burn some magic weeds and charge a thousand dollars. I might as well burn the bills–they won't stink as much."

"I knew you'd be spiteful!"

I stared at leaf shadows trembling on the ceiling. Emma was dead serious. I looked at her again. She shivered. Her eyes beseeched me. What the hell, I could afford to spend a little more. I hoped the public would never tire of the mob.

"Let's do it. But let's hire three of them for different times. Let's throw in a guy, too. Got names?"

"Yes, here."

"You actually have a written list?"

"I did a piece on psychics once. Not all of them are charlatans."

"Let's see: 'Natalka, great-granddaughter of the last czar,' 'Penelope, a descendant of the Great Oracle of Delphi,' and 'Black Witch of Haiti.' Black? Or Black Witch? What about the Great Wizard of Oz? Probably something to do with copyright."

"Don't mock! But you're not. Thank you."

"Let's get a guy for balance."

"I know a Father Ethelred who performs exorcisms. The Bishop excommunicated him. He stays a priest, though, so I'm confused."

"Me too."

"It's only four days now. Will they have time?"

"They'll have time. Don't worry. I'm sure they'll come for a crisis." They'll charge extra for an emergency, I thought. "We'll stagger them over the next four days. No collusion this way. Plus, your safe room is practically done."

I'd ordered a thick stainless box coated with cement. It weighed a ton. More than a ton. It slipped into Emma's bedroom, but I had to add steel girders on their own posts below. We cut out a door and inside installed state-of-the-art locks. The door looked like a part of the wall.

Next day the first of Emma's ghostbusters arrived. Natalka was all business and efficiency. She took one look and declared the ghosts were dead.

"Can ghosts die?" I mouthed to Emma. She shushed me.

Natalka cleansed the house with burning sage to release the ghosts' bodies. Where do the ghosts of the ghosts go? I glanced at Emma. She was focusing so hard her face was scrunched up. Natalka charged $500 for the spells and $500 for the emergency cleansing. As expected.

Next day Emma said the ghosts were still there. I wondered if a little parsley and thyme would have worked.

The Black Witch of Haiti came at noon on the dot. She was very black and covered in black from her head wrap to her pointy little shoes. She towered over me. As soon as she stepped in the foyer she shuddered.

"Black Magic. I inhale it from every corner."

Probably the sage. The Black Witch hurried through the rooms. Then she sang incantations in a high nasal voice and thrust a box in my hands.

"Candles. You must light black-and-white candles at every window, every door. The pure white will suffocate the black evil."

"You are a *Black* Witch—but isn't evil black? I'm sorry, I don't get it. How much?"

"You don't have the gift of knowing," she sniped.

I caught a glimpse of the nasty look she hid under the lofty contempt.

"Five hundred dollars for one box of candles and the spells I cast on them."

Five hundred dollars again. Probably set by a witches union.

"But this is a large house with many teleports. Two boxes of candles. I'll get more from my car."

I wished I hadn't mocked her. She was back.

"Plus $500 for these blessed amulets." She tried to hang a leather sack around my neck. "Five hundred each."

"No. We don't want them. Here's a check for $1000."

"Oh, no, you don't. Cash only or this house will destroy itself. I have spells."

And arsonists waiting for a job. I had the cash. I'd been sure someone would demand cash. I went into the bathroom and pulled a grand from my money belt.

The Black Witch waited nervously at the door. She must have worried I called the police. Not me. I'd paid enough. She stomped to her car with my money and I tossed the amulets after her.

"No emergency fee?" I called after her. I'm a fool, I thought.

She turned and spat at me. It was a gesture. I wasn't near her. She turned around counter-clockwise three times. She stamped her feet three times before getting in her car. It was a BMW. Then she threw me the finger and shot off from zero to eighty.

I carried the candles in their boxes to the basement. There were thirty candles in each. Thirty. I had to stop thinking like Emma. I'd be seeing bloody numbers, too.

Next day the doorbell chimed at noon. The Oracle should have come at nine. This must be Father Ethelred. I opened the front door. Penelope, the Oracle of Delphi, and the unfrocked Father Ethelred jostled each other coming through the doorway. They stared at each other incredulously like space aliens from different planets. Emma came to see who it was.

"My dear child," Father Ethelred laid his hands on her head, "you are consorting with Satan's minions. Only God's mercy can save you now."

I thought *he* was the conduit for God's mercy. The good Father slammed through the door and covered his head like a monk; Latin chants escaped him now and then. Well, that didn't hurt the wallet, I thought.

The Oracle was in the center of the great room. I was exhausted, not a quip left to throw at her.

"Blood and tears, blood and greed, blood and dark shadows foul the air."

That sage again.

"Is the evil in the past?" Emma asked.

"The evil is in the past, in the present, and in the future. I cry for you, Girl."

The Oracle turned and walked to the door. Oh, great. Emma was keening. That's the only word to describe her cries. Keening.

"How much?" I asked.

She was hurrying down the stairs. "I need no money from her."

"It's not from her. Did you come out of your good heart to destroy my sister? What can she do?"

"Run. Run fast. Run far. Take nothing. Leave the house to evil."

She kept going down the stairs but turned her head on the last step. "You may bring gifts."

Gifts. I knew it would come sooner or later.

"Go to Demitrios' Greek market. Buy fresh olives and figs. Leave them. I'll pick them up next week."

She gave me a sardonic look. Olives and figs. Maybe I should believe her. I'd ask Emma what she thought.

My smart, astute sister stood like a mad woman in a movie. Her hair had grown long over the last two months. It lay like tangled corn silk over her eyes. Her eyes had drifted to infinity again.

"Emma, the Oracle said to run. Far and fast. Leave everything. I'll figure out the finances later." I stretched out my hand.

"I can't. Tomorrow is twenty-nine. I must be here on thirty."

"No. Isn't that what's driving you . . . worried? Come with me tonight. We'll come back tomorrow."

Her eyes refocused. "You're lying. You won't let me come back."

She was right. "I have to get some finishing touches for your room. Come help me out."

"Nothing new will happen tonight. It's waiting for thirty."

Maybe I should have had her locked up as a paranoid schizophrenic. Or whatever. A danger to herself. I couldn't, even if I believed it.

Next day, the big twenty-nine, I rushed in as a grandfather clock tolled 5:00 a.m. Emma waited in the kitchen. She hadn't changed her clothes, hadn't washed, hadn't untangled her hair. Her eyes glowed blue from some place in her soul. She wasn't there.

"Come on, Em. I'll show you your hidey-hole. I dare any man, beast, or ghost to get to you."

Her ability to detach herself from the present and snap back in an instant puzzled me. "Okay. Let's go."

She looked at me and stretched her hand out to mine and held it. I cried. She always held tightly to my hand when we were kids but kept scolding me non-stop, because she was older and she was the boss.

I took her upstairs to the remodeled bedroom. "Where have you been sleeping this week?" I asked gently.

"Here and there and nowhere."

"Of course. Here are a futon and a quilt. I bought them. They haven't been out of my sight." I gave her a smartphone. "Just press one and I'll come running. There's music, too, and TV." I put a pitcher of water and a glass on a frilly little table next to the futon. Then I showed her the commode. "It's just one night. There is toilet paper, and hand sanitizer, and a two-gallon bottle of water."

"That's fine. Thank you. I hope you're right."

I felt uncomfortable with her clear thinking. Maybe she was coming to terms with her sickness. Maybe she would go back to the psychiatrist.

"Can you open the door?" She asked as she stared at the array of locks.

"That's my secret. I'll be there if you need me."

We came downstairs and went out to sit on the deck and stare into the woods. An ethereal green haze rested over them. Spring was here.

"Soon the flowers will burst out; the birds will build nests and fight over food."

"And angels will bear cake and honey to my lips. Shut up, Lance. Just sit." She held my hand and fell into a deep sleep.

My stomach growled. I was thirsty. I needed to relieve myself. I didn't want to wake her but at last, I couldn't stand it. I uncurled her fingers one by one. They dropped softly into her lap. I crept away. Maybe she just needed sleep. Those anonymous "they" say that seventy-two sleepless hours will make you crazy. Maybe that was her sickness.

I relieved myself and ate a messy Reuben, the best kind. I decided against beer. Too early. I had an energy drink instead and debated my next move. I decided to wake Emma. If she didn't know I'd gone, she might think I'd been ghosted away. I gave her arm a gentle shake, then a little harder. Her eyes sprang open. She was alert. No sleep befuddlement. She smiled sweetly. That made my stomach churn. Emma rarely smiled that sweetly.

"I left a peanut butter sandwich for you in the kitchen and a pomegranate energy drink."

She stood and followed me. She was nearly sprightly when she sat.

"I'll eat this. Don't worry. I might take the food to the deck. You can go. Just come by five, before dark."

She smiled sweetly into my eyes. My stomach lurched. I could understand her theatrics. This person appeared from a place I didn't know.

I kissed her forehead and left. I was confused. Why should a normal Emma, a hungry Emma, a peaceful Emma be a stranger? Maybe her meds finally kicked in. Maybe she realized she was dreaming a nightmare. Maybe she was sorry for ripping my heart out and was returning it to me. At the back of my mind, a sneaky little worm of an idea was struggling to be noticed. I ignored it.

First, I went home to pack a duffel with spare clothes and three types of camera, including an infrared motion cam. I added tape recorders, flashlights–one of them solar. I added my galleys as an afterthought and pens, pencils, and notebooks. A spare phone. I didn't quite tear the kitchen sink from the wall.

I lugged my stash to the car and was slamming the trunk shut when I remembered something: where do you imprison a ghost once you catch it? Silly, but I wanted Emma to believe I was doing my best to believe her. The Ghost Busters used some sort of cooler and dry ice. I bought a pressurized cooler and dry ice from a medical supply store. I couldn't attach a vacuum cleaner. Maybe she wouldn't notice. Again, that wiggle in my brain. Again, I ignored it.

I returned at four-forty-five in the afternoon. My heart thumped uncomfortably. To tell the truth, I did anticipate something or someone unpleasant to manifest itself at midnight. I sat in the car and

breathed deeply. I reminded myself that my exorbitant stage set was for Emma's peace of mind. I guess I got caught up in the fiction. Emma's ghosts were her apparitions, not mine.

The sun was far down in the sky. It flamed orange and ochre through the back windows facing the woods. The misty green merged into soft teal. Nothing sinister would dare disrupt such tranquility.

Emma was waiting on the deck when I came in. Her hair was glowing. She had showered and changed into black leggings and t-shirt. She could have picked a brighter color, I thought.

"The sunset is striking."

I hugged her tight. Was noticing the sunset a good sign?

"Tomorrow we'll watch it together. We'll go to a Vietnamese restaurant. I'll buy you a bright pink birthday cake on the way." She smiled a genuine smile and looked me in the eye.

"I have everything sealed tight. All the locks are wired to alarms. If you come out, I'll know. If anything touches your door from the outside, sirens will wail and 500-watt LEDs will flash. We'll catch the thing and freeze it. You are completely safe."

"Mmm."

I escorted her to the bedroom. She checked every item. "I'm fine, Lancelot. You remember the Professor Smurf I stole from you? I'm giving it back. Goodbye."

"Don't you mean good night?"

"That too."

I was closing the door when the niggling idea jumped out. *Suicide.* She was calm, she was resigned, she was at peace. She was giving away cherished mementos. Forget the ghosts. She was going to kill herself. I whirled back to her and cupped her face in my hands. I drilled my gaze into her eyes.

"You are planning suicide." I started to cry. "I love you, Boss Sister. Don't leave me alone. Live through one more night. I beg you. Tomorrow it will be over, whatever it is."

"Don't cry, little brother. I never would kill myself. It's cruel to the living. I'll be watching *Naked and Afraid* on demand. I missed episodes recently. Good night."

I kissed her on the forehead. "Thank you. Good night." I closed the door. The thunks and clangs of the locks assured me she was safe. I breathed deeply again. Not suicide. I cried again, from relief this time.

In the kitchen, I drank a beer. It was a Budweiser I'd brought with me. Just one, because I didn't want to fall asleep. I chased the beer with strong coffee, pulled out the galleys, and settled in a kitchen chair. I thought about waiting upstairs but didn't want to scare *it* off only to return another day.

Something startled me awake. I guess one mug of coffee wasn't enough. I stood up to pour another. Again, I heard a noise. It hadn't been a dream. The ceiling lights lit up on their own. The spooks were awake. A mix of clangs, bangs, and beeps walked into the kitchen. I couldn't see anyone, but the noise came nearer. Then it materialized into a mist. Another followed. They looked like The Visible Human I once put together for a science fair.

These didn't have any organs inside. They seemed male. The very visible cigars they were smoking tipped me off. They smiled collegially at me as though we'd met somewhere before. A book reading? A signing? I couldn't place them. Presumably, they were solid humans when we met.

The short, rotund guy sat opposite me. The rotund tall guy was pouring water into the kettle. He saw me gawking.

"Just a little tea for Maury and me. You don't remember us at all?"

I shook my head to clear it. They didn't disappear, so I must be having a dream within a dream. Maybe beer and coffee gulped one after another brought on hallucinations. I was having a conversation with ghosts. Were these the live ones? Would they become dead ghosts?

"Hey, Writer. *He's* Len," Maury said.

"Yes, now I remember. You looked different then. Clothed for one thing, corporeal for another. You offered to serialize my mob books on television."

"And you, Shakespeare, said you were an author, not a shill for advertisers. You wanted complete artistic control like you were a freaking Stephen King."

Maury and Len laughed heartily. Their rotundities jiggled. Belly laughs from ghosts without stomachs. The situation was getting more and more farcical.

"I'm sorry. I was young and foolish." It was true. A public television station offered me a pittance.to produce a documentary based on my books. They were true to my books. The series was so boring that I turned it off. Six months later a mob series was introduced on A&E: *The Sopranos*. That could have been my series, I thought.

Len put the tea he'd brewed at Maury's place. He used an antique Japanese cup that should never be used for black tea. The shell-thin porcelain shouldn't be used at all. I didn't dare complain to a non-entity.

"Len! Wrong cup. Give me a mug. Len doesn't understand niceties, Lance. Bad childhood."

"Get to the point. Your backgrounds don't interest me. Neither do your high concepts."

"They should. We had to produce a high concept series or we'd be out on the street," said Len. "It had to rate the highest Nielsons."

"When you wouldn't play ball," said Maury, "we busted our heads to invent a dazzling series. Something nobody would dare show."

"A reality show like no other," Len said.

I smiled. "A reality show? That's your great concept? Viewers are sick of reality shows."

"They are not tired of reality shows. They're not tired of excitement and anxiety," said Maury.

"Let's see," I said. "*Dancing With the Stars* and a half dozen derivatives; the same thing with song and voice contests, even the kids are trying to be rappers; *Dance Moms*; housewives from every state in every color and size; fattie shows; midget fatties; Amish runaways. And the latest in stupidity and titillation: *Naked and Afraid* that even my sister watches; *Naked and Afraid XL*. Who can top that?"

"We could and we did," Maury said. "Surgeons slicing up people. Live, uncensored. All the sweat and blood and tension as it happens."

"It's been done," I said. "*Trauma*; ER in Detroit, Boston, New York, Australia; *Bizarre Bodies*."

"But surgeons competing with each other? We called it *Surgeon's Cut*. Get it? They cut and then they're cut."

"No. I don't get it."

"Every week four surgeons complete an assigned surgical case. They are graded on speed, efficiency, and the client's post-surgical condition. Every week we sign up clients with the same condition, age, and health. Four pompous dopes, oops, I mean surgeons, are randomly assigned a client. That's it. The one with the lowest score gets cut, heh, heh."

"How did I miss this unbelievable reality show? You call them clients?"

Len explained. "Clients is what patients are called now. I like it. Less touchy-feely, more businesslike. The show aired for a year but shut down after the third episode of Season Two. They're syndicated now. Lots of money still pouring in." Len was rueful. "We didn't live long enough to enjoy it."

"Did practicing, licensed surgeons sign up?"

"Of course, they did. Greed, egoism, money, pride on a scale to be a Deadly Sin. Why not? We streamed the entire surgeries for addicts. We used forty-five minutes out of twenty hours for a digest."

"I don't believe it. Did they lose their licenses, hospital privileges, parking spaces, for God's sake?"

"God doesn't have that in his commandments," said Len, "the AMA does. Only one poor schmuk ran out of luck."

Maury and Len exchanged questioning looks. "What the hell. We're dead. He's already killed us," said Maury.

"Your Boss killed you, but he's still your Boss."

"You got it. His bad luck spread to us. The cancellation was punishment enough. Then he killed us. Ripped out our hearts. They weren't good ones. Heart attack country. He dragged us to his car and drove home. He committed suicide. Stabbed himself in the heart. Three times."

I jumped up. Three times? The mad doctor had owned this house.

"We started with gallstones." Maury stood up and started pacing. "The thirteenth episode was a heart transplant. Our money was on Dr.

Gideon, but he dropped the heart we gave him on the floor. He was in a hurry to pick it up and didn't put down his scalpel first. The heart was slimy. He sliced it three times juggling it. He tried to sew it together. He couldn't. Then the buzzer rang. It was over and the poor lady died. During the commercial for a new mausoleum, he ran backstage with a butcher knife and ripped out our hearts, probably thinking he could use one of them in the woman. Too late for the lady and too late for us."

"Yeah, but, Maury, before he died he said he had to search for 'a thirty-year-old, lightly used, woman's heart.' I don't know why. He can't put a heart into a ghost."

"Len, let's go. It's one minute to April 30. She died a year ago. It's her thirtieth birthday, too. Like your sister."

The clock began to toll. Maury and Len disappeared. I ran to Emma's bedroom.

The ghostly doctor was holding her dripping heart. He was smiling.

# #

About the Author

Christine W. Kulikowski immigrated to the United States in 1952 at the age of seven. She was a passionate reader and writer from the time she was learning English. She has a BSc from the College of St. Elizabeth, NJ and English, Russian, and Speech minors; an MSc in animal breeding from the U. of Hawaii, and an MA in English literature from Rutgers University, NJ. She taught biology and English at the college level and edited a hometown Forbes weekly. In retirement, she gardens and writes short stories. Readers can contact her at chrissyalicia@peoplepc.com

THE TELL-TALE SKIRT

D. K. Ludas

April 1987
New Brunswick, New Jersey

I reached the office drenched by April showers. The pouring rain prevented me from stopping for my morning coffee and newspaper on the way in. I shook off my umbrella, closed it and raced into the unusually quiet waiting area of the Social Services office. As soon as I dropped my belongings in my office, I headed for the small break room we shared with Juvenile Services.

"Good morning, JoMarie," my assistant, Kelly Carson greeted me. "You look like a drowned rat!"

"Thanks a lot." I shook my head in hopes the natural curl would spring back. "Good morning to you, too. Looks like it might be a quiet day."

I poured myself a cup of coffee and went to my office.

Kelly followed me. "The rain must be keeping the striking utility workers and the folks in need away today." She laid the folded newspaper down on my desk. "Better enjoy the quiet now." Kelly winked. "Sun's due out by noon."

"Glad to hear it won't be raining all thirty days of April." I grinned. "Thanks for the paper. I will settle in for some quiet." I picked up my coffee cup and glanced down at the front page of the Ledger.

"Oh, my lord." I dropped into the chair the same time I dropped my coffee cup.

"JoMarie, what's wrong?" Kelly asked, mopping up coffee as she put an arm around my shoulders.

"That woman on the front page. I saw her yesterday." I gulped in air, my head was spinning.

"Where did you see her?" she asked.

"While I was waiting for the bus yesterday. I heard angry voices. The traffic light had turned red, and the voices grew louder. I saw a man slap the woman seated in the passenger seat of his car. She yelped. He slapped her again."

I glanced down at her picture in the paper. "She pressed her face against the window looking at me, helpless, crying. He smirked at me as if he was challenging me to something. I just stared in horror. The light turned green, and the car sped away. That's when I noticed her colorful plaid skirt seemed to be caught in the door, flapping in the breeze, waving goodbye to me."

"Weren't there police or anyone else around?"

"No. The bus pulled up right away."

"JoMarie, didn't you report it?"

"We were so busy here yesterday, I just didn't get a chance. Now a young woman is dead." I reached into my briefcase and pulled out my pad. "Here. Here's the information I jotted down on the bus." I handed the paper to her.

"White Lincoln town car, four doors, license plate: HOTSHOT," Kelly read aloud. She handed the paper back "It must be so difficult for battered and abused women to stir up the courage to come here for help. I know how hard you try to keep them from getting hurt."

"But not this one." I pointed to the newspaper. "She wasn't twenty feet away from me, and I didn't do anything. She was only thirty years old. My age."

"Maybe you can do something now. Is there a number to call?"

I grabbed the paper and scanned the article. "The Union County Prosecutor's office is looking for tips. I've got to call them." I folded the coffee soaked paper and dialed the number with shaking hands.

"I have information regarding the dead woman found by the bridge," I told the receptionist who answered the phone. I was put on hold.

"Detective Angelo Tirado," a deep voice answered. "How can I help you?"

"My name is JoMarie Manetti," I answered, still shaking. "I'm a social worker in New Brunswick, Division of Women's Services." I told him what I could about the incident at the bus stop yesterday. He listened without interruption until I was finished.

"Are you sure about the license plate?" He spelled it back to me and I confirmed it. I thought I heard him groan.

"Is something wrong, Detective?"

"Nothing ma'am. Can you think of anything else?"

"The woman I saw was wearing a lovely plaid, lavender and gold dress or skirt. It was caught in the door of the car as though she'd tried to get out and changed her mind. Or, perhaps, he wouldn't let her get out of the car. About four inches of her skirt was flailing outside the car."

"Is there any chance you can come up to the office today or tomorrow, JoMarie?"

"I can arrange to take tomorrow off. I want that man caught and off the streets. If I'd have called yesterday, that young woman would still be alive."

The detective sighed. "Not necessarily, but I understand how you feel. Unfortunately, we know this guy. We don't save them all."

We sighed in unison. "But we still keep trying," she whispered.

When I hung up the phone, the rain had stopped, and the office waiting area was full, just as Kelly had predicted. By two o'clock we were swamped. The stack of folders on my desk seemed to be growing instead of shrinking despite the fact we hadn't even stopped for lunch. Now my clock read five-forty-five. I had six minutes to catch the last rush hour bus home. I slipped a few files into my briefcase and dashed out the door.

After I dropped into my seat on the bus, I thought of the girl in the newspaper. The same girl I saw yesterday at the bus stop. Now she was gone. Another life simply snuffed out.

Forty minutes later, I opened the front door and was greeted by the aroma of fresh basil, garlic, and tomatoes, my mother's homemade sauce. "Hello. Sorry, I'm late."

My father stood and kissed my cheek. "I was hungry, so we started without you."

My mother appeared from the kitchen. "JoMarie," she kissed my head.

"Thanks, Mom. Let me go wash up, be right back." A minute later I returned to a steaming plate of pasta. "Hmmm," I inhaled. "Your sauce is the best."

My father nodded savoring the thick mostaccioli pasta. "What makes you so late?" He twirled his fork in the air. "I hear a lot of things going on in New Brunswick. You must be careful. Drive to work."

After shoveling several bites into my mouth, I answered. "The parking is awful Dad. The utility workers are picketing, and there is so much construction going on parking is almost impossible. But I'm taking the car tomorrow. I have to go to the prosecutor's office in Union in the morning then I will drive to work." I went to the kitchen and scooped more pasta into my plate.

"You work too hard, JoMarie. You have no fun. A young woman like you should go out, meet people," my mom said.

"What kind of people do you mean, Mom?" I grinned.

My parents looked at each other, forcing back smiles. "Young men," they said in unison.

"I know I haven't had much of a social life these days, but one day I will."

"Still, you work too hard, my daughter, you can't save them all, you know," my dad muttered.

"I know Dad, but I have to save the ones that I can."

* * *

The next morning, I showed my driver's license to the security guard at the Union County office building. He checked the roster and asked me to have a seat.

"Miss Manetti?" a tall, dark-haired man asked, waking me from my sorrowful reverie.

"Yes." I stood. "Detective Tirado?" Tall, dark and handsome fit the deep voice I heard on the phone. We shook hands and he escorted me into the inner offices of the building.

"Call me Angelo, JoMarie."

When I declined coffee and removed my coat, I sat in a chair at the conference table and faced him.

"You said you knew this man." I crossed my leg. "Were you able to pick him up?"

"We have asked him to come in this morning. Could you identify the driver of that car if you saw him again?"

"I'm sure I could. He looked right at me and I was going to give him a piece of my mind, but the light changed and they sped off."

"It's probably better that you didn't. Although I'm using the term sarcastically, he's a prominent 'business' man out of the Jersey City area. Connected, if you get my drift."

"So, he gets to beat young women and kill them?"

Angelo ran his hand through his wavy hair. "Of course not. We've just never been able to prove anything or make anything stick, that's all."

My stomach turned over. "Are you telling me the witnesses disappear or something?"

"We don't usually have any witnesses. People in Union, Hudson and Essex counties know better than to stand up to him. And you aren't really a witness, but you will give us enough to get a search warrant. Maybe we can find something important in his car."

The phone rang and Angelo asked to me to face the window that made up one wall in the conference room. Seven men filed in, all about the same height, age, and coloring.

"Take your time and let me know if you see HOTSHOT in that room, okay?"

I know what I wanted to see, but he wasn't there. I looked for close to fifteen minutes. It pained me to admit defeat.

I shook my head. "He's not in that room. The man I saw was a little younger than any of these. Maybe in his mid to late thirties."

Angelo left the room. I slumped in the hard wooden chair, totally deflated. I hadn't gotten her help yesterday, and I couldn't help her today either.

"JoMarie," said Angelo as he pulled a chair to face me. "The owner of that car was in that lineup. The fact that you couldn't identify him, only means he wasn't the driver of that car. I'll still get my search warrant."

"How?"

"The skirt you described was indeed the victim's dress. She was still wearing it when we found her body. That places her in the car you saw. You've been a big help."

"Will you keep me posted, please?"

"If you'll let me buy you a cup of decent coffee, I promise to stay in touch, JoMarie."

His smile warmed my chilled bones and somehow, I felt better than I had in a few days.

* * *

Easter came and went and with it the usual increase in holiday-instigated abuse cases. The faces changed week to week, but the stories didn't vary much.

Kelly opened my door. "Your next case is here."

A young woman wearing a plaid skirt with bruises on her face and arms walked in. I jumped up and pulled a chair out for her.

"Please sit down. Let me help you." The plaid skirt reminded me of the girl in the plaid skirt, I didn't help, who hadn't lived to see thirty-one. Any thoughts I had pondered of a career change recently, were removed from my brain, as I was determined to help this battered young woman sitting in front of me. I called a few numbers and was able to have her transported to a woman's shelter immediately.

"Detective Tirado is on your line," Kelly announced at four-thirty, the first day of May. "Can you take the call?"

"Sure, thank you," I replied, my heart rate picking up at the sound of his name.

"Angelo, good to hear from you," I said, trying to sound collected and professional. He was down the street at the deli and wanted to know if he could drive me home.

"I'll be ready to leave in a half hour. I'll meet you at the Bayard Street door, okay?" I asked

Half an hour later, he was leaning against the car inhaling a cigarette, waiting for me in the NO PARKING zone.

"Cops get to park anywhere, huh?" I laughed.

He smiled as he held open the car door. "Police business, ma'am. I've got news for you."

I gave him directions to get us out of New Brunswick, then settled back to hear what he'd driven fifteen miles to tell me.

"So, what did your search warrant get you, Angelo?"

He navigated the heavy traffic easily, watching his mirrors constantly. "A killer, JoMarie. The man who killed that young woman will never do it again."

"That's wonderful. When is the trial?"

He moved into the turn lane for Woodbridge. "There won't be a trial."

"I don't understand. I thought you said you had him? Or did he plea out?" I knew all too well how many beaters walked away from jail because of space or legal technicalities. I coughed.

"I said he won't do it again, and he won't. He's dead, too."

"HOTSHOT? You said he was *connected*. You didn't mean politically, did you? Did he…?"

Angelo shrugged and placed his hand over mine. I told him where to turn and when, but we didn't speak until he was parked at my parents' house.

"Probably, is the answer to your unasked question. For Union and Hudson counties it eliminates some major problems. We don't have to worry about witnesses getting killed or about him walking away from a corrupt courtroom. And he won't kill anyone else."

I thought a minute. "You're right. It is justice, isn't it?"

He nodded. I glanced at the front of my parents' house. "You want to stay for dinner?" Meet my folks?"

He goes out of the car and opened my door, offering me his hand.

"Sure. I'll bet your mom makes a mean tomato sauce."

# #

About the Author

D. K. Ludas is a published and award-winning short story writer. A retired teacher and active realtor, Daria is the co-author of the southern women's inspirational series, Amazing Grace Trucking Company, with N. L. Quatrano. Book one, MERCIFUL BLESSINGS, will be published by Salt Run Publishing under their Two Stone Lions imprint, in 2018. For book information, visit http://nlquatrano.com/amazing-grace-trucking-series-inspirational-womens-fiction/. Daria can be reached at DLLudas@Verizon.net.

FIRES OF SPRING

David Manfre

Oliver pulled his ten-year-old Honda Civic into the Boys and Girls Club of Monmouth County's parking lot. His parents' words of concern still rang in his head. His new messenger bag with the patches he'd sewn on sat next to him.

He might have missed seeing–and thus run over–Randolph Marino, someone he knew from across the street, had he not been paying attention.

And not seeing Randolph would have been horrible. Not only would Oliver have potentially injured or killed another person– something he could never live with–but anything the legal system did to him would have been far better than anything Randolph would have done to him if he'd been able.

Randolph's friends might or might not do anything bad depending on how loyal a friend any one of them was.

Oliver had noticed a bulge on the side of Randolph's jeans where Oliver saw cops carry their guns.

"How it hangin', McRae?" thirteen-year-old Brian Kettering asked as he approached Oliver in his car and leaned his arms on the roof as he looked in the driver's window.

"What have I told you before, Brian?" Oliver asked the young man.

"Don't block you from getting out of your car," Brian replied and stepped back.

"What else?" Oliver asked, looking directly at him while still keeping Randolph within his peripheral vision.

"How are you, Mr. McRae?"

"I'm doing well. Thank you. And you're now two for three."

Brian shrugged. "Go inside as soon as I get here. And I *did* just get here. You'll walk me inside?"

"Of course, I will." Oliver snapped his fingers, remembering he forgot his messenger bag, which contained items he used for helping his students. Oliver's thoughts were interrupted by slurred words coming from across the street.

"Hey, my friend. How you? Got the good stuff? I'm looking for a fix."

Oliver could practically smell a bar coming off of Kory Ventimiglia as he approached Randolph, looking for cocaine. What a poor shame Kory was. Oliver knew from listening to him talk to Randolph that Kory was hooked on cocaine, heroin, and alcohol, often using two, or even all three in the same day, but never at the same time. He used something at least three days each week, though.

And, if Oliver was good at guessing ages, he would guess Randolph and Kory to be around thirty years old, just five years younger than him. Sad. They were young enough to get themselves clean and have a life. They might not have a great life, but it would be better than what he was witnessing, now.

As volatile as Randolph or Kory could be separate, together, they always made Oliver extremely nervous. He'd never seen anything that made him fear for his safety or that of his students, but he knew it would only be a matter of time.

Oliver just knew that someone with Kory's cluelessness and

Randolph's gun was a bad combination.

Brian headed inside and not a moment too soon in Oliver's opinion. He heard an explosion come from across the street. As many times as Oliver had heard gunshots before, he was still startled by the sound and spun around when he heard it.

Randolph was lowering his gun and Kory was on the ground, nursing his arm, looking like a child who'd just been reprimanded by a parent.

"You cheatin' me!" Randolph yelled.

"Na. I good for it. I already paid ya. Don't yas remember? We had this conversation yesterday. Yas knows I'm good for it. We has a deal," Kory cried.

"Yas not seen me yesterday. You no here yesterday. I here all day," Randolph said, then pulled the trigger again, hitting Kory in a leg. "Yas ready to pay me?"

Kory looked even more confused and in pain. "I paid yo yesterday," he grunted through the pain. "You owe me stuff."

Oliver was too stunned to do anything but stare at what was going on across the street. He did not notice one of his colleagues, much less which one, tugging his arm, urging him inside.

"Na, ya did not," Randolph said, then fired one more shot, this one in the head. Kory's head fell flat on the pavement. Randolph bent down and picked up cash next to Kory's body.

"Ya two not gonna say nothin' to nobody 'bout nothin', ya hears me?" Randolph yelled, waving his gun in the air.

"You, you, you...," Oliver stammered.

"Ya not gonna say nothin' to nobody 'bout nothin'," Randolph demanded as he strutted over to Oliver and his colleague, his gun raised to Oliver's left temple.

"We didn't see anything. We were just talking about our curriculum and enjoying the sun in the sky. Isn't that right, Ollie?" Oliver's colleague asked.

"He, he, he's dead," Oliver stammered.

"And you will be too if you don't forgot what you seen here. Gots me?" Randolph asked, a fist and his gun each raised at Oliver when he got in his face.

"We're going now," Severo Basutro said as he tugged Oliver's arm again. Oliver blinked twice at his colleague, finally realizing who was beside him.

"Randolph killed Kory," Oliver mumbled as Severo towed him toward the door by the arm.

"Shush. Don't say that. In fact, don't say anything. Just come inside," his friend urged.

"It's so horrible. No one deserves to die like that. He could have done something with his life. Randolph could have done something with his life," Oliver mumbled as Severo led him into the building.

"There's nothing you could've done. You just have to let it go," Severo said, weak confidence in a voice that was normally as iron-pressed as his dress shirts.

"We could've done something for them. I could've done something for them. That's what we're here for."

"I have been here longer than you have and we've tried with them. Their parents did not want them or their siblings to have anything to do with us. They and their siblings have all been raised to live that lifestyle. And I don't see how you could've done anything for them. You're only five years older than those two are—they have no respect for you as a teacher."

"So, Randolph just gets away with it? No one takes any responsibility for any of it?"

"No. The cops know them. We will call them anonymously in a few minutes, just as soon as Randolph leaves, and we'll let them deal with what happened."

"I don't want to die. You heard him. He will *kill* us." Oliver sat on a chair, almost missing it. Then, he dropped his face into his hands.

A crowd of people, adults and children alike, gathered around Oliver. "Give him some space, everyone. Go back to what you were doing," Severo's shaky voice ordered.

* * *

Oliver sat at home in his recliner in the wee hours of the next morning, contemplating what he had witnessed. He'd spoken with two Asbury Park police officers about what happened and given them his statement, but that didn't mean he'd gotten over what occurred.

He didn't know how to articulate what he'd experienced. The police barely got the story out of him. Whenever he closed his eyes to sleep, he could see Randolph standing over Kory, his gun pointed at the young man he'd killed.

However, morning arrived, the sun shining through the shades. Had he fallen asleep and not even known it? Either way, the memories still haunted him and additionally, his back hurt, probably from sleeping in his recliner.

How was he going to handle his day? Luckily, he did not have any responsibilities, thus there was no one to disappoint if he stayed in his apartment all day. That way, he could figure out the benefits of what he was doing in Asbury Park.

There was a difference between working with children to keep them on the right path—and watching a man killed. Watching drug transactions was bad enough, but murder? That was something else.

Oliver's phone rang, startling him. How long had he been sitting there since waking? "Hi. Um, yeah, hello," he said into his phone, still groggy.

"Hi, sweetie. Thank you so much for the lovely anniversary plant! We just love it. Next spring, we'll plant those lilies in the back garden."

"I'm glad, Mom. Listen, I had a really rough day yesterday and I didn't sleep too well, either. Can I get a shower and a cup of coffee and then come over?"

"Sure. Why not pack a bag and just spend the day with us? Get out of Asbury for a night or two?"

Oliver didn't need to be asked twice. Getting away was exactly what he wanted to do. He might not even come back....

* * *

Though he was usually confident in his abilities to get over any situation, no matter how difficult, Oliver was badly shaken. Sure, he might need help sometimes, but he could always acclimate himself. But this situation was different. He didn't know if he would ever get over it, much less how. As he drove toward Old Bridge and the home he'd lived in for many years, he thought about how he'd tell his parents about the shooting.

He pulled into their driveway, grabbed his backpack and then headed up the steps to the porch and through the front door, a door that he remembered was seldom locked. On his apartment door were *three* locks and he didn't feel safe.

"Oliver," gushed Maura, his mother, wrapping her arms around him.

He dropped his bag and hugged her back, holding on a bit longer than usual. She pulled back and searched his face.

"What's wrong? Your color is terrible and you're trembling. Are you sick? Should we call the doctor?" she gushed.

He smiled and took a deep breath. He was safe here. He looked at her a long moment. "I'm not fine, but I'm not sick. Well, not in the way you mean. How about we join Dad in the kitchen? I could use a cup of your coffee and maybe some toast?"

He waited until the toast was in front of him and they all had mugs of steaming hot coffee. Without looking at either of them for too long, he gave them an abridged version of what he'd witnessed the day before.

His mother turned the color of a sheet of paper and his father went sort of gray. "Oliver," his father, Conrad, said, "that's horrible.

You need to get the hell out of there and do it today. The cause is noble, but not worth your life, son."

"I'm thinking about it, Dad. But I don't want to make that decision right this minute. I thought some sleep, good food, and celebrating your anniversary might allow me some space and perspective. My life is there, you know? My job, my apartment, the volunteer work at the club."

Maura nodded. "We understand that, but we don't want you in danger. You can stay here as long as you like, you know that. And, if you need to talk about this, we're here."

"I know you need me to talk to someone about what I'm going through. You've always taught me that," Oliver said, finishing his coffee and pushing the chair back as he got to his feet.

"Not *someone*, sweetie. Me. I am your mother and I love you and want the best for you," Maura said. "Your volunteering in such a dangerous place just worries me. You explained why you volunteer there and why the club's there, and I get it, but I still don't like it."

"I know, Mom, and I do appreciate it. Maybe I should transfer to the Red Bank location. I know where it is, but I do not remember whether it's in or right near downtown, but that location's safer, and that's an option."

"It's good you're thinking like that because it means you're not thinking to run away and hide, but you might want to give it some thought. You don't want to quit the first time things go sideways. It's not like you to quit anything that easily," Conrad said, trying to sound hopeful.

"Would you like to talk to a counselor about this? You don't have to feel embarrassed by it. People who've earned lots of success and respect often talk to counselors about their problems and, as much as we love you, and we do love you, professionals do this for a living. They know how to help people with traumas like this," his mom suggested.

"I'll think about it. Thanks, Mom." Oliver rinsed his coffee mug in the sink and then turned it over in the drainer. "I'm going to go take a nap if that's fine," he said. "I'll take you two out for a late lunch, how about that?"

Maura glanced at Conrad and covered his hand with hers, then smiled at her son. "That sounds lovely. We'll see you later."

* * *

In a shopping center near Old Bridge's municipal complex Maura, Conrad, and Oliver had just placed their Early Bird orders when Oliver looked straight ahead and gasped.

"What's wrong, honey?" his mother asked.

Oliver pointed but didn't speak, though his mouth formed words. He thought it entirely possible he was going to be sick right there.

A man wiping down a table looked around the room nervously. He seemed to know something was wrong.

"What? You recognize him? He's a harmless young man. I see him here a lot. He came to America a few years back and he's trying to make a living," Conrad said to Oliver before he turned to the young man and called him over.

"Oliver, this is Arturo. He usually keeps to himself, but he helps customers when we ask him. Who did you think he was?"

"He looks like someone I know from Asbury—from the side. Sorry for getting so freaked out." Oliver struggled to smile. "Nice to meet you," he said.

Arturo's smile was kind. "My pleasure. Have a nice meal."

* * *

"You don't have to do this, Dad. I do appreciate it, but it's unnecessary," Oliver said as he and Conrad walked down Cookman Avenue in Asbury Park's downtown on Sunday evening in search of a place to eat dinner.

"I respectfully disagree, son. You're still scared and I want to show you that you can be in Asbury Park and remain safe. Not too many years ago, this part of town used to be dangerous. Look at it now. It has come back to life with shops, restaurants, and some people raising families here as well as those who don't live here bringing their families for the day or on vacation. You suppose the section where you volunteer could, one day, become as nice and family-oriented as this one?"

"It's always possible, but I don't see it now because of my frame of mind."

They stopped walking when a shrill voice broke the comfortable quiet of the evening.

"What you talking about you can't release my brotha? He didn't do nothin' wrong. Plus, he be my brotha and nobody disrespects my family because that be my family," an irate woman screamed at a police officer.

"Listen, Audrey, we can't release anyone just because his family loves him. He was given bail, I'd imagine, and you or he may pay it if he was and you can afford it. Until that point, he'll have to remain in jail. As much as I'd like to help, I cannot." The officer remained as calm as any officer Oliver had ever seen.

Oliver's stomach rolled over, then lurched. The coppery taste of fear almost choked him. He grabbed his father's arm.

"Come on, Dad. I think that's Randolph's sister. I'm almost positive of it. I know he has a sister and she looks more like him than that guy did yesterday. I need her to not see me. I don't know what she knows about me, including whether I said anything to the cops," Oliver almost whispered to his father.

"I agree. Let's get out of her line of sight. We'll step in here," Conrad said as he led Oliver into Downtown Workout, a fitness store.

Normally, Oliver would have picked up on the irony of entering a fitness store to avoid being attacked, but he was so frightened that his mind was still outside with Audrey and flashing back to The Boys & Girls Club murder. It didn't help that, as he and his father entered the store, he heard Audrey call out to them. *I've got to get out of here.*

Seconds later, the door flew open and she stood within a foot of Oliver, looking as though she'd tear him apart. "Hey, you the one who saw what my brotha did. Go on, tell them cops he didn't do nothin' wrong and was only defendin' himself," she hissed.

"Come, Dad. Let's move away from her," Oliver said as the police entered and confronted Audrey for reasons Oliver didn't want to know about.

"Na, coppers. Talk to him. He be tellin' the truth about what my brotha Randolph did to that guy. That guy be cheatin' my brotha and he had to defend himself," Audrey said.

How does she know who I am? I didn't tell anyone other than the police, and they have to keep that stuff confidential.

"I'm sorry, but I don't know you. We've never met before," Oliver said, remaining calm because the police were there.

"Na. Don't be lyin'. I know who ya be. You be da guy from The Boys & Girls Club who snitched to them cops about what my brotha be doin' on Saturday," Audrey said, hostility in her voice. "Tell them he no killah. Tell them he be defending himself."

"I think you should leave my son alone, ma'am. He's one of the most honest people I've ever met, so, if he says he's never met you, he's never met you, and, if he told the police a thing about what your brother's done, good or bad, your brother's done it," Conrad said, standing between Audrey and Oliver.

"It would be better if you let us handle this one, sir. We're the ones trained to handle situations like this," one of the officers said to Conrad as the other made an effort to peacefully remove Audrey from the store.

Oliver didn't know what to do. On the one hand, Audrey might be dangerous, possibly as much so as Randolph, in which case getting on her bad side was a mistake. She might have access to a weapon. Perhaps violence ran in the family.

On the other hand, not doing anything would allow her to walk free, potentially getting access to him. Who knew what she would do if allowed to walk free? She might, for example, make a false claim about him, if he didn't do as she wanted.

"But, I be tryin' ta help my brotha. I be doin' this on his behalf," Audrey cried.

"Either get away from him now or I'll place you under arrest," an officer said.

"On what charge?" Audrey demanded.

"Intimidating a witness, if I can verify that fellow is a witness. And, disturbing the peace to pick two," the officer said, her partner standing next to her, each one almost in Audrey's face and not backing down.

"Your brother will have a chance to tell his side and present any evidence he has during his trial. Don't make things worse for him or you by doing this. Go about your day as you were before you ran into us and if you really want to help your brother, hire a lawyer for him. I urge you to leave this guy alone," the officer said, apparently noticing that Audrey was going to say something.

Audrey slammed back out through the doors, fuming over the injustice she apparently felt her brother was facing over being arrested for killing someone because of a drug deal.

Oliver took a breath to calm down. The nausea had passed, but his knees still felt like they were made of rubber. "I appreciate what you did, officers. I did witness her brother kill someone and it was *not* in self-defense. I don't know how she found out I witnessed it. I was told you guys wouldn't give my name or contact information to anyone."

"We don't give out that info, sir. The perp must've told her he suspected it was you, if he saw you," one of the officers said.

* * *

Oliver's paid job in the produce department of the grocery store wasn't as rewarding to him as volunteering at the Club had been a week ago, but he knew it was important. He used to dream of becoming the manager of either the produce department or the entire store, with his preference being the general manager.

But the violence he had witnessed on Saturday eclipsed his every thought, let alone his dreams. Would he even have a future?

"Talk to me, Ollie. I can tell when something's wrong, and I'm seeing it now," Trevor Austin, his general manager, said when Oliver was on break the next day.

"Did you hear what happened over the weekend in Asbury Park?"

"Yeah. A couple people said you mentioned it yesterday. Pretty rough. I would have approached you yesterday had it not been for all the suits from corporate coming here, fine tooth combs in hand. I've seen a couple fights in my day, but nothing like that. Those were just some drunken fools in bars or kids on playgrounds. How are you holding up?"

"It's rough. My parents have been helping me, and I appreciate it, but I still feel like I shouldn't have said anything. Not to anyone, especially the cops."

"I have seen you with the kids at The Boys & Girls Club, and you're so great with them. You teach them the difference between right and wrong. What would you tell any of them now if one of them were to bring this problem to you?"

Before he could answer, someone called him from outside the door. He felt the color drain out of his face.

"Oliver, get outside now. Someone vandalized your car," cried Suzanne Ray from the meat department as she burst into the break room.

"What? Are you sure?"

"One hundred percent. I recognize your plate and car magnets. Come look and see if you don't believe me."

Oliver, Trevor, and Suzanne exited the store and approached

Oliver's car, and Oliver saw key scratches and spray paint covering portions of it. The word "snitch" was scrawled across the car magnets that proudly displayed his volunteer passions.

Oliver was so numb at the moment that he didn't realize how numb he was, and a part of him was frightened because of that.

* * *

Officer Shotwell took Suzanne's and Oliver's statements and he recommended a body shop to him. Oliver thanked Shotwell and started for the store.

"Are you sure you're up to finishing your shift?" Trevor asked, a false sense of sympathy in his voice.

Oliver wasn't thinking about finishing his shift. He hadn't even made up his mind about how he would finish his day. However, he was not surprised Trevor wanted him to finish his shift. Trevor had a one-track mind and for the good of the store, he needed all his employees to work no matter what.

"You've got to be kidding me, dude. My car's been vandalized and you want me to finish working?"

"I've always worked, no matter what I've had going. My fifth marriage is collapsing because I'm so dedicated to work and I've never taken a day off. Not for a wedding, child's birth, a divorce, or anything else, except when my boss has threatened to fire me if I didn't," Trevor said proudly.

Oliver began to shake. "I'm not you, dude. Fire me if you must, but I'm going home." Without saying anything else, Oliver went inside, clocked out, and got in his car, graffiti and all.

* * *

He was relieved to find his apartment had not been cleaned out. Two possibilities were that either Audrey and anyone else doing Randolph's bidding did not know where he lived, or that they did but they had their limits. Either way, he was still safe, at least for the time being, in the one place where he should be safe.

Oliver couldn't get over how his life had changed in the blink of an eye. He'd witnessed a murder. He had heard others say that Kory, Randolph, and those like them were blights on society and that they all should be killed or locked up forever. He knew better and preferred to get them help. After all, addiction was a disease and addiction to drugs and alcohol were the worst kinds, as far as Oliver knew.

He didn't know Kory's or Randolph's specific stories. However, he did know the specific stories of many people living in poor areas. Asbury Park, outside of downtown and the Oceanfront section, was a perfect example. The undereducated turned away from low-paying, often sporadic jobs to more lucrative ways to make money and most of those ways were illegal and dangerous.

Starting to feel depressed, Oliver fell onto his recliner. He normally felt inspired to take action to better the world when he thought along those lines, but not today. Maybe he needed to face the fact that many wouldn't be saved.

Oliver's phone rang and he jumped. Would it be Audrey? Who else was connected to the murder? There was Randolph, but he was locked up in the Monmouth County Correctional Institution. Could he be calling? What would he want?

Oliver checked the caller ID and saw a familiar number he couldn't place, so he answered it. "Hello?" he said after a moment's hesitation.

"Hi, Oliver. Suzanne called and told me what happened. That's terrible. Is there anything I can do to help?"

While Melinda Coryell was not Oliver's favorite person since he'd caught her cheating on him, part of him was relieved to hear her voice.

"I don't know what to do. I've called the police once and behind the back of the guy who killed the other guy and the killer's sister threatened me yesterday and, if I'm right, vandalized my car today. I don't know if I did the right thing by calling the police today. And I am damned scared still."

"You did the right thing. You know you did the right thing. However, you are smart to be scared. My sister is engaged to a prosecutor she met after you broke up with me. I'll call him and see what I can do about helping you. That is if you'd like."

"But I don't want to end up hurt or killed."

"You won't. Have I ever let you down? I mean, besides..." Melinda's voice trailed off.

"No, never. Not even after we broke up."

"I didn't think you knew about that. In any case, maybe my sister's fiancé can get the police to protect you. Has to be something they can do. I'll be right over."

* * *

Oliver waited for what felt like thirty hours but was probably more like an hour or two at most for Jack Bennett, the prosecutor assigned to the Kory Ventimiglia shooting, to call him into the courtroom to testify, still as nervous as anything. He had followed the news in the papers and online and Randolph still looked as much like a thug as the first time Oliver had seen him and was glad for the police presence in the building. "The prosecutor's ready for you, Mr. McRae," a bailiff eventually said.

"Thanks," Oliver said as he got up to follow the bailiff, wondering why he felt as though he was walking the last mile.

"I know you can do it," Oliver's mother said with a smile and a gentle pat on his shoulder in her usual motherly way.

He smiled at her as he entered the courtroom, appreciating the support he'd received from his parents and ex-girlfriend. He'd made a point of telling them as much from the start. Again, he wondered who he might be if his home and parents had been different, less stable. Would he be like Randolph, maybe?

Oliver sat in the witness seat, between the judge and the jury, and allowed himself to be sworn in, making sure to look the bailiff in the eye. His business with the bailiff done, he looked Jack Bennett in the eye, purposely avoiding looking at the defendant.

He felt more confident than he had while waiting in the hall, felt as though he was able to testify without being intimidated. Though it was the first trial he'd ever attended, let alone testified in, he paid attention. He knew that he'd have to testify in at least one more unless Audrey pled guilty to vandalizing his vehicle, which she had yet to do since her arrest.

Oliver kept in mind the fact that he had no control over what others did or did not say or do. Everyone made their choices. Sometimes others had to pay for those choices, but that is just how it worked.

He concentrated on his testimony only, drawing strength from Bennett, ready to honestly answer any question he was asked about the events he'd witnessed, his confidence high.

# #

About the Author

A lifelong resident of Central Jersey, David Manfre loves writing stories taking place in locations familiar to him because he believes that placing characters and events in familiar places helps to make his writing immediate and lively.

David also believes in living peacefully with as little violence as possible but knows that not everyone agrees with him.

He can be reached via email at trantor1701@yahoo.com *or on Facebook at* facebook.com/david.manfre1

LAST DANCE

Chelle Martin

The fiddle player traded licks with the electric guitar player on a popular country hoedown song while Amanda Smith's boots pounded the straw-covered patio in the midst of a barn dance atmosphere. The Smith home saw many a theme party and Amanda was the queen of charity balls. This ball, however, served a two-fold purpose. The first was to raise money for a newly proposed therapeutic riding center in Wall Township, so her immediate thought was to do away with champagne and caviar and opt for blue jeans and more down-home fun. Hay bales took the place of fountains and scarecrows and farmhands served drinks. The second was to celebrate her and her husband Mel's 30th wedding anniversary. At least for appearance sake.

Her dance partner husband matched her moves as a line dance instructor led the energetic crowd through a series of boot-scootin' dips and turns. But Amanda's eyes kept stealing looks at the singer of the band, Walt Bell, a handsome man she'd known many years ago while she worked as a barmaid part-time while attending Monmouth University in West Long Branch. She hadn't thought of him in years and had no idea he fronted this band. She'd hired The Santa Fe Riders solely on word of mouth reviews and knew they drew large crowds to their shows. Her arrangements for them to entertain were done through their booking manager over the phone.

"Okay, we're going to take a short break," the singer announced. "Grab yourselves a beer and we'll see you in a bit."

The partygoers applauded before dispersing in search of food, drinks, and mingling. "Honey, can I get you something from the bar?" Mel asked his wife.

Amanda's fingertips rubbed her temples. "No, I feel a headache coming on. I think I'd be better off with an aspirin and a club soda. But I should probably make the rounds like a good hostess. I'll find you in a bit." Mel placed a perfunctory kiss on her cheek and set off in the opposite direction.

Her husband had just about departed when her neighbor Eileen Radcliff grabbed her by the arm and pulled her aside. "Oh, honey, you've outdone yourself tonight. This party is fab and that singer...." She waved an imaginary fan at herself. "In a word—hot."

Amanda smiled, though she felt a twinge of jealousy. Eileen was wealthy, ten years younger, and had a Pilates-perfect body that accentuated her tight jeans. She was also divorced and available. Normally, Amanda wouldn't care who Eileen set her sights on, but when it came to Walt, she suddenly felt protective of their history as if she had some unspoken right of ownership to him. Only she couldn't bring up the past to Eileen. For sure, Mel would find out and think she'd invited the band for that sole reason. As it was, Amanda and her husband were trying to get over a rough patch in their marriage that she was determined to keep hidden from prying neighbors and those in their social circle.

Eileen's eyes looked past Amanda's shoulder, "Don't look now, but he's headed this way."

Then like that, Walt's eyes were staring into Amanda's. "Hey, you," he drawled in a tone that brought up old feelings a married woman shouldn't be having. He reached for Amanda's hand and his large musician's fingers closed around her delicate ones in an envelope of warmth. "Good to see you again," he said.

"You two know each other?" Eileen said, her eyes darting from her neighbor to the handsome band leader and back again.

"Oh, no, no, no," Amanda covered. "Mr. Bell and I met at a...a...wedding demo. Remember when my niece was looking at bands? That's where I got his card," she lied.

"You don't say," Eileen purred, not sounding totally convinced.

"Maybe you'd like a card," Walt said, producing one from his pocket and handing it to Eileen.

She reached for it, Amanda noticed, letting her hand linger a little longer than necessary, to accept it from Walt's fingertips.

"I'll definitely give you a call," she said and winked. For effect, she stuck the card inside her bra which peeked from her red and white checkered country-girl shirt. Satisfied with her prize, she smiled at Amanda and walked off.

Before Walt got too cozy into the conversation, Amanda whispered, "We can't talk here. I-I-didn't know you were with this band. I'm surprised you even remember me."

Walt laughed and threw a hand to his heart. "Not remember you? You are not a woman who is easily forgotten. Believe me."

Amanda felt the heat rise in her cheeks. She wanted to wrap her arms around Walt and be transported back in time to happier days. From the look in his eyes, he felt the same way.

"It was so long ago."

"The heart doesn't tell time. Remember all those songs I wrote about us way back then? Well, I still write songs, but now they're about you, the girl who got away."

"Walt...my husband..."

"Later tonight," he said, "at the gazebo." He nodded in the direction of an intricately lit structure located on a far corner of the elaborately sprawling property.

Before Amanda could speak, the bass player and Mel joined them from opposite directions. The bassist, Nate, hadn't changed much from the lanky chain-smoker that Amanda remembered. He was always the practical joker of the band.

"I hate to break up your reunion," Nate said, but Tiki's here." Amanda noticed Walt's posture become rigid at the mention of the name. Could it be the same Tiki from years back? She couldn't scan the crowd with her husband present. "And you'll never guess who else," Nate said. "O'Reilly's here, too."

"Excuse us," Walt said to his hosts. "Just about time to start the next set." He grabbed one of the beers the bassist was carrying, shot Amanda a parting smile, and moved to the stage.

"Tiki? I know it's not Tiki Barber. Where do I know that name from? And how do you know this singer?"

Amanda's head pounded at the onslaught of questions and no immediate fabrication presented itself, so she acquiesced with the truth. "It was a long time ago. I…"

"Wait, I remember that jerk. He's the one you were going with when we met. I knew he reminded me of someone. I can't believe you hired him."

"It wasn't intentional. I haven't seen him in decades. I had no idea he was with this band." Amanda could protest the innocence of the situation to the ends of the earth, but there would be no convincing Mel. His trust issues started in childhood after being abandoned by his father when questions of his paternity arose. Rather than succumb to a DNA test, his father chose to leave Mel and his mother for a woman in his office.

"Here," Mel said through clenched teeth. "I got you an aspirin and a club soda." He shoved the glass into Amanda's hand causing its contents to splatter onto her clothes.

Amanda sighed, but took the white pill and swallowed it. If she argued, the situation would escalate even more. "Thank you," she said, touching his arm. "Really, this is all a big misunderstanding."

Mel yanked his arm away from her and stormed off. So much for appearance's sake, she thought. The encounter didn't really worry her though. They'd clear it up in counseling like so many other arguments. It was Tiki's presence that scared her. Which of her guests had brought a notorious drug dealer to her party?

* * *

The band played its final set a little after midnight, but the crowd was still going strong. The dancing continued even when the crew started breaking down the equipment and packing up the truck. The music now switched to contemporary tunes pouring from a very expensive outdoor sound system wirelessly programmed from the interior of the home. Sinatra crooned a love song and all partners were moving in time to a slow, sensual tempo.

Amanda made the rounds, thanking her benefactors for their generosity. The new riding center was sure to make a difference in their community, and everyone in attendance was invited to the eventual ribbon-cutting ceremony to announce its opening, hopefully in a few short months. Between hugs and handshakes, Amanda's eyes darted toward the gazebo in the distance, her mind weighing the consequences of going there. Her marriage was in shambles, but it was also comfortable in a way. Granted, she and Mel had issues. All couples did. Thirty years of history. Like the rusty car you keep patching and fixing because you aren't ready to part with it.

Initially, it started with Mel working late and spending time away on business. Amanda had had her suspicions. She'd watched enough daytime talk shows to recognize the signs of a cheating spouse. Once she discovered the truth, it had devastated her, of course. She'd never actually met her rival; she just saw a text message with a photo of a woman in a negligee wearing a fancy Mardi-Gras-type mask. The woman, judging by her firm body, was probably ten years younger, much like Eileen, with perky breasts and flawless skin. Marriage counseling was getting them through it, convincing her it was a mid-life crisis on her husband's part. No big deal; all men do it.

Their counselor advised them that things wouldn't go back to normal overnight, but Mel had been getting home at a reasonable hour after insisting he'd ended the affair. The hang-up phone calls had ended, and he no longer arrived home reeking of hotel soap or another woman's perfume. Amanda, still learning to trust again, periodically checked his phone while he was in the shower. No improper pictures or texts were anywhere in sight.

But Walt. Walt was a different threat altogether. He hadn't been a fling. He'd been her soul mate, or so she'd thought in the innocence of youth. She had convinced herself that their love was forever. He was passionate and fun and their nights reflected a bright future together. Only Walt never grew up. The band, the parties, the music. It had consumed him more than she ever could. Recreational drug use had become routine. Amanda hated being around the stuff. She hated the sight and smell of it.

And then there was Tiki, providing a steady supply of pills and powder, lighting up the band and slowing them down so they could keep a steady schedule. If he wasn't supplying, O'Reilly was. Crosstown rivals. Things turned deadly with a band member's "accidental" overdose. The case was never proven otherwise; the truth buried with its victim.

Amanda had needed stability, someone with ambition and an attainable goal that would ensure a life of status and comfort. Even though she considered herself a strong, independent woman, she yearned for security and someone who could take care of her financially and emotionally. She needed a partner, an equal, someone on the same page, with her same drive.

Mel had been a business major at Monmouth who began his studies on a sports scholarship. Amanda had met him through his mother Victoria when she happened to be sitting next to her at a Hawks basketball game. "That's my son," she'd said proudly. After the women had shared a pleasant conversation during halftime, she insisted upon introducing her son after the game. Amanda had been impressed by Mel's work ethic in addition to his boyish good looks. He could be a bit cocky at times, but his old-fashioned good manners like opening doors and putting down the toilet seat won her over. The little things. Mel had been a polished stone compared to Walt's diamond-in-the-rough personality. Walt's potential was there, but he never seemed to get beyond the partying and band nights with the boys. And even though he'd been faithful to her, Amanda had grown tired of groupies, the drugs, and the fear that one day Walt would move on and she'd miss her chance at a good life. After Amanda found Mel, she left and never looked back.

She set her soda down on a table and rubbed her arms which shivered in the cool breeze. People buzzed around her, sauntering in and out of their esteemed and grandiose home, all having a wonderful time. If not her relationship with her husband, at least her fund-raiser was a huge success.

To top off their evening, she'd hired a fireworks company to set off a dazzling display. The first loud bang startled her and some of those nearby, but once the gathering saw the explosion of colorful sparkling light, the dancing stopped and everyone cheered.

Amanda glanced again at the gazebo with its sparkling white lights beckoning her toward it like a great lighthouse in a dark sea of blackness. With everyone's attention focused on the fireworks, now was her chance. She took a step in that direction, then another. Her head felt a bit woozy, even though she hadn't consumed any alcohol. The aspirin had dulled her headache, but suddenly she couldn't stop yawning.

Her conscience told her not to go, but her heart was winning out. She needed to speak to Walt, if for no other reason than to prove to herself that she had made the right decision in choosing Mel. As the gap closed between her and the great structure, her mind whirled with the many possibilities of where this conversation could go. When she had felt his familiar touch tonight, she'd been transported to the happier times, the days before the band, when life had been just the two of them.

As she reached the gazebo, Amanda saw him sitting there in shadow, reclined against the seat, long legs stretched out in front of him. She stepped up onto the structure and sat beside him, but he made no move to greet her. Then she saw it, the needle sticking out of his arm. Her body tensed and her hands flew to her face.

"Oh, God!" she cried. "Walt! No!" Amanda felt for a pulse but found none. His eyes were unfocused, staring blankly into space. Walt Bell was clearly dead. She started to cry inconsolably as she flung her arms around his neck. The weight of his body sagged against her, his arm brushing limply against her leg.

"Isn't this touching."

Amanda started at the sound of her husband's voice. "Mel, call an ambulance!"

Her husband stepped from the shadows of some Arborvitae along with Eileen. "I will, but first we need to tend to you," he said.

"What? I don't understand." Amanda shivered. Was she going into shock?

Then she spotted the syringe Eileen was holding, but her mind refused to believe her husband and her neighbor could be capable of such a heinous act. Murder was something you heard about on the news, not something that happened in your own neighborhood, much less your own house.

"How's your head, darling? I think I might have mixed up your aspirin with an Ambien. There may have been another in one of your club sodas. I didn't realize you needed enough to down a horse."

"What have you done? And…Eileen, you helped him? Why?" The light played across her neighbor's face and reality smacked her hard. Eileen not only resembled the woman in her husband's text message, she was that woman. They'd played her all along.

Eileen shrugged. "Sorry, Amanda. But we needed a way to be together."

Amanda had been a fool to believe her husband would drop his mistress in order to save their marriage. He must have continued his affair behind her back while playing the remorseful husband. She hadn't even thought he might have another cell phone, a phone he must have bought to keep in touch with Eileen.

"Mel, I forgave you. I thought you loved me," Amanda said, still absently clinging to Walt.

"Ha! And yet here you are with your lover," he said, feigning hurt. "After all these years, one last chance for a reunion. Too bad you both gave into temptation."

"No!" Amanda sobbed. "You know I never did drugs. Nobody will believe you!"

"We don't need to prove anything," he said, as Eileen handed him the syringe and he began to scrutinize its readiness. "You won't feel a thing," he said. "For what it's worth, neither did your boyfriend."

Amanda grasped the gazebo's railing to stand, struggling backward, as her feet slipped awkwardly and she fell off the platform. Eileen and Mel pounced on her together and she struggled to escape. Fireworks still exploded above, muting Amanda's muffled cries for help.

Eileen held Amanda's arm in a vise-like grip while Mel fumbled with the needle. One push of the plunger and it would be over soon.

Amanda struggled to stay conscious, but the Ambien overtook any hopes she had of escape. With a half-hearted attempt to overthrow her assailants, Amanda depleted her last ounce of strength. Knowing there was no escape, she silently prayed to God for mercy. And then an extremely loud firework exploded much closer than the others.

"Get away from her or one of you gets the next bullet!"

Amanda felt Eileen's grip loosen and she went limp, her breath coming in shallow gasps.

"Move away from her. Now! On the ground, both of you! Face down. Move!"

Suddenly, someone was at Amanda's side, speaking. "She's okay. She's alive. Where's the damn ambulance?"

At the mention of the word, a siren wailed in the distance.

"It's okay," Nate said, as he helped Amanda into a sitting position. He cradled her back and held her hand supportively while checking for a pulse.

Through what little awareness she still possessed, Amanda saw a familiar face, that of O'Reilly, his weapon trained on her husband and mistress.

"You okay, Mandy?" he asked. Amanda forced a weak smile, then collapsed into the bassist's arms.

* * *

O'Reilly was the lone visitor in Amanda's hospital room. When she awakened, he held up a shield. "DEA," he said, sporting a big grin.

"Really?" Amanda managed a small laugh. "You decided to join the good guys," she said. Her voice sounded hoarse, strained. "If anyone would have told me that thirty years ago, I never would have believed them."

"Be glad it's not thirty years ago."

"Where's my husband?"

"Monmouth County, awaiting arraignment. Eileen Radcliff, too. You know his accomplice?"

Amanda snorted. "Our neighbor, his lover," she said, barely audibly, breaking eye contact with her long-ago acquaintance. "I'm such a fool."

"Hey, don't do that to yourself," he said. "If anyone's a fool, it's your husband. He thought he had a perfect plan to collect your insurance and get you out of the way. At least that appears to be his motive. It wasn't just to be with his girlfriend."

"Life insurance? He took out a policy on me?"

"Found it sitting plain as day on your dining room table. As I said, he's a fool."

Amanda pondered that a moment. The night had certainly been full of surprises. "Tiki," she continued, "What was he doing at my party?"

"He was Eileen's guest. She saw the band name on the invitation and happened to Google them with your husband present. He immediately recognized Walt Bell in the band photos. I guess that's when he decided to drug you. A simple plan to garner sympathy for himself: the poor husband trying to put his marriage back together, only to have his wife run into an old lover and take up where they left off, ending in an accidental overdose."

"I never did drugs. He'd never get anyone to believe it."

"A needle in your arm and no witnesses? People get away with things. Heroin has become so prevalent now. I'm sure you've seen the governor's ads on TV telling people how to get help."

Amanda nodded as she shivered involuntarily. "But I don't understand how Tiki came to be at my party."

"Further conversation with Ms. Radcliff revealed that your husband hired a PI to find Tiki. He lured him to the party with a big cash payoff. Told him some old friends wanted to reconnect."

"And Tiki fell for it?"

O'Reilly shrugged. "Cash talks. Plus, he clearly remembered Walt and you."

Amanda silently processed the information for a few minutes. Her husband had hatched an elaborate plot to kill her so he could be with his mistress and cash in on a life insurance policy that she wasn't even aware of.

"Eileen told you all of this?"

"That was the statement she gave. She jumped at the idea of confessing if she could reap the benefit of a reduced sentence. Apparently, Ms. Radcliff has no real love for your husband."

"And you," Amanda said, "How did you get invited to my party?"

"I didn't. I was undercover with the catering company. Though I thought my cover was blown when one of the musicians recognized me. Tiki had been under surveillance for a while. We were hoping he'd lead us to some bigger offenders, but...." He shrugged.

"Thank you for saving my life," Amanda said. Her eyes welled up at the thought of how close she'd come to being murdered. "But, Walt..." She couldn't hold back the tears any longer. He didn't deserve to die like that.

"Hey," O'Reilly said, moving closer to her bedside. "You might want to wipe those tears," he said, handing her a tissue from a nearby box.

He moved to the door and tapped on it. A bedraggled looking Walt Bell walked into the room with a nurse assisting him with his mobile IV unit.

His voice was faint, but it was still music to Amanda's ears. "As I started to say at your party, Amanda. Good to see you again."

# #

CHELLE MARTIN

About the Author

Chelle is a member of Mystery Writers of America where she has served on the NY Chapter's Mentor Committee, and a member of Sisters in Crime where she has served as President and Vice President of the Central Jersey chapter. She's published in numerous mystery anthologies and is currently working on a novel. More information can be found on her website: www.ChelleMartin.com.

HAPPY 30TH BIRTHDAY, MY DEAR

Nicki Montaperto

Curled up and comfortable, Jane slept deeply, totally unaware of the thin, vile mattress on which she rested or the ugly dinginess of the room in which she reposed. Her rare peacefulness and satiny full-length shirtwaist gown highlighted her delicate features, making more shocking the disheveled, torn apart state of her once carefully-coifed golden hair.

Suddenly, her breath started to quicken in short, harsh bursts. Her beautifully manicured hands began to clench and unclench. Her eyes fluttered wildly under closed lids until with a sudden, frightened thrust, she bolted to her feet. Her eyes swept the room frantically, then instantly relaxed. Her breath slowed, replaced with a relieved smile.

"Safe," she whispered, gratefully. "I am safe. There is no one here."

Slowly, her eyes swept the faded, dirty surroundings with incredulous pleasure. Relaxing fully, she joyfully slid her hands up her arms to hug her shoulders in a warm self-embrace.

"Finally. A refuge," she whispered. "More! A haven. At last, I have escaped."

Turning slowly to further view her surroundings, a sudden bolt of fear stopped her cold. Sensing without seeing the mirror on the wall behind her, she felt an unexpected pull. She resisted, but it continued to beckon. Strongly. Irresistibly. From the moment she had entered the room, she had instantly felt its threat. Still, it drew her, pulling with the force of a magnet, as it had from the moment of her arrival just hours ago.

"But why?" she asked herself aloud. "Why? This time you will not win. This time I will not give in. I must not give in."

But would this work? Thoughts piled one on another in her mind. Would fighting the pull be the answer to breaking its hold? What about mirrors in other places? Would she need to avoid them too? Was it even possible not to peer into a mirror ever again? If not, how could she ever consider herself completely free?

Slowly, she realized that she had to take control of her life. This was the final hurdle she had to conquer. The question was simple. "If I do not conquer this fear now, how can I ever trust this new freedom?"

With a reluctant force of will and fascination, she turned to the glass and gazed deeply into her own eyes. Her trembling fingers touched her hair, making her aware that it was no longer thick, shimmering and gold. It now drooped dull and limp. Her hazel eyes, once bright and lively, looked haunted and hollow.

"Who is this stranger peering back at me?" she asked, feeling the horror beginning to grow.

Frantically, she closed her eyes, then opened them and looked again, her heart full of hope. With a fierceness that frightened her, she tried to make the image go away. But it would not.

Suddenly, she thought she heard a knock.

Frozen, she listened closely. At first, it was just a soft, tentative tap—more felt than heard. She turned her back on the mirror, pressing her body against the dresser. The tap at the door came again, a little louder.

"Discovered again?" she whispered frantically. "No. No. I was so careful this time. It cannot be. I will not answer."

But then, insistent and against Jane's will, her visitor entered—as silent and accusing, as ever.

At first, Jane stood paralyzed. Then, hatred slowly seeped into her, followed by a sudden calmness. With the calmness, a new feeling entered her being—a confidence she had never before experienced. This was a new plateau. She had never reached this far in her plans. Suddenly, she knew. This time there would be no surrender.

Her words became measured. Even to herself, her voice was surprisingly sympathetic and in control. More than in control. She felt in command.

"So, you've found me again," she acknowledged. "It's been so long and yet I knew you would."

She tilted her head playfully to the side. "Oh, my dear. So solemn? So silent? After all this time? But then, you always did your best—or should we say your worst—in silence.

"Come, sit down." She pulled a chair away from the table and gestured toward it.

"It must have been difficult for you to come. Especially here." She swept the room with her hand.

"Well, this time I am pleased that you have come. It is time for a long-awaited talk."

She motioned toward the table. "Please, have a seat. Let me get you something. Some tea, perhaps?" Jane started toward the stove but stopped abruptly.

"What's wrong? Oh, I see. You do *not* want tea but you're afraid to refuse. Afraid I'll suspect that you don't trust me." Jane smiled again, sympathetically. "Ah, if someone had tried to kill me twice, I wouldn't trust her either."

Jane stamped her foot in mock petulance. "Oh, don't look so uncomfortable. You see, I have always understood *you* even though you have never understood me."

Determined to stay in control, Jane crossed to the table, pulled out the other chair and sat down. Her eyes became bright and lively. For just an instant, her glance darted involuntarily to the mirror. Finding it no longer disturbing, she sighed thankfully and relaxed against the back of the chair. Cupping her chin in her hand, she eyed her visitor smugly.

"Well, then, what shall we do? Shall we just visit? No, don't protest. I have so much to say."

Deliberately sitting taller to match her newfound confidence, Jane took control of the situation sweetly but firmly.

"Well, dear, you haven't spoken all this while. For once, let's keep it that way. You see, I *want* to talk. I *need* to talk and this time, I need you to listen.

"Correction! You *will* listen. And you won't speak until I'm through."

Punctuated by a long, tense silence, the command hung in the air until Jane, expecting challenge but receiving none, continued.

"You know, you wouldn't believe it but, all my life, I've had feelings, too. Oh yes, you've tried to ignore them, suppress them— you've even tried to change them. But nothing ever worked, did it?

"Perhaps, part of the problem was what I said before. You know, that I always understood you but you never understood me.

Oh, I don't blame you entirely. Father was in it, too. In fact, I think sometimes I could have handled you if he weren't always there. With the two of you teamed up against me, I was helpless.

"Perhaps—perhaps if Mother had stayed—but no, *his* laws, *his* expectations—who could live by them? Only *you* were willing to try.

"My struggles with the two of you began quite early too, starting when I wanted to play with those children who father said were 'beneath my station.'

"In Paris, I wanted to visit the small cafes with adagio dancers and torch singers. Yes, I even yearned to know what it would be like to have a Frenchman make love to me. Maybe even many Frenchmen!

"But was *I* to have *my* way? Hah! As usual, you had other plans. You and our dear father.

"Instead, we visited the Louvre and dined with the ambassador.

In Italy, we saw the Coliseum and ruins of a civilization long dead, while the world of the living surged by us in the gondolas of Venice and in the back streets of Rome.

"And so it went for the rest of our stay.

"I returned with you from Europe more desperate than before I left.

"But did you notice? Did you care? You, with all your rules and regulations and self-control. Could you ever hope to understand that I was ready to live life? Could you?"

Jane slapped the table with her hand. "Of course not! Instead, you decided it was time to chain my spirit even more. It was time to squeeze the unruly, freely-shaped piece of clay even tighter into the mold. You both decided I should marry. And quickly.

"Did you think I'd forgotten my musician?"

As she uttered the word "musician," a sudden memory slammed into her mind. Her hands flew to her face, her fingers pressed hard into her eyes and against her mouth until she was almost cutting off her own breath.

Frozen, she sat with her eyes tightly closed, her hands still pressing her face until she could press no harder. Finally, after a long moment, she released a harsh breath. Her shoulders relaxed. A stillness gradually poured itself into her, bringing a serenity she had not felt for what seemed like an eternity.

* * *

Surrendering totally to the new sensations, she opened herself to what was happening. It was more than just a memory that came to her now. She suddenly found herself in a place where she had lived the only moments of happiness she had ever experienced.

She heard the music. She heard laughter. She sensed movement and excitement. Daring to open her eyes, she smiled in disbelief. Was this a memory? A fantasy? No, neither. She was here. It was real!

She looked down at herself, not surprised that she was wearing the cut frock of a simple peasant woman. In fact, completely gone was any memory of the conservatively designed gown she wore just a moment ago. It simply did not exist.

Nor did the quiet somber room in which she and her visitor had sat. Instead, music swirled about her, moving her feet with its rhythm. Her body swayed and relaxed, becoming part of it.

Through the sounds surrounding her, a woman's voice called out, "Jane, Jane, come join us!" Jane's eyes swept the room. Now seeing it more clearly through all the smoke and dim lights, she found herself surrounded by people dressed as she was. Not caring. Just laughing and calling to her to join them.

"Are you all right?" asked a beautiful, dark-haired young woman as she sat down next to Jane. "Where have you been? Jonathan's been looking for you. We've all been helping him."

Jane tried to answer but the young woman pulled her to her feet. "No matter," she laughed. "You've been found now and..."

She was interrupted as Jane felt a hand on her arm turning her completely. In an instant, she found herself folded into the arms of a tall, muscular man with laughing blue eyes and a full head of tawny-colored hair.

"I've been looking for you everywhere. Where did you go, my beauty? Have you been evading me?"

Before she could answer, his lips came fully on hers, cutting off her breath as his arms pulled her tightly against him. For one involuntary moment, Jane tried to pull away but, in that instant, full recognition came back. Time dropped away and she had no awareness whatever that she had ever left. It was as though she had been in this place forever, even after her dreams about her father discovering her. Suddenly deliriously happy once again, she surrendered herself totally into his arms, returning his kisses with a fervor she remembered with joy. Now she knew absolutely where she was.

"I am here. I have never been gone," she said, completely believing what she was saying. "But if I was, I promise I will never go missing again—not even for an instant."

And so, the evening wore on as timeless as ever since she had first arrived in this place. She laughed, she danced, she kissed and was kissed back. At last, her lover said the words she had been longing to hear.

"It is late, my lovely," Jonathan whispered. "It is time. I want you all to myself."

They walked in the happy silence of the moonlit night. Jane followed without question for he had led her this way before and she knew what awaited her alone again with him. As they reached the cottage, he caught her up lightly in his arms and carried her inside. Her urgency matched his as they entered and he wasted no time.

Crazed and hungry from the deprivation caused by the separation he still believed, they fell upon the bed. Jane surrendered herself to him again without a thought about anything else.

As the dawn broke the next morning, she lazily turned to him under the heavy quilts and nestled against his chest.

"Where *did* you disappear?" he asked. "I looked for you everywhere."

Have I really been away? Jane still wondered, for she truly could not remember any separation. Not knowing what to answer, Jane touched his lips, his face, his chest. "I still do not feel as though I have ever been gone. But, it does not matter," she whispered. "I am here now and will never leave you again."

"I had the priest ready to marry us," he told her. "I didn't know what to do, where to look for you. Suddenly, you were just gone. How did it happen?"

"Hush," she said again. "I am here to stay. Just you, me and your beautiful music."

"My beautiful music?" he repeated her words. "For a long time, my saxophone stayed silent. When I started to play again, it just cried out for you. I didn't know what to do."

For the next few days, Jane reveled in the life she was living. She was still wondering why he believed she had been gone. Truly, to her, she had never left. Their life together had never been interrupted. She did have some sense of a dream—a nightmare really—about a separation. But it never really happened. Her father had never found her. He had never kidnapped her and taken her from the life she had always wanted. Their plans for marrying had never been arrested. No separation had ever occurred.

But then unwanted, an uneasiness began to stir in Jane. If no separation had ever occurred, why were these other memories haunting her? How had her father entered the reality she was now living? He had never even met Jonathan. Nor would he have cared that she loved him and he loved her. That they were already lovers. That they were planning to be together forever.

Nothing mattered to her father except for the now growing thought that he had really found her in the marketplace one fateful day. Had it really happened? Had he really kidnapped her and taken her back home?

Suddenly, Jane jolted upright in her chair. The harshness of the present reality bludgeoned her senses. Incredulous and distraught, once again, she found herself once again sitting at a table with her visitor in this dingy room. She looked wildly about her to be sure, her heart breaking with the return of reality.

She sat forward in her chair, a look of heartbreak in her eyes. "How could I forget leaving Jonathan? How could you have taken me from him? Neither you nor Father ever even knew his name. I don't even believe you knew he existed. How much he meant to me. Or that we had planned our future together."

Now, once more totally back to reality, Jane stared into the eyes of her visitor.

"Were you envious that I had found the kind of love I wanted instead of the sterile relationship you and Father planned for me?

"Once you had me back, you arranged my marriage, you and Father.

"John Dexter Harris! He was your choice for me.

"And the man behind the name? I cried out that I did not love him! Warned you I would not have him. But you tuned me out!

"So, I stayed quiet and you were fooled into thinking I had accepted my fate.

"Let's see, was it two days, or three days, before the wedding? Well, no matter. That was the first time I tried to kill you.

"I locked us in that small, dirty room in that small, dirty hotel— how I laughed to see you cringing even to sit upon the gray sheets.

"It was a horror, I'll admit. And I could have used a drink just then myself. But for your sake, I ordered only tea, hoping it would make things just a little bit easier for you.

"But even to this day, there is one thing I have never figured out," Jane said, her brow furrowed with a question.

"Such a large dose of sleeping powder. And its work already was begun. How did you fight it?

"Dear God! Why didn't you just go to sleep and die?" She slapped the table again.

"Instead, somehow you knew I'd drugged you and you called our darling father.

"Of course, he rushed to rescue you and, though neither of you would listen to me before or then, I *did* accomplish something."

Jane uttered a long, exaggerated sigh. "Father stopped the wedding—but decided that I needed to go into a rest home for a while. And supposedly, 'for my own good,' you agreed."

She smiled with mock understanding. "Oh, you both kept it very hush-hush and proper. *You* signed the papers and Father signed them, too. You knew better than to ask *me* to sign.

"For a year, I lived in that dreadful, unreal world. We ate on schedule, slept on schedule and even talked to the doctors on schedule. And finally, you both decided I was subdued enough to be allowed to live in the real world again, and you let me out. Out into what?

Jane shook her head slowly. "Another world of plans and schedules, all neatly regulated by your version of proper behavior and proper living?

"Living. Hah! How long did you think I'd take it? Again, I fooled you. Behaved for a whole year and when you and Father began to relax, I struck again!"

Jane tipped her head with a calculating look. "But, by then, I knew that in order to be free, I would have to kill not only you but Father, too.

"Remember? The servants were off that night when I had finally found the courage. That is, all except Joseph. Miserable wretch! I thought he was off, too. but he had only gone to the post office.

"When he returned, I told him a call had come that his mother had become desperately ill. He believed me and left immediately.

"You and Father had gone to bed early, as usual, for what I thought would be your final sleep. It would have been, too, if Joseph hadn't decided to call his home from the station to check on his mother. He found out about my lie and came back and saved you both from the gas."

With a slap of her hand on the table, Jane eyed her visitor with anger. "And again, you and Father put me away.

"How long have I been gone, my dear? You see, I've lost track of time. And how did you find out I'd escaped?

"I knew you'd find out, of course. Somehow you always seem to know what I am doing and when. It's almost as though you have an 'in' to my mind—as though you were my other self."

Jane waved her hand nonchalantly. "But no matter. You're here now and we've had our little talk. Now, how about that tea?"

Jane viewed her visitor disdainfully. "Don't look so frightened, you fool! You see, I've finally realized it's useless for me to try to kill you. You just seem to go and on, like one of those toys with sand in the bottom. Every time I hit you, you pop up straight again and I'm the one who gets knocked down."

As Jane poured the tea at the stove in the corner, she kept her back to the table and emptied a small vial of powder into one of the cups. Carrying the cups across the room, she set them on the table, placing the cup containing the powder in front of herself.

Smugly, she took a sip, replaced the cup and sat back in her chair. Suddenly, a look of sympathy crossed her face.

"Oh, you're still anxious, my dear. You'd like to trust me but you're still afraid. I guess I can't really blame you."

With a sudden movement, she switched the cups.

"Here, take the one I've tasted. Maybe then you'll believe me. And look…"

With a look of satisfaction on her face, Jane raised the cup she had just placed onto her own saucer to her lips. Feeling her visitor's eyes upon her, she sipped until the tea was gone, then set the cup down, and waited with an expectant look.

But the other cup stayed in its place on the other side of the table. Her visitor made no move to touch it.

With a sudden cry of fury, Jane jumped to her feet and stood hovering over the table. Her fingers gripped the edge, whitening. Her voice became a hoarse, incredulous whisper.

"You bitch! A lifetime I have done your will and still, you hesitate? Oh, no," she said, her voice low and menacing. "This time you shall do as I say. Father cannot help you now. Oh, yes, I've seen to that. You stand alone. Obey my will. Or by God! I'll kill you now."

Slowly, Jane lifted the cup and carried it to her own pale, trembling lips. She drained the contents and replaced the empty cup on its saucer.

For a moment, her shoulders slumped with relief, but suddenly, she straightened, turned and crossed to the mirror.

With a look of triumph, she stared at her reflection.

The image before her eyes became young and neat, prim and proper.

"You fool," she said, speaking between her teeth. "It's done. It is really done."

With her eyes closed, she drew her breath in deeply, deliciously, held it a moment, then expelled it slowly. A satisfied smile illuminated her entire face as she peered into her mirrored reflection.

"Happy 30th birthday, my dear. With you gone, I'm free to live the life I want to live at last."

With a victorious smile on her lips, Jane collapsed to the floor.

# #

About the Author

Nicki Montaperto has been writing stories since she was seven years old, and sold her first story just before her fifth child was born. She is a freelance writer, author of three other books, as well as many short stories and magazine articles. She has taught courses in fiction and non-fiction. Nicki has five grown children and lives with her husband, Richard, in New Jersey where she is writing a sequel to Witness to Treason. She can be reached via email at nickidm@verizon.net

THIRTY YEARS TO LIFE

L. A. Preschel

All of Gunther Hauptmann's numbers added up precisely for me. Thirty years old, worth thirty million dollars, and given thirty years-to-life for first-degree murder.

A perfect *trip three-zero.*

The prosecution's summation of evidence convicted an American Aristocrat proving Lady Justice is blind and fair. Catherine, my employer, refused to believe the math. She was well-acquainted with the Blueblood's corollary: remove Lady Justice's blindfold, glare into her eyes while wielding a blank check, and any conviction can be overturned. Aristocratic entitlement prevails over integrity, earning a social injustice no average citizen could ever secure.

The circumstantial evidence against Gunther appeared conclusive. He shot his mother with the gun he filched from the gun club only ten days before. He claimed he returned the Ruger to his brother's lockbox at the club prior to the murder. According to the manager's documentation, brother Rupert signed the weapon back in four days after his mother's death. A mystic feat, since Rupert was two-days post-suicide at that time.

A jury of twelve peers, none owning a villa in St. Bart's, gave Gunther a chance for parole on the thirtieth anniversary of his incarceration.

My boss, Catherine, a lawyer of high esteem and renown knew the family from attending D.A.R. luncheons, cotillion balls, and going to the same prep schools. Gunther's smiling face on the Times' society page made him incapable of murder. His conviction rocked the *noblesse oblige* center of Catherine's brain.

In my cerebrum, there was not even a tremor. As a prominent lawyer's low-class no-class gumshoe, my non-Aristocratic brain is devoid of a *noblesse oblige* center.

My opinion? Justice spoke. Let him wear the school colors of Sing Sing Correctional University—orange with black block letters "G. Hauptmann." A Harvard MBA or not, he will receive an egalitarian education while attending the institution at Ossining.

Catherine reminded me of my definition of opinions and added her own genteel flair to it. "They're flatus, they hold no substance. Everyone has them, but polite people hold them in, to spare others displeasure."

To make matters worse, Lilith Hauptmann-Vanderbilt, Gunther's sister, called our meeting a *High Tea.*

Detective Samantha Cochran at a High freakin' Tea? "You gotta be kiddin' me. I've worn two dresses in my whole life; one to my first communion and the other going solo to my prom."

Catherine, who in my heart would always be the D.R.B. (Damn Royal Bitch), and I held opposing malodorous opinions on my attendance at the so-called High Tea. Neither of us tightened our sphincters sufficiently to prevent the others' displeasure.

"I do not attend social events," I repeated as I took off the Dior gown for the fifth time that afternoon. "Got it?" I asked Catherine with my fiercest glare.

Clarice took the gown to re-stitch the bodice to my shape.

Catherine laughed. "You will attend. Clarice, tighten that waist. She is not Ms. Sponge Bob, square-dress."

"*Impossible a faire*, Madame, no waist has she." In the salon of Catherine's townhouse, three mad female monkeys prepared to throw dung. "Her build is meant to lifts the weights."

Nothing new about a ruckus between the Damn Royal Bitch and her in-house peon of a private investigator. Since we met, we have bonded by backbiting, but in those four years, we became besties.

So, Clarice, Catherine's housekeeper-seamstress attacked Catherine's ten-year-old Dior, tailoring it from fitting Catherine's curvy five-foot-nine-inches to my five-foot-one-inch fireplug figure.

Torn Wrangler jeans and a tee shirt wouldn't pass the dress code at High Tea. I swallowed a sigh. That would feel too much like surrender for me.

After an hour of bicker-fitting, I needed to escape Catherine's ire so I lit a cigar. It served its purpose–she left. My blood pressure returned to mildly high. I resisted the urge to flick live ashes on the pink silk. I'm not a silk person. Nope, I'm pure Irish biker babe. *Where's my Guinness*?

After another hour of on-and-off's, the dress was good enough. My wide black-leather belt secured it at the waist. The buckle said *Harley-Davidson* in script.

I own no high heels-too dangerous. Instead, Catherine, dressed like Oz's good Witch, waved her hands and poof, my lace-up cop boots were "retro-chic."

She loaned me a Chanel shoulder bag to hold my wallet, blank index cards, and a Walther PPK, my backup weapon.

"Don't pack any death torpedoes," Catherine ordered, referring to my smokes.

The scent of even an unlit cigar nauseates her.

Dressed like Elly May Clampett, I accompanied Catherine to the Winchester Hotel to interview Lilith Hauptmann-Vanderbilt.

My boots echoed on the mosaic-tiled floor of the lobby as if it was a cave.

Catherine scolded. "Do not stomp. This is Polite Society. Walk like a lady. Dainty."

She sighted Lilith and skipped ahead. Her high heels clicked as she rushed like an excited child to an empty swing.

"I'm a dainty damsel," I mimicked as I tiptoed behind her. Making a soft *swoosh*. "Catherine, is that my dress?" I asked.

"Sssh." Catherine raised her hand and blocked my path. "My friend, as a damsel, you are *not* in distress, you are a carrier. Quiet."

"Got it." I followed her into the Tearoom.

The well-padded carpeting on the restaurant's floor thwarted my stomping. An enlarged copy of *The Last Judgment* by Michelangelo, the carpet rivaled the electric candelabras hanging from the fifty-foot-high ceilings for garishness. Wheeled teacarts filled with pastries squeaked across a bookless library filled with overdressed inert silver-haired librarians.

Hidden behind a rolling service tower of petite fours sat an emaciated brunette in a Givenchy chiffon dress. A single strand of pearls encircled the whiter-than-ivory stovepipe-neck of a bulimic Amanda Seyfried. Lilith, the daughter of the victim, was the sister of Gunther and Rupert Hauptmann.

"Lilly, you look so wonderful." Catherine gushed in a mouse's whisper.

Even so, two obese great-grandmothers, jowls rippling from chewing their pastry-cud, lowered their teacups and their noses to disparage the uncouth youth whose emotions were so obstreperous.

The seated living-skeleton offered a limp-wristed hand. "Glad your mundane work did not detain you. Working is such a bother." She grimaced and sipped her tea.

"I relish my work," Catherine answered. "But I haven't agreed to handle your case yet."

"You simply must. Who better to work for than a true friend? Working is so drab anyway. And you choose to? Me, I'd starve and go naked rather than work."

"Or kill?"

Lilith ignored my whisper. Catherine nudged me. I shut up.

"I work because I can." Catherine sat on the remaining chair and asked the white-gloved server to retrieve a third. "I bring justice. I don't sit on my assets and play Duchess of Windsor."

"Tsk, justice?" Lilith sneered. "What a charade. Justice begot what for my brother?"

The manservant retrieved a red-velvet cushioned chair. The gold scrollwork on its back was raised, ornate, and truly annoying. *No wonder the rich sit erect at tea.*

The table was minuscule. Frequent collisions of knees prevented crowding the third chair around it. *Like holding a Shriner's convention in a coat closet.* I wedged in, and remembered Catherine's suggestions: purse on lap, knees together, sit up, shallow breathing, and calm, tacit respect.

Lilith squinted at me. Catherine's hired hand who'd invaded her soirée. Her look asked, why had a scholarship student sat at her sorority's table?

"And you are?"

"A working person by necessity. I'm protection," I answered.

Lilith looked more perplexed. I endeavored to enlighten her.

"Catherine's a sap. I stop the world from screwing with her."

"Such language. Catherine, you associate with that?"

Catherine's I-win smile spread across her face. "She proves people innocent." It was a pat on my back for "splendid" work. She added, "Sam Cochran meet Lilith Hauptmann."

"Hauptmann-Vanderbilt," she corrected. "Charmed."

Although she was anything but. Instead of offering her pasty hand, she picked up a triangle of rye bread covered with a creamy spread. With a small spoon, she slimed tiny black balls on it.

"Ever seen Caspian Caviar?" She did not offer me any. "Thought not. It's yummy." She spoke with her mouth full. "Gunther is miserable in jail. He is innocent. Free him."

Catherine retrieved her Mont Blanc pen from her Fendi purse. I reluctantly removed the rubber band from my index cards. Catherine handed me the black pen. At NASCAR, the race starts when they drop the flag. We initiated the inquiry into the Marilyn Hauptmann murder by the passing of Catherine's pen.

"Please start before your mother was murdered," I said.

"Am I supposed to communicate with *her*?" Lilith pointed at me as if identifying her Water Spaniel's fresh poop so the butler could scoop it up.

I countered. "After eating that whole slice of bread, you must be stuffed." I pushed the little urn of unborn beluga sturgeons aside. I placed a mini-tape recorder where it had been. "Talk to this. Better?"

"I talk to real people." Lilith snapped her fingers at the server and directed him to move the cart of petite fours away from my side.

He obeyed with a nod and gave us space, but stood at the ready. His posture, silence, and distance embodied Lilith's role model for me.

I ignored her wishes. "Start before Marilyn's murder."

"When I talk, *real* people listen. I'm a Hauptmann and a Vanderbilt." She turned toward Catherine, showing me her back. "These are nice." She offered the petite fours to my boss.

Catherine's raised hand refused the offer. "Sam interviews. I know the law. We are a team. Hire me, hire her. So?" Catherine turned Lilith's chair back my way. Golf gave Catherine great arm strength.

Lilith scanned me up and down. She glowered. "I will need a shower with sanitizing soap." She wiped her hands with her napkin. "There. That will have to suffice." She faced Catherine. "What was the question?" Lilith sighed loudly. "Am I truly required to talk to her?" She looked at Catherine, receiving no response. She gushed, like a punctured balloon.

"Rupie's gun shot Mother, but the police fixed the evidence to convict Gunther. It's smoke and mirrors. Rupie owned and controlled the gun. Rupie asked Mother all the hard questions. Rupie was mad. Irrational. He spoke of an investigation into all our trusts. Imagine the embarrassment."

My gut agitated like the needle on a lie detector. "If Rupert did it, no Hauptmann does time, because Rupert is dead. Gunther goes free." *She's playing us.* "How convenient."

"Penitentiaries were never meant for a Hauptmann. Rupie's murder-suicide proclaimed his guilt." She dabbed at the corner of her dry eye. After a suitable silence, she continued.

"The only evidence that Gunther had been in her office were his fingerprints on the desk and papers. As our financial advisor, he sat at her desk working most days. His prints? Please. He signed a few papers that were on that desk, too."

"No other evidence?" Catherine asked.

"Nothing. Rupie needed money. Quarreled with Mother that day."

"You're kiddin' me! His net worth was multiple millions," I said.

Lilith disregarded me. "Gunther graduated Harvard with an MBA at the age of twenty-one. The genius ran our trusts since Father's demise. Legally, Mother had the final approval. I signed papers and spent money. It was Eden. Our half-sibling Seth Hauptmann had the most reasons to kill Mother. 'Strange Seth' never was very social. Mother disbursed the money. He got less than his share. Gunther's fund was robust. What's his motive?"

"Seth?" Catherine asked. "I don't remember him."

"Father's first wife bore Seth. He avoided us. Pure jealousy. The loner-outsider visited once a year to claim his trust's dispersion. He spoke with Mother minimally. Father loved all his children, but he favored us. We showed him our love."

"Your mother controlled Gunther's trust too?" I asked.

"Legally Mrs. Hauptmann controlled the trusts until each heir reached forty years old," Catherine said before she took a sip of her tea. "At forty, they could separate their funds and manage them privately, or opt to remain commingled under Marilyn's management."

"Seth was thirty-nine when Mother died," Lilith said. "With her dead, maybe the courts grant him a larger share? Seth's motives were obvious."

"We've reviewed trial transcripts, too," I said.

My voice startled Lilith, though she still didn't quite face me. "Oh, I forgot you were here."

She turned further toward Catherine. "Really Catherine, how can she–*her*–understand our type of people? Mother distrusted Rupie's frivolous nature. His money maintained bad habits. Single and thirty-four years old, he lived to excess: women, wine, and cocaine. Mother demanded the final say-so on all investments because of Rupie. She trusted Gunther. Mother always followed his instructions. What would killing her gain Gunther?"

"Rupert started a hedge fund?"

Lilith smiled over her shoulder at me. "More research? Aren't you the one?" She faced Catherine. She fussed over selecting another canapé.

"Rupie had trouble figuring the tip for a cab ride. His name drew money to the fund. A gun hobbyist, he belonged to a Gun Club. Bought and sold weapons. He owned the murder weapon."

"The fund has his name," Catherine said. "Hauptmann-Karcher Capital Security."

"So it does." Lilith leaned to capture another *petite four*. Speaking open-mouthed, she displayed the cake's progressive demolition to crumbs as she talked. "Why would Rupie write a note admitting his guilt, or murder himself, if Gunther killed Mother?"

Catherine said, "Gunther sued for absolute control of the funds without supervision, because of Marilyn's early dementia. Was there bad blood?"

"Oh, you know of that." Lilith changed gears. "Alzheimer's, but only moments of confusion. Mother was humiliated. It affected her philanthropic image. She agonized about her command over her personal accounts, and my father's charities, but they reconciled. He dropped the suit well before her death. The suicide note confirms Rupie did it."

"Did Gunther gain control of her fund, too?" I asked.

"That's not our way of thinking." Lilith's look patronized me. "Rupie wanted to use insider information from his hedge fund. Mother would not taint our trust with insider trading. We—our type of people—even though you work, Catherine, you understand; killing for money is so banal." Lilith crossed her arms over her chest. "Dear girl, we don't do tawdry. Refined and elegant are the words associated with the names Hauptmann or Vanderbilt."

Before Catherine could speak, I replied, "Human nature, as vulgar as it is, kills for money or power all the time. The great equalizer crosses class lines, ethnic groups, and if you watch the Animal Channel, even apes and lions kill for power. Are the Hauptmanns not human animals?"

Lilith's stare was smug. "Dearie, you don't get it. We've evolved."

"Calm tacit respect?" Catherine whispered to me. "She'll dismiss you."

"Will she, please?" I begged as I pinched and twisted Catherine's forearm. "I hate you."

She scraped my hand off. "Rodent, I hate you right back." She patted my hand.

That drew my laugh. Time to carry on. "With your mother dead and Gunther jailed, who controls the trusts?"

"Gunther manages them, period." Lilith gave me the you-are-dog-poop look again. "I sign, I have money. I spend. Life is perfect." She lifted her white gloves and pillbox purse from her lap to the table; then neatened them. "As I said, it is like living in Eden."

She straightened her shoulders and narrowed her eyes as she addressed Catherine. "Get Gunther out. The law protects our people and serves our purposes. Gunther found Rupie's confessional suicide note and the police ignored that. Why?"

"You have seen the documents?" Catherine asked.

"Gunther's lawyer holds all the paperwork proving poor Rupie borrowed against his trust. Unable to repay, or extend his loan, he killed Mother, then committed suicide." Lilith gave a passable imitation of sorrow without tears.

"Police don't miss things like that," I said.

"Unless it's on purpose. Find out why Rupie committed suicide, you get Gunther a new trial. As your patron, I order you to discover Mother's true killer. Liberate Gunther." Lilith's face turned ruddy.

Catherine glared into Lilith's eyes. Her blue eyes' glowed iridescently; her cheeks reddened. With her new perm, she was Medusa's daughter in the flesh.

Lilith turned to stone under a gorgon's heated stare.

Catherine huffed. "Working on this case is a challenge." Her tone dismissed friendship. "As to laboring for you, let's just say, justice is what is utmost. The possibility of re-opening this case is slim, but you hired us."

"You better get the answers. I have lots of acquaintances who–"

"You will be billed," Catherine said quietly. "The free rides you mooched off my sister when she was alive, are over. I remember no reciprocation."

Blushing deep red, Lilith was quiet.

"Sam?" Catherine offered me a macaroon. "These are quite excellent." She inspected my notes.

I am blunt to the point where sometimes it earns me grief. I refused the macaroons. "Thanks. I'm busy."

I wrote: review crime book from murder, investigate Rupert Hauptmann's death, suicide note, method of death, Seth Hauptmann? & Lilith's motives and alibi? I underlined the last phrase twice.

Catherine scanned my index cards. "I suppose Marco can help with the police reports."

"Marco?" Lilith coughed as tea went down the wrong pipe. "The detective? Don't like him," she sputtered. "His partner, Detective Ryan, was in charge and even less personable."

"Wonderful." My confrontational history with Ryan was famous. My relationship with Marco was completely different.

"Is there a problem?" Lilith rolled her eyes. "You should be in your element, talking to them. They've no polish, either."

"I'm polished to a shine." I stood over Lilith. I contemplated shaking sense into her noggin. It would not help. "I don't create problems Mrs. Hauptmann-Vanderbilt."

I snatched a macaroon, and inches from her nose, snapped off half in one bite. "I solve them. Ma'am." I chewed with my mouth open, and sat down, disregarding her flabbergasted face.

Catherine ignored us, reading my underlined notes. She tapped my shoulder urgently. "Sam, pack up." She motioned to hide my cards. She glanced at her unexposed wristwatch. "Oh, look at the time. Sorry, we must leave."

"I want answers quickly." Lilith regained her autocratic tone. "That's why Sherwood and Crothers L.L.C. no longer work for me. You have ninety days. I want a progress report in weeks."

We Ubered it back downtown. "Glad friend Lilith was cordial," I said.

"The years have mellowed her," Catherine snorted. "Another D.R.B. from the D.A.R."

I whispered. "As a D.R.B. she is the queen; you're only a P.I.T., a princess in training."

We reached the townhouse on 33rd street, our offices and living quarters. I rushed to my basement bedroom and reclaimed sanity, changing into black jeans, grey tee shirt and a sweatshirt with "WTF?" printed across the front.

On my leather belt, I hooked Nana, my 9 mm Beretta Nano. I resumed living in my version of Rousseau's state of nature, as an armed woman.

Wasting no time, I called Marco's cell phone.

Marco answered. "Yeah Sam, what is it?"

"And hello to you, too."

"I'm working a case. No time for no social call."

"Which case?"

Marco paused. "You know I can't tell ya. So whatcha want?" Marco snickered. "Like I have a choice, my blackmailing *marone* of an ex-partner. Aarrh." He must have been biting his finger.

"I need to see the Marilyn Hauptmann casebook and evidence box. You available?"

Marco always had an excuse.

"Part of dat case is still active. You can't see it."

"Part? Active? C'mon Marco spill."

"I'm working dat case, so drop it. Unlike you, I like working for the NY PD's."

"The Rupert Hauptmann murder? Isn't that a suicide?"

"Ok, Sammie. Here's your best deal–come in tomorrow afternoon. Ryan's visiting his three daughters and his second ex in Schenectady. Won't see ya nosing around. Any help you give is only ta me and off da record. Different eyes may see some-tin' new."

"About two?"

"Perfecto. The techies have Rupert's laptop."

"Two it is. I'll be there and bring my toys."

I climbed the stairs to Catherine's first-floor office. By then, she had secured lunch at Jean-Georges with Gunther's half-sibling, Seth Hauptmann.

* * *

At the restaurant, the maître d' led Catherine to a table in the corner behind a temporary screen. Seth stared out the window at Columbus Circle as Catherine approached. She invaded his field of vision; he slid his hips forward and twisted to evade eye contact.

The maître d' whispered, "Mr. Hauptmann." Seth remained fascinated by traffic. "Ms. Worthington has arrived." The man walked off.

"Ah." Seth nodded and peered over Catherine's shoulder. Without standing, he presented his hand. "The knights in the middle ages initiated the convention of shaking hands. Shows we're unarmed. We both come in peace, right?"

"Of course," Catherine said. Seth's apathy caught her off guard.

"The bottom of medieval beer steins were transparent glass to enable you to watch your enemies while you drank." Wearing a stern expression, he inspected his tumbler. "All glass. Modern overkill? Or do my enemies surround me?" He remained emotionless. "Even family? Their prodigious self-interest shan't dishearten me. The cosmos is my oyster, I search for the pearl."

Catherine sat across from Seth. "Mind if I sit?"

"I am harmless. Killed no one." His words were hollow, an accountant's announcement of a sum of added numbers.

"The meekest of humans, sufficiently provoked, kills," Catherine stated.

Seth remained stoic and spoke softly. "My nature is otherwise, I assure you."

Seth's eyes had yet to meet hers, allowing Catherine to uninterruptedly inspect the forty-two-year-old clean-shaven man. Six-two, lean and sleek, he wore a custom-tailored silk suit and shirt. His left fourth finger had no ring or tan lines. Did his asocial personality prevent relationships, or was his manner to mask his hostility?

Forty awkward seconds of silence passed. Seth finally said. "Academic, not physical, my nature will never allow violence." He rocked in his chair, sweated, and looked at his feet.

More silence obligated Catherine to speak. "A shame we've never met. Worse yet, I must ask about your step-mother's murder."

"No other logical reason for contact between us." He spoke to his lap. His eyes roamed back and forth like a snake looking for prey. "Cannot lie. I am not remorseful. They don't like me. We're not family." His fingers played in his lap, doing a cat's cradle without any string. "My condition precluded any relationship. Marilyn augmented my alienation." He looked sideways at the bar, tapping his fingers on the table.

His behavior *was* peculiar. "Why?" she asked.

His gaze found her face but quickly departed. "Father tried to include me, so I am forced to beg for my trust money from them. My half-siblings shunned me. I'm a joke. Mother Marilyn was the head comedian. I have no remorse, but still, I believe sadness is appropriate."

"I don't understand."

"Asperger's syndrome. I lack *pragmatic language skills*, have a *low social quotient*. Illiterate to social cues, I transmit inappropriate ones. I'm not the debonair Hauptmann image. I'm flawed."

His contemptuous commentary held no venom.

"You are over forty, why let them manage your fund?"

On the other side of the screen, a waiter dropped a tray. *Berrangggg*.

The noise startled Seth. He ejected from his seat, ready to flee. "I should go." He stepped hesitantly toward the exit.

"Please stay." Catherine reached for his arm.

Frozen in place, Seth avoided contact. He stared at her hand. "Must get this over. So, I stay."

"We'll finish now. I promise." His discomfort gave Catherine empathy.

"Repeat your question?" He wilted to his chair.

"Your trust is controlled by your enemies. Why?"

He studied the ceiling. "Investing money becomes a distraction. The trust dispersions are for taxes and contributions to my Autism foundation." He ventured a quick glance at Catherine. Satisfied, he looked away. "I am the classic cliché. A brilliant scientist, twenty-two patents in medical technology. My Hauptmann trust pays the income tax on the royalties. Too busy in my lab pursuing quantum particles with their entanglements, or firing electron guns, to bother firing a handgun at such miserable humans." He paused. "As you witnessed, loud noises affect some autistics extremely. I refrain from sporting events; they shoot off cannons. I hide on the Fourth of July. I have a list in my wallet." He sat forward to retrieve it.

"That's not necessary."

He focused on the ice cubes he swirled in his drink. "Like planets around the sun, or electrons around a nucleus. Interacting energized particles, see them spin. Forces of the universe, I must bring order to this chaos," he mumbled to himself. The three cubes circled his swizzle stick.

He took a long drink. "I have too many equations running around in my brain to worry about Hauptmanns, living or dead. They pay my taxes. Their sole contribution to society's well-being."

"On that night...." Catherine took a deep breath. "Where were you?"

"Detective Ryan asked eight times, threatening me as if my answer would change. That Marco man pulled Ryan off me after he slapped my face to compel me to look at him. The alibi is embarrassing. I'm forty-two years-old."

"You need an alibi. Tell me."

"I supped with my mother at Le Perigord from seven-thirty until eleven. Mother monitors her man-child once a week. Jacques was our waiter. Det. Ryan has not harassed me since."

Seth wrung the napkin tightly. "Have to leave." He looked out the window unfocused. "Must get free. My lab needs me now. Are we done?" Seth abruptly stood. "Yes, we are." He strode around the screen. His footsteps trailed off.

He was gone.

Catherine called for the check.

The maître d' arrived at the table. "Oh no, Ms. Worthington, Mr. Hauptmann runs a tab. This is his spot for lunch every day but Monday. The bill is his. We appreciate your concern. He is a kind and gentle man."

* * *

At breakfast the next day, Catherine explained her strange interlude to me. My Internet research confirmed Seth ran a foundation and he held patents. A world-renown scientist, and a member of Mensa, Wikipedia categorized him as a high-functioning Asperger's syndrome, as if that single phrase could tell everything about a person. How horrible. A label, more than his ailment, trapped Seth.

The maître d' at Le Perigord confirmed his alibi. He had a reservation into perpetuity for dinner each week. Brilliant Seth succeeded in creating order out of his life's chaos.

* * *

The station house hadn't changed in the eight years since I'd turned in my gold shield. Marco the Metro, my former partner greeted me.

"Sammie, how's it wit-chew?"

I tolerated the arm he slung over my shoulder. "How's it wit-chew, Marco?" Funny we were buddies now, but I quit the force because of him.

"Shush, I gotta sneak ya upstairs. You're an off-da-record consultant. Can't be looking at no active files."

"The Marilyn Hauptmann file is inactive."

"Trust me, you want *both* files: Marilyn's and Rupert's. C'mon upstairs. Rupert was murdered; can't get the DA to see it our way. Need a better sales pitch."

We climbed the back stairs to the second floor. The homicide room's two tables were a mess: two loose-leaf notebooks, a large and small evidence box, and a locked gun box.

"Here. Dis one's Marilyn's murder book and dis Rue-burp's book." He laughed. "Named him after regretting a belch. Rue burp."

"Get serious. Rupert left a note?"

"A note was dare, but…," He shrugged. "Rupert ain't no suicide. Never was. Never will be."

"Don't get frustrated with me, Marco. Show me the books and the note."

"The note, look Rupert was left handed. The experts said a rightie wrote that note. Lefties inject bullets in their noggins wit da weapon, squished against the left side of the old squash. Use da left hand. Rupert's entrance wound was over his right eye. Nowhere on his sheet does it say he's a contortionist. The gun club manager said he shot exclusively left-handed." Marco snatched a blank sheet of loose-leaf paper from the table.

"That's good work, Marco."

"There's more." He crumbled the paper and slam-dunked it in the trashcan. "Yeah. Two points. No matter what, the hand that holds the gun wears GSR. Neither of Rupie's did. The gun had no prints. None. How many suicides blow their brains out and den wipe the weapon clean? Suicide my ass, Sam. Needa lock this case down. It's Gunther from now until the cows come home."

"You're that sure?"

"The jury got it right, killed his mother; he offed his brother, too. Rupert's office was completely clean, no prints. The same weapon killed dem both. Needa motive, without it, Gunnie-boy may skip on dis. I don't hear no moos nor see no cows. Cows ain't come home yet. He did it." Marco danced with excitement. "Sammie you're da best, help me get justice here."

I laughed. "Same old Marco."

"I feel it in my bones girl, in my bones." He grabbed my shoulders and shook me.

"Easy boy. If Rupert did'em both, that ties it up."

"Yeah, and maybe a bear craps in a public toilet at Starbucks after downing a mocha latte. Maybe the milk for dat latte came from dem same cows. Get real, Sammie."

"Still elegantly persuasive," I said. "And twice as stubborn."

"Gunther has a temper. Three shots to make sure his Momma was fully dead."

"That's cold," I said. "But he did publicly embarrass her."

"He is a psycho. And den, who killed Rupert, huh? I'll work over here. Knock yourself out with dat stuff. Be a pal. Help me bring the cows home." He uttered a long loud. "Mooooo, in my bones, Sammie."

Marco put his feet up on the other table, and read the Daily News.

I spent the afternoon until five scrutinizing both books and the evidence boxes. I wanted to search Rupert's computer. The forensics tech guys left at six. They had to proctor me while I broke down the computer. So, I gave the weapon a quick once-over. A Ruger 22/45 Mark III, a sportsman's pistol, the magazine was full.

The magazine was full?

We have an obsessive-compulsive murderer. Interrogating the bullets may rat out the culprit.

Rupie's hands bore no gunshot residue. Here come Marco's cows. We snuck into the techies' lab.

Sol, an asthenic black-haired Eurasian tech greeted us. "Hey Marco, is this the famous Sammie Cochran? The brains of your partnership?"

"The one and only. But you got that wrong, she was the brawn."

"Both brains and brawn." I flexed for Sol: a five-feet one-inch tall woman imitating Hulk Hogan.

"Den I have the good looks." Marco laughed and combed his bald dome with his fingers.

"Pleasure to meet you, but that's scary. I'm puny." Judging from the five losing lottery tickets on his work desk, Sol's exercise program involved vigorous and repetitive scratching.

The techies had already discovered Rupert had an appointment with his Mother the afternoon of her death. They made Rupie a full-blown suspect.

"The crime book had nothing about Marilyn's schedule for that afternoon," I said.

"That page was AWOL," Marco answered. "Strange huh?"

"But non-specific."

"What have you here?" Sol had rifled through my computer mechanic's box full of disks for retrieving information. Each one worked on a different operating system. Some I had written myself.

A nerd wiz-kid in high school, I probably should have become a programmer-gamer. However, virtual reality is not real. Make-believe does not provoke my adrenaline, so my talents are used bullying CPU's to spill their beans and tattle on the guilty.

"Wow," Sol plucked a disk from the box and held it up like a hooked fish. "How did you get this one?" Red Chinese letters were written on it.

"My friend bootlegs to China. They don't observe patents or copyrights so well."

"Do you know what these words mean?" He brandished his prize.

"Have no freakin' idea, but we'll get answers."

"It translates to 'Appear,' but it sort of means to un-erase." He leered at Rupie's laptop as if he was about to make love to it. "Can I watch? Thought New York outlawed your disk."

I slipped the disk into the laptop. "New York laws say: it's legal if no one knows you used it. Watching makes you my accomplice."

"I saw nothing." Sol watched the screen blur with lines of data. "Wow, it's ripping through that drive. Go, baby."

"Outlawed?" Marco the Metro made a constipated face. "Sammie, what're you guys doing?

"Retrieving documents from the hard drive that were recently erased. Catherine will get them in evidence."

"Oh, Sammie girl, I don't like the sound of dis no how. Is there legal reaper-concussions from stuff like dat dare? Need reasonable suspicion and a warrant."

"You wanted help to bring home those cows so your bones can relax?"

"Yeah," Marco gave a sheepish nod. "Dem bones is screamin' ta me, but...."

The laptop made a grinding noise. A decision box, in Chinese, appeared on the screen.

"Holy crap," Sol said. "It's asked how far back to start *re-appearing* the data?"

"Marco, get us two bagels from the Deli." I tapped the chair next to me. "Sol sit. Type in three years, five months. Marco go."

"Get my usual schmear," Sol said.

"For me, an Everything with scallions."

Marco grabbed his coat. "I see nut-ting." He covered his eyes and ran.

When you erase documents from a hard drive, you disassociate the entrance pathway from the program. That blocks access. The information remains until it is overwritten. Most modern laptops have enough memory to keep years of information. It stays locked behind unopenable doors. My program creates keys to those doors. 'Open says me.'

A cache of information on the hard drive made everything clear: "Report from Mr. Malcolm Edelman C.P.A."

In the past, Catherine had employed Malcolm as a forensic accountant. His cell number was in my contacts.

Marco returned. "For Sammie, one toasted everything bagel with scallion cream cheese. And for my man Sol, a bialy with shrimp salad. Sollie, that ain't kosher."

"Kosher shmosher, my Shanghai-Bubbie taught me to eat'em that way. They're delish."

I said, "Marco, since the gun's handle had no prints, dust the magazine and do touch-DNA on all the bullets in order. When the killer reloaded, he made your case."

* * *

My appointment the next day with Mal was in Catherine's name. When my backpack Nana, and I appeared at his office, my presence unsettled him.

Catherine hires the helpers to find answers; I persuade wise guys to give them up.

If he saw the guest in his vestibule, his mind would race past unsettled to anarchy.

"Hi, Sam." With his back to me, Malcolm shut down his private laptop. "Be right with you." He secured it in a draw of his ebony credenza using a built-in combination lock. "Confidential client stuff. Hush-hush." He spun and faced me over his tan modern wood desk. "You understand." I received a faux smile. "Ready to do business. Talk to me?"

"You seem jumpy, why?" I placed my backpack on the floor and unzipped the main compartment. Several folders were inside.

"I have no reason to be." He perused the folders' coded labels. "Do you have a case for me?" He tugged at his hand-tied bow tie. "So? What can I do?" He straightened papers on the desk and looked at me. "What gives?" He rubbed his hands together as if to warm them.

A DA once told me, "Tension besieges the mind, strong-arming the release of answers held hostage." Waiting for the hammer to drop makes tension build.

He cleaned his horn-rimmed glasses. "Speak, already. You're here for something?"

He waited, while I fished out a manila folder.

"I can help, only if you ask me." His hands shook as he put on his glasses.

"We need help on the Hauptmann murder case."

"How?" He stammered. "I've heard rumors, but know less than you."

"The trust funds need a forensic evaluation. Were the accounting practices on the up and up? We'll pay the usual per hour fee."

"Oh, so you're here to hire me." He took a deep breath and regained some color in his cheeks. "I'm very busy. It's the season. I can look sometime early next month." He stood. "So, we're good." He stepped toward the door.

I remained seated. "It happened over three years ago, but your mind is identic. How did the books look right before the murders?" I glowered at him.

"Murders?" He went ashen. "Oh my Lord, I thought this day would come. Sam help me." He shuffled to and closed the door. He walked back like a schoolboy going to the principal's office, then he collapsed into his chair. With closed eyes, he took a deep breath. "Oh Sam, I can't. If he knows I told what I know, I'm dead. He is colder than a crocodile. They eat their young."

"I have your summary report. Lifted it from Rupie's hard-drive." I waved the folder and dropped it on his desk. "Catherine's subpoenas will work. It's in. Testifying as a private citizen, for a private attorney, the police won't offer you protection. Hope you live through discovery. The police will want the originals."

"He said he erased Rupert's drive...how did you—"

"Oh, also, the police know, you knew what Gunther was doing. They are interested in finding out why you, a forensic accountant, did not come forward. They call it withholding material evidence or aiding and abetting in murder after the fact. For that, they can charge you with murder. So many options."

"I'll talk to them only when they make me. Goodbye, Sam." He stood.

Now I stood. "Wait a minute." My hand on his chest stopped him at the door. His heart thumped at a hundred thirty beats per minute. I opened the door and waved Marco in. "He's all yours."

"Stay Sammie. It's really your collar. Mr. Edelman, sir." Marco's free hand slapped his copy of the report. "Is dis here report accurate, as to when, where and how Gunther embezzled money from his brother's and sister's trust fund?"

"In my best interest, I cannot answer that question. I take the fifth."

"The fifth is for self-incrimination. Did you kill or embezzle here?" Marco asked.

"No, but ...." Malcolm shivered. "He'll kill me."

"Withholding evidence, interfering with the prosecution of a murderer, dem charges are not in your best interest no how. Answer to me, you don't need no fifth. The DA is playin' used car saleswoman. She'll deal a plea for information. A short-term opportunity, ya don't wanna miss."

I added, "Sell Gunther out to buy yourself freedom, Mal. You've no choice."

Malcolm said. "I reported to Rupert that his brother stole him and Lilith blind, using service charges sent to shell management corporations and other techniques. Collectively, their trusts were on the brink. Rupert said he would discuss that with his mother that afternoon. By midnight she was dead."

"Do you know who met with whom and when?" I asked.

"Rupert left directly to his mother's. The next day the papers said she was murdered. Rupert called me that evening. Forget we ever met, he said. Everything was all right, he said. I was to destroy the report ASAP, he said. No worries, he said."

"Dat report's evidence. You didn't destroy it," Marco demanded.

"Original's locked in my safe. I can't legally destroy my work for seven years. It might have tax consequences."

"Oh, it mighty-might." Marco pranced and gave me a high-five. "Gotcha, Gunther. Moooo."

"After Rupert committed suicide, I assumed he killed his Mother." Malcolm sobbed into his hands. "Then Gunther came to my office, he told me it was an assisted-suicide and winked.

"He asked me, 'Are you feeling depressed too?' His frigid glare into my eyes, while displaying the gun tucked in his belt, terrified me. He demanded to watch me destroy the reports. I shredded the copies. He whispered in my ear. 'I'm watching you forever. You're alive only because never three on the same match, too close together. Haven't seen him since."

"I am serving you, personal-like, with this here subpoena and a subpoena *Duces Tecum*." Marco dropped the paperwork on Malcolm's desk. "Gimme the original report. You will testify at a Grand Jury. By voluntarily providing these reports for our discovery, the D.A. could drop the obstruction charges. Testify truthfully, verify dees events, and the DA might reach a deal on the aiding and abetting charges, too. Don't know about your CPA's license. Huh?"

"Just protect me. He is a murderer."

"He's jailed," I said.

"His sister Lilith isn't. She's mental. Could be involved."

"You know that for a fact?" Marco took out his pad.

"Her only thought is money. Was the most selfishly avaricious of the three. She threatened me. Said I knew something I wasn't telling. She has an agenda. Protect me."

Marco answered. "Maybe a change in address, or apply for the witness protection program. Should've come forward sooner. Withholding evidence in a murder case is three years."

"I'll deal today." Malcolm dropped to his knees with folded hands. "Arrest me. Please."

"It doesn't work that way." Marco patted his head. "Maybe we should videotape your deposition today. For your protection, den Gunther has no reason to murder you. C'mon stand and turnaround so I can put on dees bracelets." Marco jingled the cuffs. "We're going downtown for da videotape. We'll buzz your lawyer to meet us dere."

* * *

Catherine took it amicably when I told her a member of her bluebloods' fraternity had committed matricide and fratricide.

Catherine is nothing, if not a realist. "The logic is clear and undeniable. Good work, Sam."

Gunther generated phony fees to cover his embezzlement. Marilyn's dementia did not allow her to appreciate his stealing. While Gunther accrued money, his siblings' accounts dwindled.

Malcolm's report commissioned by Rupert caught Gunther. During a lucid moment, Rupert informed his Mother. Marilyn confronted Gunther, and he killed her. His need for a fall guy necessitated Rupert's death. He stole the printed report from Marilyn's office, along with her appointment book page. He erased the report from Rupert's computer after his *suicide*. When Malcolm's shredded his copies, Gunther thought the evidence was expunged.

The pieces of the puzzle interlocked successfully. Rupert probably spoke to Malcolm while Gunther aimed the Ruger at him. After cleaning up the second murder scene, Gunther appeared at the wake. He conspicuously announced Rupie's absence and his brother's fight with his mother on the afternoon of her murder. Dramatically, he exited the wake to retrieve his disrespectful brother, only to find him "dead of a self-inflicted gunshot wound." The note laid on the desk.

Gunther's fingerprints were on the magazine case as well as his trace DNA on the top four bullets in the magazine. The rest had Rupert's DNA. Gunther had replaced the bullets that he used to kill Rupert and Marilyn. That evidence brought Marco's cows home, and his bones stopped aching.

Nailed, Gunther pled guilty.

His second sentence for first-degree murder, to be served consecutively, assured incarceration for the rest of Gunther's natural life, no parole.

* * *

I did not have to accompany Catherine to a dinner at Per Se with Mrs. Hauptmann-Vanderbilt and her significant other, Mr. Vincent Vanderbilt. I weighed dining in that expensive and reportedly fabulous restaurant against being in the company of Lilith for more than fifteen seconds.

I dined solo in the townhouse's dining room. Chef Paulie cooked me an aged American Wagyu porterhouse steak from Lobel's, with sweet potato fries in a cabernet sauce.

I smoked a victory Cohiba after dinner in my office.

As Catherine told me over her Bloody Mary at breakfast the next morning, Lilith took the proof that her brother killed her mother and brother too well. Her smirk confirmed she employed us under false pretenses.

Catherine explained the evidence.

Lilith replied, "He's guilty of both murders? What a disgraceful scoundrel." A short laugh burst from her. "Who would believe my brother Gunther a killer?" She beamed at Catherine. "Certainly not *moi*. I guess, all the money in the trusts, except for Seth's, is mine. Even dear dead Mother's money. What surprising good fortune for me."

According to Catherine, Lilith had smiled like a circus clown. "Oh Catherine, I have a blank check for your fees, what number do I fill out in reciprocation? Always good to do business with someone who has class. I will pay for tonight's meal too, including the tip. After your labors, I can more than afford it."

# #

About the Author

L.A. Preschel is the author of the Samantha Cochran–Catherine Worthington mystery series. The first novel in the series, LYIN' EYES, is to be published soon. The second mystery, GENDER THEFT, is in the draft stage. L.A. is a member of Mystery Writers of America and Sisters in Crime. L.A. Preschel has an author's page on Facebook: NoirMysteries. His email address is <u>Lew0309@aol.com</u> *or visit his website at LAPreschel.blogspot.com*

COLD AS ICE

N. L. Quatrano

New Jersey 1987

It was lung-burning. Vicious.

Eight below zero is too damned cold to be hanging around outside. What survives in this kind of howling, grueling cold, anyway?

The body I was standing over hadn't. Of course, by the way the ice pick still stuck up out of her full-length rabbit-fur coat, obviously, the cold had nothing to do with her death. It would account for the unusually small pool of blood beside her lovely blonde head, however.

"Hey Detective Holmes, we can go in the house, right?" the patrol cop called to me. He'd been standing around for the better part of a half hour waiting for me to get to the scene, so he was possibly colder than he'd been in his entire life.

"No, you can't. Why don't you sit in your patrol car? I'll do the photos and wave down the coroner."

He nodded and ushered the dead woman's bereft husband into the back of his car. Then he climbed into the driver's seat and started the engine to get the heat running. Folks from Wisconsin or Winnipeg might be acclimated to these temperatures, but people in New Jersey certainly were not.

I pulled the instant Polaroid camera out of the oversized pocket on the inside of my arctic parka and snapped a few pictures of the victim. As fast as my gloved fingers could manage it, I stuffed the photos into my shirt pocket so my body heat would help them develop. When I'd shot the first eight frames, I headed back to my car to load a new cartridge. The wind screamed at over thirty miles an hour, driving the snow sideways.

I was in the car and had just ejected the spent film pack when my cell phone rang. I glanced at the number and decided I didn't need any more aggravation tonight. After the third ring, a lovely disembodied voice from the phone company would take a message for me; my ex-wife, *Her Royal Pain-in-the-Buttness*. It was the third time she'd called today.

I snapped the film into place and pulled the photos out of my pocket to take a look.

Mrs. Daphne Oberhauser was a lovely corpse. Long lashes graced her translucent cheeks like those on an expensive porcelain doll. Her lips were full and perfect if not just a touch bluish, her hair thick and shoulder length and the exact color of clover honey, spread out on the snow-covered ground beneath her like it would be on a satin pillowcase.

I glanced into the rear-view mirror but still no sign of the coroner's office. I tossed the photos on the seat of my car and headed back outside to finish the body shots. When I was happy with all the angles, I trudged through the snow toward the house. The cop in the squad car started to open his door, but I waved him off. I pushed open the front door of the house and stood in the quiet hallway, listening.

I pushed the heavy door closed with the toe of my snow-covered boot and pulled off my leather gloves, replacing them with clear latex ones. The foyer was amazing. The lights glistened off the Austrian crystal chandelier overhead, like moonlight on an ice-coated lake. The black and white tiles made me think of Alice in Wonderland. Where was that strange rabbit now? Was Daphne's husband the Mad Hatter?

After almost twenty years in homicide, the last ten of those with the NJ State Troopers, I knew what to look for. There was no sign of struggle here. I glanced into the parlor to my right and looked longingly at the inviting fireplace which was, of course, lit and burning warmly. A book lay flattened, its spine broken, on the plush gray sofa, a discarded blanket beside it. Someone had been cozy as a bear in a cave.

My cell phone rang again. I pulled it out and glared at it. "Holmes."

The coroner's investigator was a bit breathless. He was still at least twenty minutes away. The exit at the Route 9 turnoff was closed with an overturned tractor-trailer.

"Anyone hurt?" I asked, hoping he wasn't going to get sidetracked at the accident scene.

The injuries seemed to be minimal, but the required detour meant they had to go back to Egg Harbor and go around. He asked if we needed anything.

"We're fine. The vic is still out there in the snow with a patrolman watching over her. I'm in the house trying to determine if this is part of the crime scene."

"The way this wind is whipping around, the snow will have her and any other clues covered up in no time."

"I know, Bill," I sighed, understanding his upset. "We parked the cars to block as much as we could–it's too damned cold to do much else."

He agreed and signed off, needing to concentrate on his driving so he would eventually arrive, investigate, and transport the then-frozen Mrs. Oberhauser to the morgue.

I returned to my task. There was no blood trail, inside or outside the house. If there'd been an argument in this house, someone had been very quick to cover it up. But then, that was not at all in keeping with what our tipster had relayed.

The kitchen was likewise, spotless. I moved to the door that led to the garage where the dead woman's car would have been parked an hour ago. Nothing to indicate she'd been stabbed in there either.

The house was so clean it made me grimace. I'm not a complete slob, but even on cleaning day, my place didn't sparkle like this one. I sniffed the air; no bleach, no detergent, no spray cleaners had been used recently. A faint scent of vanilla hung around…

By the time I'd walked through the entire thirty-five hundred square feet of house and garage, the coroner's truck was outside. I closed the door behind me and hiked back to the road and the puzzle at hand.

I knocked on the window of the patrol car which by now was so steamed up the cop couldn't see an ax murderer if he was standing next to him. The window rolled down a crack. "Yeah, Detective?"

"Why don't you take Mr. Oberhauser back inside, Officer? Maybe put on some coffee? Stay in the kitchen if you wouldn't mind."

"Yes sir, I will," he said, scrambling to get moving. Undoubtedly the idea of hot coffee had made the man nearly delirious. He opened the door and let Daphne's husband out of the inescapable back seat of the cruiser.

"Knight, would you mind taking the husband's statement for me? And I'll want your report by tomorrow at quitting time, understood?"

The rookie almost stood at attention and saluted, and I nearly laughed, but then my face would have cracked because I was so damned cold.

"I'll try, sir. He hasn't answered a single thing I asked him. He's either in major shock or he's deaf."

I sighed. "Give it some time. He'll come around in a little while."
I shooed him toward the walk. They disappeared in the blowing snow
to the big house on the hill with the darkened windows.

I stomped my feet, kept my gloved hands stuffed as deep and
tightly in my coat pockets as I could and tucked my chin into my
chest to hide in the parka hood. Bill moved around as though it was a
chilly fall night, not eight below. However, he wasted no time. He
took her body temp, checked her gorgeous blue eyes for broken
capillaries and examined her alabaster throat and wrists for bruises.
He took more photos, finally stood up and closed his bag of tools.

"How long's she been dead, Bill?"

He shrugged his shoulders. "With these temps, who knows? I
have to get a liver temp back at the lab—that will give me a better
idea."

"Give me a guess? An hour? Two? Ten?" I was walking beside
him, tossing out my smartass remarks as we moved to his truck.

"She's not frozen stiff, or completely buried in snow, so I'd say
she's been laying there less than two hours." He grabbed a folded
sheet and looked Daphne's way.

"Help me get her into the truck, will you? I told the assistant I
could handle it so we weren't both out in this awful weather."

I nodded. We carefully rolled her and her bloodied fur coat to the
side and slid the sheet beneath her. We repeated the procedure in the
other direction. Bill tied the ends of the sheet, and we lifted her easily.

"What is she, maybe a hundred twenty pounds? No defensive
wounds. She knew whoever it was that killed her."

Bill shook his head. "Or she didn't see him coming."

"Or her."

"Or her," he agreed quietly.

I hadn't corrected him to be politically correct. It was important
that we both remembered not to make assumptions. We'd made that
mistake years ago and a serial killer still roamed free.

* * *

He jumped down from the back of the truck and slammed the doors. I double checked them. We didn't want to lose our corpse before we'd discovered what had happened to her.

"Did you get a call this time?" he asked as he stomped his feet to get off some of the accumulated snow.

"Sure did. A woman called it in. Hung up before the dispatcher could get any verifying information."

He thought a moment and nodded his head. We'd been at this point before. He climbed into the SUV without another word and drove off.

What he didn't say terrified me.

I watched the taillights on his van disappear down the long, tree-lined lane, then turned to join the others in the house. I was too tired for another long night. I needed to get this done.

Interviewing Joseph Oberhauser seemed straightforward. He looked to be shattered by his wife's demise. He was her senior by almost fifteen years, but by his account, they were devoted to each other. He pulled out photos of happy times; several black tie and evening gown affairs that showcased how perfect they were for each other. They had no children although he had two from a previous marriage. One lived in Ocean County, the other all the way across the country in California. Where it was warm.

Officer Knight had finished his coffee and left after I'd come in. He was going to knock on the doors of the other homes on the lane just in case anyone had seen anything. We doubted it, but it was protocol. We needed to locate our tipster if we could. And the tow truck still had to pick up Mrs. Oberhauser's car.

"When can I have Daphne back?" the husband asked quietly.

"The coroner will call you to make arrangements as soon as the autopsy is done, Joseph. He tries to be quick about it. Usually, twenty-four to forty-eight hours if he's not worried about toxicology or anything."

"I still can't believe she's dead. How do I go on without her?" He asked me as tears streamed down his face.

I never have an answer to that question, and it's been asked of me dozens of times in all the years I've been a cop. I shook my head. "Have faith that time will heal, Mr. Oberhauser. That may sound empty right now, but it's my experience that it is true."

He looked me in the eye. "Has time healed your pain, Detective?"

I didn't answer him and he waved the question aside. I let it slide by me like a smelly dog that wasn't mine.

"Can your daughter stay with you tonight? You probably shouldn't be alone. I can call her for you if you'd like."

"We are not on speaking terms. She disagreed with my marriage to Daphne. Some nonsense about being unfaithful to her mother."

"And her mother is where?" I asked, taking notes as fast as I could.

"She's been dead for fifteen years. You'd think Jenny would get on with life, wouldn't you?"

I shrugged. "Kids handle things in their own way, I guess. At least you'd hope she'd want to see you happy again."

"She doesn't. She believes I should be miserable my entire life. And now I will be."

"How does your son feel about it all?"

"David's in the Navy. San Diego almost ten years now. He felt he should devote himself to one career and he didn't choose a family. I gave my children horrible legacies, Detective."

"How so, sir?" I asked.

"My daughter thinks I killed my first wife. Not literally of course, but by not being around enough. I was fighting to keep the family business alive, amassing the money it would take to care for them in style. It required a lot of hours and travel. Jenny feels Mandy died of loneliness."

What the hell could I say to that? After all, my marriage had been a victim of too many hours and days absent, too. Not for money maybe, but I was responsible none the less. I stood quietly and concentrated on not shuffling my feet. "When did you become a minister?"

"Ten years ago. After a certain point, the money lost its sparkle. After Mandy died, I took a good look at my life. The company was strong, and I made sure that the family would be taken care of in the sale. I can do the Lord's work, now."

"No vow of poverty, huh?" I asked, realizing why I'd recognized the man when I saw him at the kitchen table. He traded salvation for personal checks three nights a week on the local cable stations.

"It isn't money that's the sin, Detective. The sin is what we are willing to do for it." I was usually wishing I had more, so I couldn't relate to a man who collected millions from blue-collar people like me every week.

"Is there anyone who can stay with you, Joseph? You shouldn't be alone right now."

He shook his head, his hand on the gleaming brass door handle. "I'll be all right, Detective. The Lord is with me. And with you. Thank you for your time and your compassion. You've made this somehow bearable."

I shook his hand, pulled on my gloves and shoved through the heavy door into the blistering wind. My head down, I forged through the snow toward my car. I turned the key and let the engine idle for a few minutes. When I looked at the house, I could feel sorrow reaching out to me through the arched Tudor windows. Secrets. The fireplace flickered in the parlor, the only light in a house of many windows.

* * *

"No Elise, I'm not giving you any more money. I'm paying you what the judge ordered and I'm paying you on time. That's it. Get a job if that's not enough." I was having this conversation at seven-fifteen in the morning, after four hours sleep and no coffee. If I hadn't been sound asleep when the thing rang, I wouldn't have answered it. Even after eleven months apart, my ex-wife could still push my buttons.

I listened for another minute and swung my legs out of bed. "I'm not angry with you. I'm just tired of this whole thing. I've moved on. It's not my fault your boyfriend did, too. Don't call me again." I closed the phone and turned it off. If the station needed me, they would call the unlisted house phone.

After a trip to the bathroom, I crawled back into bed. The dawn was not bright and glorious, so my bedroom was still dark. When I woke next, it was eleven o'clock.

I started the coffee, took a hot shower and dressed for doing nothing. Coffee mug in hand, I put down tuna and whitefish dinner for my three-legged feline companion, collected a soggy paper from the front porch, and settled in at the kitchen nook to read what was dry enough to decipher.

The kitchen phone rang at one o'clock. "Mike Holmes."

"I finished the autopsy on Mrs. Oberhauser," said Bill. "You might want to see some of this."

"Fair enough. I'll be there in forty minutes."

We signed off. I changed into jeans and a sweater, my partially dried boots, and my parka. "Bye, Cat," I called to my independent but pretty housemate.

I strode into the coroner investigator's office and tapped on the door before entering. Bill was typing at a feverish pitch. I peeled off my coat and gloves and dropped into the worn, black swivel chair on the other side of his desk. By the look of him, I'd had much more rest than he had.

"You sounded like you found something that surprised you, Bill. What's up?"

He handed me a clear plastic bag with my current business card in it. On the back of the card, in neatly printed letters was a warning. "SHE'S NUMBER 5."

"So, we're right, huh? He's back." I dropped my head in my hands. "*Why* is he back?" I asked Bill who knew exactly who I was talking about.

He patted my shoulder. "I don't know, but we have to catch him this time. You know how bad this will get."

And that was the truth. I did know. Too well. This guy had a signature that nightmares were made of. "Why her? She doesn't fit his old MO at all."

"He's been out of action for five years, Mike. Maybe his MO has changed. Maybe he's been locked up someplace and learned new tricks? I have no idea. However strange it is, he's got your new business cards and he's connected to you somehow. This guy knows you better than you know him."

That was probably what terrified me most. He'd always seemed to be a step ahead of me. Facing him scared me to death and yet I'd been obsessed with catching him. Obsessed with making him pay for killing that young girl....

But I hadn't made it happen. When we'd busted through the door to his cold-water flat in South Trenton, all that was left was a note for me. In that same, meticulous handwriting he'd written: "I'LL BE BACK."

"You okay, Mike?" Bill asked quietly, pushing a cup of what he called coffee into my hands. I nodded but didn't trust myself to open my mouth.

Years of psychotherapy down the drain with one dead woman and three little words. My nemesis had murdered four people before he suddenly disappeared. I'd celebrated by marrying Elise. Somehow a musky perfume like hers had been in the air at that run-down apartment and I'd taken it as an omen of good things to come. A year for major errors, it would seem.

I sipped the hot liquid and ran my fingers through my hair. "Okay. I'm better trained, have better resources and don't have a family to worry about this time around. This time we win, Bill. I promise."

He nodded, knowing how painful the whole thing had been for me. The killer, who'd become the "Ice Man" to us, had almost destroyed my life. My very own Jeffrey Damler. Just what I needed.

I stood and looked at Bill. "Can I have a copy of that report when you're done? Today I'll get clear to handle this. Tomorrow I start to track down Damian Harbinger."

He nodded and looked at me like an older brother who knew I was headed for a broken heart. "Promise me you'll ask for help with this. You were way too close to the edge last time." "Sure, Bill. Don't worry. But I'm going to get him. That's a promise, too."

* * *

The Captain called me in, and I stood at parade rest before his desk. "Close the door, Holmes, and have a seat."

I sat in the chair, resting my left ankle across my right knee. "Yes, sir?"

"Judging from this autopsy report and the evidence collected from the victim looks like the Ice Man is back in town. Should I put someone else on this case?"

My heart just about jumped out of my chest, but I kept the Captain from seeing it. "No sir, I want to work this case. I wouldn't mind some help this time, though. The only thing that counts is that we catch him before he murders again."

I looked at him closely and knew I was already too late for that sentiment. The Ice Man had been a busy, busy man. I hung my head. "Who and where?"

"Just before dawn, we figure. Your ex-wife's next-door neighbor.
"

"Not, Marge! Please, tell me it wasn't Marge." My resolve to stay professional oozed out through my slumped shoulders.

"I'm sorry, Holmes. We've put your ex in protective custody, but she's not happy about it."

"Tough shit. Does she know about Marge? Does she know how lucky she is to be alive?"

"Doesn't sound like she considers herself lucky about anything if you ask me. Will your talking to her make any difference?"

"Yeah. It would probably make it worse."

"Try. Next time she calls your cell phone, answer it. Get her calmed down."

I shook my head, but there was no use arguing with the boss. "What do we have on Marge's murder?"

"Ice pick to the throat and a few other places. Mutilated breasts. The killer's one very angry fellow."

I ran the old files back through my brain like a worn out black-and-white slide series. "By the time the killings stopped last time, I wasn't so sure our killer was a man."

"You did the work at Quantico, Holmes. You know women serial killers are few and far between."

"But not altogether absent. And we both know this is personal. It's connected to me, somehow."

Cap waved me out of his office and reached for the phone. "The press will be all over this Oberhauser murder. I expect the FBI will be sniffing around the end of the week." He picked up a pen and pointed it at my chest. "You be careful and take Cyrus with you. You'll need a partner. A sharp one."

I closed the door behind me and wondered how the day could get worse. Ordered to talk to an ex-wife who would like to see an ice pick sticking out of *my* anatomy and enlisting a partner who had a chip on her shoulder like Mike Tyson. *Damn.*

* * *

"I know, Elise, but this is for your good. Do you want to become the next corpse on this guy's list? It's possible that could happen, you know. You need to calm down."

I held the phone away from my ear so I could retain my hearing. She ranted at full steam about her freedoms and how unfair it was that someone was after her when I was the bastard. I had no defense that would work with her, so I just waited her out.

"I can't come up there right now–I have to work this case. You'll be fine. The officer with you will see that you have all you need."

She switched to whining which was almost worse than the screaming. However, I knew her well enough to know she was about out of energy. "I know. I agree it stinks. Just try and be patient a few days, okay?"

I closed the phone and wished for coffee, too drained to go find some. The desk phone rang and I hit the speaker button without opening my eyes. "Holmes."

"Mike, I just spoke to the Bergen County coroner. The Myers woman was killed in exactly the same way as the Oberhauser woman. That prompted me to do some trajectory studies. You want to come take a look?"

I declined and Bill forged on. "Killer is left handed for sure. Thrust measurements indicate the probable weight is between one forty and one fifty pounds. The entry wound is almost straight in. I'd have to say the killer is about the height of these women. Around five-foot-seven or eight, maybe."

I listened and jotted some notes. "I'm back to thinking we may have a female killer here, Bill. This info's good, but I need more. I'm going to call Bergen County. Keep me posted, buddy."

The speaker went quiet and I got up to pace. I think better when I'm pacing for some reason. My phone rang and I reached for the receiver. It was Joseph. I put him on speakerphone.

"Good afternoon, sir. What can I do for you?"

He paused a moment. "I have a question for you, Detective. Do you have a moment?"

"Sure. Go ahead." I crossed the office to close the door.

"I was going through the desk drawer tonight to find the checkbook to pay the funeral home for Daphne's burial."

"I'm sorry, Joseph."

"I know Detective. And I, for you."

My cop radar went nuts. "How so?"

"Do you know an Elise Holmes?"

"Why do you ask?" I hedged, trying to swallow around the lump in my throat. What the hell had she done now? Now it was my turn to wait for that other shoe to drop.

"Do you?" he asked me again.

"Not anymore. We've been divorced for almost a year. How do you know Elise?"

"Oh, I don't know her, Detective. But apparently, my wife did."

"What makes you say that?" I wiped my palms on the knees of my slacks.

"Daphne handled the finances. In the drawer is a birthday card, obviously made out to her lover. There is a carbon duplicate of a check made payable to Elise Holmes. For two-hundred-fifty-thousand dollars."

I sank back my chair. Lovers? *A quarter-million dollars*? What the hell was going on?

"Detective? Are you there?"

This was like something from the Twilight Zone. None of this could be true. I swallowed hard. "I'm here, Joseph," I replied. "Confused as hell, though."

Someone knocked on my closed door but I ignored them. I waited to see if Joseph had anything else for me.

"Will you need these for your case, Detective?"

I blew out a long sigh and wished the answer was no, but of course, it couldn't be. "Yes, I will. Please put them in a plastic bag and I'll have them picked up from you. Thank you, Joseph."

"I'm sorry, Detective. We will speak again, I'm sure. Goodbye."

I stood there listening to the dial tone for a half a minute. I looked up to find Megan Cyrus stationed in front of my desk, Glock on her hip, coat slung over her shoulder.

"Where do we start?" she asked in her smoker-husky voice. I shook my head.

* * *

I'm assigned to the Toms River State Police barracks. The good thing about that is that it's in Ocean County where the Sheriff's department has one of the best crime labs in the country. The downside is Toms River is a long way from Bergen County.

I left my partner to research the Oberhausers and get as much background on Elise Kenney Holmes as possible. I apparently didn't know the woman at all.

It took me two hours to reach the county courthouse and find the coroner on Marge's case. He pulled out the file and photos and pushed them in my direction. "Since you had the first murder, you're a primary on this investigation. The County boys said to cooperate."

I looked at the photos. Poor Marge. A bright, energetic woman in her early thirties who thought everyone deserved to have a friend, even Elise. It's always tougher to look at crime scene photos when you know the victim personally. I swallowed the knot in my throat.

"Do you think a woman could have done this?" I asked Amos Schultz without preamble.

The coroner brushed his deep brown mustache with his index finger. "Sure. A pretty pissed-off woman, but the height and weight of your perp could be that of a woman. Of course, it could just as easily be a slight man."

I pulled out some photos of my own. "This is Damien Harbinger. We were really close to nailing him last time—would you have any records on him?"

He took the photo and left the room. Five minutes later he was back. "I've asked Paula to run it through the databases. We may learn something."

We discussed the file and findings for another hour. A tall, dark-haired woman with glasses popped into Amos' office and dropped a report on his desk. Without a word, she vanished.

He picked up the report and scanned it. "Well, if it was Harbinger last go around, it isn't him this time."

"Why not?"

"Take a look." He handed me the report and leaned back in the chair.

Harbinger, arrested, tried and convicted of child molestation in Texas, had been murdered while in the prison exercise yard. Over a year ago. *Crap.*

"Can I keep this?" I asked as I stood. He nodded. I put everything in the folder he'd given me when I arrived. We shook hands and parted company at the door.

I was on the Garden State Parkway, aptly named since you are mostly parked in traffic when you are on it. I came upon the rest area and pulled off to call Cyrus.

"When you going to be back here?" she asked.

"At this rate? Sometime before my forty-fifth birthday. Why?"

"We have a lot to go over. And you aren't going to like any of it."

I sighed. What the hell? I didn't like any of the rest of this case. Why should I be surprised now?

* * *

Putting aside her strong feminist instincts and not biting my head off for suggesting dinner, Cyrus and I met at The Grill for something to eat. It had been a long time since breakfast for me. We ordered, and over tall colas, we compared notes. I ticked my findings off first.

"How well did you know your wife before you were married?" She led with a right uppercut.

"Not very, I'm afraid. We met in a jazz club that I frequented. She was lovely, willing and quite smart, so when we weren't in bed, we could actually have conversations that were challenging."

She let my sexist comment slide. "What happened?"

"You doing a profile on her or me?"

"You each relate to the other. Need to know both, don't I?"

Of course, she was right. A recent grad of the FBI academy for law enforcement members, Cyrus knew she was on the scent.

"I worked a lot of hours, spent a lot of time alone. Elise needed company as well as money to keep her in a manner she wanted to become accustomed to. She took up gambling and sleeping around. I wasn't happy about either hobby, to be honest with you."

"How long before you caught on?"

I sat back to let the waitress put our orders on the table in front of us. "Almost four years. We split up for a couple of months, tried to put it back together once. Our divorce was final eleven months ago."

"I read the divorce decree. You were pretty generous."

"I didn't want anything. She wanted the house—I still help pay for it. She can manage the rest, even though she says she can't."

"Okay. Well, aside from her financial records which she hasn't consented to let me see, I've got about as much as I could find. Did you know she'd been arrested?"

I almost spit my Greek salad in her face. "Arrested? When? For what?"

"Prostitution. About six months before you two were married. Hope you got tested."

I was speechless. Who'd have thought I should run a background check on my future wife? Now I was wishing that I had. "That the only time?"

"The only one in NJ. Seems she's been picked up in Vegas, too. Apparently, she was running a scam of some sort out there. She was busted with a guy named Otto Josephson. Got six months for that one."

"You're a thorough investigator, Cyrus. The bad guys don't stand a chance."

"By the look on your face, neither do the good guys."

I washed down my food with soda. "What do you have on Oberhauser?"

She shrugged, took a bite of her chicken sandwich and chewed a few times before swallowing. "He was tougher, believe it or not. Info trail doesn't even really start on him until about eleven years ago. Where did you say he got his money?"

"He claimed it was a family business of some kind. Nowadays, he makes his money selling God to people who watch too much television at three in the morning."

"I couldn't find anything in industry or any of the business directories on Oberhauser until he became a minister. Found a marriage announcement to a Lisa Needham. No record of death or divorce that I could find. Nor could I validate the marriage."

"Where were they married? Someone would have records."

"Vegas."

"Aha. Well, the marriage may have been real or not; annulled maybe when everyone sobered up?"

"Maybe. But if he was married to Lisa Needham and never divorced her, then his marriage to Daphne would be null and void. And how would it look for the good minister to be a bigamist?"

"Wouldn't look very good, that's for sure. The donations might slow down a bit if that got out, I guess. Good work, Cyrus."

We finished our meals and paid the check. I sat over coffee to think before I headed for home. "Can you get any proof of that marriage? I'd like to have a big stick in my pocket when I call on Joseph Oberhauser."

"I don't right now, but I'll have it for you by tomorrow if it exists. I promise."

I was sure she would.

* * *

I called Elise at the hotel. I was secured in my office. The officer assured me the ex was still safe and sound. And asleep. I asked her to have Elise call me in the next half hour.

When the phone rang, I braced myself as I hit the speaker button. "If you haven't called to tell me I'm free to go home Michael, you should just hang up now."

"Sorry, Elise. I called to get some answers. The nasty part about being involved in murder, even remotely, is that everything about everyone gets investigated." I heard an intake of breath on the other end of the line.

"I want permission to access your bank records, Elise. Some interesting facts have been brought to light."

"Like what?" she hissed.

"Like your arrests for prostitution and fraud. You neglected to mention those to me at any time."

"So? You were a cop for god's sake, Michael. You didn't ask and I didn't tell. Those things were misunderstandings, anyway. I didn't do much time. You knew damned well I wasn't an angel."

That was true enough. From the first time in the back seat of my Monte Carlo, it was evident that Elise was no virgin. Hell, the sex was always so hot–not to mention interesting–that I didn't even care.

"Fair enough. Anything else you omitted in your background, Elise?"

"You know, if you want my permission to look at my finances you'd better change your tone, Michael. I don't know what you're inferring but I don't like it."

"I don't need your permission, Elise. My partner is getting a court order in case you decide not to cooperate."

"On what grounds?" she growled. She'd learned a few things during the years she was a cop's wife.

"On the grounds that your name was found in a murder victim's checkbook."

I filled the silence with a smirk. The woman was finally speechless.

"That's impossible," she offered weakly.

"That's what I thought. But I'm looking right at it. A quarter of a million dollars and you're calling *me* for money? What was the money for, Elise? You gambling again?"

"My life is none of your business. And my attorney says I don't have to stay in protective custody if I don't want to, so I'm leaving. You are out of time with me, Michael Holmes."

"You are no longer in protective custody, Elise. You're the suspect in a murder investigation which means you're now under arrest. Better call that attorney again."

I hung up the phone when I heard the knock on the hotel room door. Elise would be on her way to the Ocean County Sheriff's office, if only for a few hours. I hoped it would buy me the time I needed to get more answers.

* * *

I pulled up to Joseph Oberhauser's house and parked on the side of the large oval. The snow from the other night had been cleared. Cobblestones dried in the sunlight. I rang the bell.

"Detective," Joseph said, taking my hand in his. "I knew we'd meet again. How are you doing with the investigation?"

"That's why I'm here, Joseph. Some confusing things popped up."

"What can I help you with?"

I smiled and pulled off my coat. Although I wasn't happy in the shirt and tie, I played the part for this man. "Who are you, Joseph?"

His smile only faltered a second. "You know who I am."

"Sure, I know who you are *now*. Who were you twelve years ago?"

"I'm sure I don't know what you are asking, Detective. Do I need my lawyer? Am I under suspicion in the death of my wife?"

"The husband is always a suspect. My job is to put profiles together on everyone in the case. My research on you starts eleven years ago. Can't find any family business or any family at all for that matter. We did locate a Joseph Oberhauser, but he's been dead almost sixty years. Know anything about that?"

Joseph's robust color drained from his face but he remained silent. He got up and poured himself a brandy, then sat down on the couch across from me.

"You are going to have to come to the station to have your fingerprints processed, Joseph. We need to account for all the prints in your wife's car. We'll find out who you really are anyway."

The good Reverend Oberhauser stood up and walked across the Alice in Wonderland floor and reached for the door.

"My attorney and I will be there, this afternoon, Detective. Until then, you and I are done talking."

* * *

Just as I'd cleaned up the last of my lunch and tossed the brown bag in the trash basket, Patrolman Knight stopped in. "My report, sir."

I took it and thanked him, but he stood uneasily in the doorway. "Anything else, Officer?"

He nodded, shifting his hat in his hands. "Yes, sir. I saw the pictures of that woman. I know her."

I smiled. "A lot of people know that face, son. Daphne was a professional model for years. You've probably seen her on magazine covers or television."

"No sir, that's not it. I saw her here. Just a few weeks ago."

I stood up. "Are you sure? You saw her here in the station?"

"Yes, sir. She was sitting outside in the waiting area when I came in with a transport. When I went back out front to see if she was being helped, she was gone. Nobody else had seen her. I thought maybe I'd imagined the whole thing."

"Thank you, Knight. You've been a big help."

The young man left my office and then I had even more to chew on. As they often do, the puzzle had more pieces than I originally suspected. Cyrus appeared next.

"Safe to come in?" she asked, not waiting for my reply.

"What do you have?" I pulled out a fresh notepad and got ready to jot down more questions.

"Elise Holmes has quite a portfolio. She'll be able to retire long before you can."

"What was the last deposit amount and when?"

"A hundred thousand dollars. The large dollar deposits don't go to her bank account. They go directly into an investment account."

"Is she using a fund manager or picking her own stock?"

"About half of it is stock. A publicly held corporation known as In God We Trust, Inc."

"Damn. And let me guess, J. Oberhauser is the CEO."

Megan smiled and the room lit up. I almost told her she should do it more often, but sexist comments like that ended many a career these days.

"Not exactly," she said.

"Then who?"

"Daphne Oberhauser."

* * *

I sat in the observation booth while my partner interrogated Elise. I watched with admiration as Megan came right to the point.

Elise didn't blink an eye when confronted with her growing fortune or her association with the dead woman's company. Her attorney sat quietly by her side, taking the occasional note and nodding yes or no to indicate authorization to reply.

Her attorney allowed the questions to go on for twenty minutes, then stood and piled notes and pencils into her briefcase. "My client has answered your questions. She bought stock in the company of a good friend. That's not illegal. She has not traded nor obtained that stock illegally. Do you intend to file some charge against her? If so, let's get on with it. If not, we're leaving."

Megan stood and faced the seasoned lawyer. "If we can put your client at the scene, we'll be charging her with murder, Counselor. I recommend you get the facts from her now."

The lawyer pulled on her overcoat and laughed. "Witnesses? In a raging snowstorm? I doubt it. However, if you are interested, my client does have a suggestion."

Megan headed for the door but remained cool, aloof. "And that might be what? That her ex-husband did it?"

Elise laughed with glee, and I grit my teeth. "Don't be silly. Daphne's husband did it."

"Counselor, you may not be aware, but a second woman's been murdered. By ice pick, no less. The next-door neighbor of *your client*. Think the good Reverend killed her, too?" Megan pulled open the door. "We'll be in touch. Don't go on any trips."

* * *

I entered the conference room to speak with Joseph Oberhauser and his attorney. I was waiting for the fingerprint information to come back. If he'd been arrested any time in the past twenty years, we'd get a hit.

We shook hands like civilized men and took seats. The lawyer indicated, for the record of course, that his client had come in of his own free will and would cooperate in any way he could. He was, after all, grief-stricken and desperate to find his wife's killer.

"Joseph, can you think of any reason why your wife would have been here in the barracks a couple of weeks ago?"

"I'm sure I have no idea. I didn't know she was."

"How much do you know about your wife's life, Joseph? I was surprised to find out you'd entrusted your earthly gains to her."

"It's purely a matter of corporate structure, that's all. Daphne was the CEO, I was the CFO. George here," he said, nodding toward his lawyer, "is on the board, too. He's the Secretary and Legal Advisor. It's all quite legitimate, I assure you."

"We'll see. I'm waiting for the financial statements now. Even privately-held companies must provide them for investors, right?"

The lawyer spoke up. "Of course, but you are not an investor, Detective. You could, of course, obtain an Annual Report."

I smiled. "Yes, I could. But my ex-wife is an investor, isn't she, Joseph?"

"I'm sure we have many investors, Mr. Holmes. I don't know about your ex-wife."

Megan appeared at the door and signaled thumbs up. Then she slipped me a piece of paper. My knees almost gave out. I turned to his smug counselor.

"Counselor, let me introduce you to Otto Josephson."

* * *

I had nothing to hold Josephson on since name and career changes weren't illegal, and I couldn't prove his religious movement was a fraud. However, I did intend to have the IRS take a good look at his books and warned his attorney to make sure the man stayed in town.

I headed for the Captain's office where I found Megan Cyrus waiting for me. I dropped into the remaining chair, the tension in my six-foot-tall frame emphasized by a killer headache. "Well, I don't know what we've found except a lot of people playing a lot of games."

"I'll say," Megan muttered, looking at the Captain. He nodded.

"What's up with you two?" I asked warily. "Another murder?"

"No, no more murders. But we did Elise's fingerprints when she came in. Her name is not Elise Kenney."

"Sure, it is. We had to have raised seal birth certificates when we got our marriage license. I saw it."

"Yeah, probably paid for by Otto Josephson. So much cheaper than divorce."

"Spit it out, Cyrus," I growled.

"Elise Kenney Holmes is really Lisa Needham. Wife of Otto Josephson."

What?! I'd married a prostitute and a bigamist. *Nice going, Holmes,* I thought. *At least she wasn't a murderer, though.*

"Should I continue?" asked Cyrus in her clipped, chip-back-on-her-shoulder tone of voice.

I didn't bother to answer since the question was rhetorical. She handed me a copy of the marriage certificate issued by the City of Las Vegas.

"Bergen County Sheriff's office got a lead. A neighbor saw Daphne at Elise's house last Friday afternoon. Also saw the other victim come out of the house. Looked really upset."

I leaned over and settled my elbows on my knees. I was so tired every muscle in my body ached. Did Daphne kill Marge? Did Josephson kill Daphne? How the hell did we prove anything? The snowstorm had eliminated the crime scene and most of the forensic evidence. Elise's fingerprints would have been in Marge's house, but Daphne's shouldn't have been. Unless unknown to me, they'd all become friends....

"You know, I have no idea where to go with this. I'm going home. I'm going to bed for eight hours and in the morning, I will try to sort it out."

A commotion in the hallway caught our attention. Trained to react quickly to shouting voices, the three of us ducked to floor level, pulled our weapons and belly-crawled to the door. I opened it a crack. Then a little further. Most of our coworkers were hiding behind furniture.

I made it across the hallway to an interview cubicle. I could hear Elise. Josephson gasping for air. I rose up on my knees, Megan beside me. I whispered in her right ear. "I'm going closer. Maybe I can talk her down."

"She's not only a killer, Mike, she's gone over the fine line. She won't hear you."

I looked her in the eye. Some of this was my fault. I hadn't had a clue and I should have. "I have to try," I growled before I darted to the desk closest to the commotion. I could make out Josephson lying in a pool of blood, his attorney's arms around him. A letter opener stuck out of his chest.

"Elise, talk to me. It's Mike."

She cackled and held the dispatcher's gun to her attorney's graying head. "I know who you are, Mike. You're a piece of shit. You never thought I was good enough for you. Well, you were right, weren't you?"

I lowered my weapon in hopes she'd lower hers. At least nine other guns including a shotgun were aimed at her. If she got me, she and the attorney would be toast. The attorney and I would be collateral damage. Like Marge. And Josephson. And maybe even Daphne.

"Tell me why, Elise. You killed the other four before Daphne, too, didn't you?"

"Got your attention, didn't it, Mr. Supercop?" The lady lawyer gasped as Elise jerked her head back even further. "No one has ever thought I was good enough. Well, the almighty preacher can just explain this to his Maker. We were going to be rich. Then he runs out, changes his name, leaves me in jail, and marries a model who better suits his new image."

I moved a few steps closer. "Why Marge, Elise? She was your friend."

She nodded, the heavy handgun wavering in her hand. "I know, but she walked in the house when Daphne was trying to get me to take the quarter mill to get lost. Marge was making me crazy about how I should go to the police. She was going to go *for* me. Thought she was helping." A tear coursed down her cheek.

I dove in and dropped them both to the floor, knocking away the Glock in the process. Troopers of all ranks, size, and gender piled on. When we were untangled, Elise was in custody, the attorney was in the arms of the Captain, and Otto Josephson was as dead as his beautiful Daphne.

Megan Cyrus was visibly shaken as she stood at my side. "She's the coldest woman I've ever seen, Mike."

"Yup," I said as I turned toward my office. "Cold as ice."

#

About the Author

N. L. Quatrano is the award-winning author of short and full-length fiction. MURDER IN BLACK AND WHITE, and STILL SHOT, Books one and two of the Point and Shoot Mystery series, are available wherever books are sold. Another award-winning manuscript, MERCIFUL BLESSINGS, written with co-author D. K. Ludas, will be released in March of 2018 by Salt Run Publishing. Email: nancy@NLQuatrano.com

GONE ON THE 4TH OF JULY

Kristina Rienzi

The canvas room billowed in the ocean breeze summoning dark and painful memories from decades ago. Gemma sipped her freshly brewed Kona coffee on the modest porch she loved so much. Brightly colored plants hung from the awning above, and an American flag swayed in the wind. Her town looked more like a county fair, but she wouldn't have it any other way. Tent City was her home, and she loved every inch of it.

She cradled the bouquet of thirty dark red roses and rocked comfortably in her lavender rocking chair. The kind stranger had left them on her doorstep again this year. They appeared every year on the anniversary of Georgia's disappearance, one for each year she'd been gone. Gemma had no idea who would make such a concerted effort to honor a lost little girl, but she was grateful for the generous soul who did, and she cherished each and every flower. Her heart beamed with love that someone random person, who didn't want to be known, had never forgotten her sweet sister.

Life went on in Tent City. Kids rode their bikes, people walked their dogs, and not much had changed there over the years. It was a time warp at the Jersey Shore in many ways, not only for the residents but for Gemma, too.

A sense of eerie calm engulfed her, and she breathed it into her soul, making it a part of her as her sister had always been. The best years of her life had been her summers in Ocean Grove with Georgia. Sand between their toes, collecting shells on the beach, and nightly barbecues, Gemma and Georgia weren't only sisters, they were twins, soulmates, and the same person in so many ways. Mirror images of each other on the outside, they were also similar in personality. Even at only five years old, Gemma knew she had a lifelong best friend in Georgia.

A cold breeze brushed Gemma's face, and she reached to touch it before it evaporated. Perhaps it was Georgia's ghost lingering; a guardian angel beside Gemma on a day she needed it most. She welcomed any sign of her twin today.

Her cell phone buzzed on the arm of the rocking chair. "Hey, Mom."

"Hey, Sweetie. How are you?"

"Hanging in there. How are you guys doing?"

"Dad refuses to acknowledge Georgia's disappearance today. Of course, I lit a candle for her, and said a prayer." Her voice cracked. "It's all I can manage to do. If I do any more than that, I'll get stuck in grief and I may never get out."

"Grieving is cathartic. It's your love for her that has no place to go now. Don't hold it in, Ma. It's not good for your health." Gemma worried about her parents being so far away and getting to them quickly if anything happened to either of them. They'd wanted her to join them in Virginia Beach when they retired, but she refused. She felt terrible saying no since she was their only living child, but Ocean Grove was her home.

Light sobs, followed by a cough came through the line. "I'm doing the best I can." Her mom swallowed hard. "I honor Georgia daily, and on always more on special days, but today is so hard. I don't want to remember it because when I do, it's all-consuming."

"All of her anniversaries are tough, but this year seems worse to me, too."

"Thirty years is a milestone. It's a lifetime ago, yet it feels like just yesterday."

"It does to me too, Ma."

"It makes it worse that everyone is celebrating."

"The holiday could be an easy distraction if you let it."

Her mom sighed. "I know you're right. I just can't bring myself to celebrate. How can I eat hot dogs and marvel at the fireworks when I know my baby vanished on this same day? She's still out there, and she needs me."

"You need to live a little. You can't change what happened."

"I don't even know what happened."

"We have to believe Georgia is somewhere safe and happy, even if it's in Heaven." Gemma knew being so blunt would upset her mom, but she hated for her to live in despair. "The roses came again."

Her mother sighed. "I know you think it's sweet, but it bothers me. If someone's sending them in good faith, why isn't there a card attached? Why aren't they handing them to you themselves? Why all the secrecy?" She huffed. "Who would honor her disappearance like this? It doesn't make sense, Gem. I think you should tell the police."

"You're overreacting. Can't I just enjoy the flowers?"

"I suppose you can. Be safe anyway. Love you." Then her mom hung up.

She wished life was different and she could be with her parents today, but they'd never visit. She'd made a good life for herself in the haunted little town, but her mom and dad refused to return. She couldn't blame them. Their memories of Tent City were too painful. Their family would never be complete again, and for parents, it was torture. Once Georgia vanished, they'd spent their lives searching for her to no end. After years of no leads, her missing person's case went cold. When her parents finally accepted that their daughter was never coming home, they left Ocean Grove and never looked back.

Gemma made her way inside, through the brightly decorated canvas sitting room where she liked to read and relax, and into the efficiency kitchen. She pulled a purple-hued glass vase down from the shelf above the sink. She added tepid water, and then put the freshly cut roses breathing their sweet scent in before putting them back in the vase. They were perched beautifully in front of the window overlooking her neighbor's yard, and lush garden. She considered scoping out her neighborhood to see whose yard was missing roses.

Unlike her parents, Gemma couldn't stop looking back. Tent City was Georgia's home, and it had become Gemma's, too. She held out hope that the truth would come out in the very place Georgia's mystery began. Her town had the answers. Maybe the roses did, too, like her mother said. Gemma would enjoy them, but she wouldn't forget why they sat, both beautiful and sad, on her shelf.

Even if it took another thirty years, Gemma would find out what happened to her twin all those Fourth of Julys ago.

* * *

Ocean Grove was jam-packed for the holiday. Gemma strolled down Beach Ave feeling naked with only her tank dress, flip-flops, sunglasses and cross body bag on. Her free arms were swinging because she had nothing to carry, except the pain in her heart. She zigzagged in and around beachgoers who mobbed the streets carrying overstuffed backpacks, giant beach bags, clanky chairs, awkward umbrellas, and coolers full of God-knew-what. They couldn't buy booze locally so it was highly likely they'd smuggled it into the town. Ocean Grove may have been a dry town, but spirits, in several forms, roamed freely.

She shook her head. *It's the beach, not a mission into space from which you'll never return.* So much stuff!

Cars slugged by on the tiny streets already lined with parked cars. The drivers were scoping out every inch of every street. Parking was slim to none, especially on a holiday.

When she finally reached Bath Ave, she turned left toward Thompson Park. The beach was to her right, where most people were going, but she had no desire to beach it today. The whole town buzzed with energy and activity. Locals kept to their porches with their company, and visitors commingled in the common areas and storefronts wasting time until the festivities began. Ocean Grove was the place to be in Monmouth County on the Fourth of July. The otherwise dead quiet and mysterious town brimmed with life that day. There were endless secrets hidden in her old beach town, but ghost souls outnumbering those with a heartbeat wasn't one of them. She'd always hoped Georgia wasn't one of the ghosts in her paranormal town, but her gut had told her otherwise.

There were no empty benches at Thompson Park. Gemma didn't mind. Her black maxi dress was long enough to sit on so she dropped onto the grass. She took in the scenery, which was a pinch of relaxation with a pound of chaos. It entertained her and got her mind off of the thirtieth anniversary plaguing her heart.

She drifted off, creating a story in her head about a nearby family eating their ice cream when a tap on the shoulder turned her around.

"Hey, Gemma." A handsome man who looked to be around her age stood over her. He looked familiar, but she couldn't place him.

"Hi." She pushed up to standing and brushed off the back of her dress. "I don't mean to be rude, but how do we know each other?"

He smiled and it gleamed. "Stupid me," he said. "I shouldn't have assumed you'd remember me. It's been a long time since I've been back. Too long."

Then it hit her. "Aaron James." She winked. "Don't tell me I have a bad memory." His elderly father, Quincy still lived on her street but Aaron had moved away long before Gemma moved back. She hadn't seen him since they were kids.

He gave her a tight bear hug and lifted her off the ground. When her feet hit the grass, she felt a little woozy. She wasn't sure if it was the old kiddie crush, foggy memories, or something else.

"How are you, kiddo?"

"No complaints. How's your dad? I haven't seen him in a few weeks now. He's usually outside in his chair drinking tea when I go for my morning run."

"Well, age hasn't been kind to the old man. He fell last week and injured his hip. He needs surgery, then rehab, and then he's bound for senior living. It's just not safe for him to live home alone anymore."

"I'm sorry to hear that. It must be hard."

"Where are your folks?"

"Virginia. They moved years ago and rented our place here for a while. Then I moved in and haven't left the OG since." She pursed her lips. "Kinda sad, huh?"

"Not at all. OG is the best. Tent City rules, of course."

"Of course." She felt her cheeks blush and prayed she wasn't crushing on him again when he'd just leave in a few days. "What about you? Where are you these days?"

"California. I travel for work so much that I haven't gotten back home as often as I would have liked. I'd fly Dad out to be with me on the holidays because the weather was much better for his arthritis." He put his hands up. "Now, I'm back for good."

"You can't be seriously trading out California for this one-horse town."

"I certainly am. I'll be helping Dad through his surgery, then I'm moving back into my old house so I can be closer to him. Guess we'll be neighbors again, huh?" Aaron grinned.

"Awesome." The thought of it set her heart on fire. There was an obvious connection. Even as kids they were close, but it might be too much for her to even have a friendship with him after all she'd been through.

"Sure is. I'm excited about it."

"What about a wife...any kids?"

"Nope. I never got married. I didn't have time for a family with my career taking me all over the country and then it sort of slipped through my fingers. But, hey, I'm not that old, right?"

"Never too old," Gemma said.

"You?" He tilted his head.

"Not yet."

"Maybe there's hope for both of us." He put his hand on her back. "Ice cream?"

The pang of a memory hit her heart. Before she had a chance to answer, they were already walking toward the popular ice cream shop around the corner. "Sure, why not?"

An hour later, they had their treats in hand. She took a bite of her chocolate fudge sundae and visions of the day Georgia disappeared came rushing back.

She and Georgia were playing in Aaron's backyard when his dad brought them ice cream. She remembered it so clearly. The butter pecan was dripping from the sugar cone and the girls squealed with happiness. They preferred strawberry, like their hair, but butter pecan was the only kind of ice cream at Aaron's because it was his dad's favorite. Aaron had been annoyed and it set him off in a bad mood, so they finished their ice cream and went home.

She shook the memory away. "How's yours?"

"Are you kidding? A waffle cone with peanut butter cups on vanilla ice cream is the epitome of a Jersey Shore summer. I'm thrilled to be back."

They made their way to her house. "Guess this is where we part ways."

Aaron bit his lip. "You have any plans to watch the fireworks?"

Gemma looked down. "Nope. I'll just sit on my porch and see what I can see. I can't handle the crowds of people. It gives me major anxiety. I'm at peace here."

Aaron smiled. "Well, then you must come to my house. I

smuggled in some wine, and I make a mean pasta and meatballs."

"What about your dad?"

"He's staying with my aunt in Neptune until his surgery. When everything happened, we started making the arrangements for me to move in. So technically, the place is mine now."

Her heart thumped. "All right. It sounds great then."

"Perfect," he said. "Stop by around eight. We'll do dinner and then hit the roof for the light show."

"Works for me." Gemma waved goodbye.

Aaron seemed to skip off, but Gemma had mixed emotions. Tonight was her night to honor her sister, alone. But he was a part of that time in her life, and now he was back. Maybe this was the sign her sister was sending. She had no choice but to find out.

* * *

The James's house looked exactly as she'd remembered all those years ago. It hadn't been updated since they were kids, and still had the old beach house feel to it. The exact same seashell lamps she remembered sat on the whitewashed end tables in the living room, with cream canvas couches that had to be a hundred years old. Everything was in meticulous order, which Gemma assumed was Aaron's doing.

Gemma sipped her glass of Chardonnay at the round, glass dining room table. The light blue starfish dinner plates made her smile. They looked new, and she loved them. "The place looks great, still. Not much has changed."

Aaron dimmed the dining room lights and lit the mini candelabra on the table. "I've done a few things since I've been here. I still have work to do, but I want to keep the beach house's integrity. This town has character and I'd like to think I could be a part of that living here."

"It sure does. It's one of the reasons I moved back to Tent City. There's nowhere else like it and no place I'd rather be in the world."

"The other reason was Georgia, wasn't it?"

Aaron's mention of her sister's name sent Gemma zooming back to 1987 and the day her twin disappeared. A day she'd spent in the very same house she was in right now before her life had changed forever. Her pulse quickened and her mouth went dry. She sipped her wine again.

"Memories are all I have left, and they live here."

His expression shifted slightly and Gemma wasn't sure if he was upset or afraid. "They do. This is exactly where you should be," Aaron said and then he headed into the kitchen. He opened the fridge and then peeked his head above the door to look at Gemma. "Is Ranch dressing okay?"

"Absolutely." It was her favorite and Georgia's, too.

Aaron served two bowls of a colorful salad. It was clear he'd been food shopping and had read her mind. It had all of her favorite ingredients, and nothing she picked out. Maybe he was a match made in heaven for her after all. Gemma tried not to think about that too much. It was inappropriate given the day.

He lifted his glass of wine. "To Georgia–and to you, my long-ago friend."

They clinked glasses and took a sip. "Today is the thirtieth anniversary of her disappearance." Gemma looked out to the backyard as she spoke. "I can't believe how much time has passed. It feels like yesterday."

"I know. It does. That's why I wanted you here tonight." Aaron put his hand on hers. "I've never forgotten little Georgia or you. And being back in town, I knew today was the perfect day to be together. Don't you agree?"

Gemma left her hand under his but felt the urge to pull away. It wasn't that she didn't want to hold his hand. The chemistry between them was palpable. It was more that she wanted tonight to be about honoring Georgia, and somehow that had been lost on her when she looked into his cobalt eyes.

The bungalow stuck in time and the mention of her twin's name brought it all back to the front of her mind. Gemma knew she should leave–her gut told her so–but it would be rude. She'd get through the night and try to have some fun, then she'd honor her sister at home, alone, later.

"I do. Today's about Georgia for me," Gemma said, with a slight crack in her voice. "Although this is a nice distraction."

Aaron smiled wide. "I knew you'd say that."

They finished their meals making chit-chatty conversation, but nothing of substance. They both seemed to be in a trance of one kind or another. Maybe they were reminiscing about the past or pondering about the future. Either way, they were in their own worlds.

After the table was clear and the dishes in the small sink, Aaron came to her side of the table. She expected him to pull the chair out, but instead, he stood behind her gently massaging her shoulders. For once in a very long time, against her own strong will, she relaxed under his touch. Then he leaned down, his lips next to her ear. It tickled and sent goosebumps all over her body. She felt ashamed to be so attracted to someone on a day she should be in mourning, but she knew Georgia had sent her there, and so she was going to go with the flow.

"Let's sit out back, yea?" Aaron whispered the words in a romantic tone she hadn't expected. The night was turning in an entirely different direction than what she had expected.

"Sure," she replied breathlessly.

He gently pulled her chair out. She stood slowly and turned to head outside. Behind him was an old wooden buffet with an intricate lace table runner on top. She was surprised Aaron hadn't swapped that out as soon as he'd moved in. It was very delicate and feminine for a single guy in his late thirties. The candlelight flickered off a silver heart frame and Gemma lost her breath.

She picked it up, holding it in both of her hands. "Where did you get this?"

Aaron opened his mouth to speak, but took the frame from her instead, admiring it. She watched as expressions of pain crossed his face. "I don't know. It just sort of appeared one day, a long time ago. I don't remember when exactly, just that it's always been here."

"It's a picture of us, me and Georgia. That was in my bedroom growing up." She stumbled back a few steps. "I'd forgotten all about it until now."

He massaged the frame in his hands. "I love this picture. It's everything."

"It's everything to me, Aaron." Her voice and an anger inside of her rose slightly. "May I have it back?"

He reluctantly handed it to her and seemed to snap back to the present day. "I'm so sorry, Gemma. I don't know what to say. I must have taken it when we were kids. I loved Georgia, too, you know."

Gemma immediately felt guilty about her reaction. He was only eight when Georgia disappeared. He'd already lost his mother, and then one of his best friends. She exhaled a deep breath filled with angst and relaxed. "No, I'm sorry. I shouldn't have reacted that way. You were only a child. We were just kids. Who's to say what was right or wrong back then? We dealt with things the way we did." She put her hand on his arm. "It warms my heart to know you cared for her so much." She placed the picture back on the buffet.

"No, please, you were right. You take it. It belongs to you," Aaron said, his expression disturbed.

"It's yours. Keep it. She'd want you to have it." Gemma smiled warmly at Aaron. She put it back on the buffet, at peace with her decision.

Aaron's expression relaxed, along with his shoulders. "Let's go have that drink on the back porch."

They sat in side-by-side padded wicker chairs, a plastic table and a bottle of chardonnay between them. Aaron refilled her glass, and then his.

For a moment, she felt safe and comfortable, as if nothing in the world could take away her peace.

Then she saw the garden of red roses, just like the ones left on her porch every year on the anniversary of Georgia's disappearance and she stiffened.

Gemma swallowed hard. She contemplated asking about the roses–if they were the ones left on her porch–and then she momentarily reconsidered her decision. She was sure it was a coincidence, one she'd be embarrassed to mention, yet she couldn't take her eyes away from the garden. Surely his house wasn't the only one to have a rose garden, especially not in Tent City where flowers ran rampant. But it was an uncanny coincidence, almost too uncanny. She couldn't let it go.

"Beautiful rose garden you have there," Gemma said. She took a sip of her wine and watched Aaron's reaction through her peripheral vision.

He twitched slightly. "I'm so glad you think so," he said. "They grow for Georgia."

Her heart rate increased. "How sweet." Her palms began to sweat. "They look eerily similar to the ones someone keeps leaving on my porch on the anniversary of her disappearance. Any idea who might do that?" She tried to play it cool, but her stomach churned.

Aaron chuckled. "I have an idea."

She turned to face him and it felt like her head weighed a thousand pounds. "I don't feel so good."

Aaron stood in front of her. "No, of course, you don't."

Gemma dropped the wine glass and it shattered on the concrete patio. She pushed up to stand but fell back down into her chair. "What's wrong with me?"

"Oh, sweet Gemma," Aaron said. "You made it too easy." He laughed with a sinister tone and shadows danced behind his black eyes. The image of him began to blur before her and she blinked to correct her vision but failed.

"What did you do to me?" Her voice sounded like she was under water and panic began to set in.

He lifted her up and threw her limp body over his shoulder, carrying her toward the garden.

"Little Georgia put up a fight. But not her twin sis. You walked right into my arms." He dropped her on the ground and she felt the pressure of her body hit the dirt, but all of the feeling was leaving her.

"Now, you'll join your sweet sister right where you belong, and thirty years to the day when I became the taker of life."

Gemma tried to scream as Aaron lifted the shovel over his head and brought it down on top of her.

* * *

When her eyes opened, fireworks shone brightly above. For a moment, she thought she'd fallen asleep on the beach, but Gemma was far from paradise. Hog-tied with her mouth duct taped, she watched in horror as Adam stood inside of a hole he must have been digging for hours. He'd opened the rose garden up entirely.

Tears began to stream from her eyes, and as quiet as she wanted to be, hysterics set in. She began to scream at the top of her lungs, but barely any sound came out. Only muted moans escaped her as the booms and bangs of the festivities exploded above. Her tears only made her face swell, and harder for her to breathe.

"There's no use, Gemma," Aaron said. "The time for you to join your sister has come. I've been waiting a very long time for this day. I've been dreaming about it for years." He flung a pile of dirt over his back. "I just never imagined the reward would be so sweet." He began laughing uncontrollably.

"It was way too easy. It almost wasn't worth it. But, I'd already drugged you by the time I considered letting you go." He dug into the ground further. "When I saw the look of horror on your face when you figured out what was happening…man, it was worth the wait."

Gemma struggled to roll from side to side to try to get free, but it seemed impossible.

"Don't make this harder than it needs to be. Georgia gave up in the end, too, and it was for the best. She died in peace, at least that's how I like to imagine her as I buried her alive."

He pulled himself out of the ditch. "I'd prefer to see you take the high road and die with dignity in her honor." He pressed his hands together in prayer, then leaned over her. "Now, if you promise not to scream, it will all be over soon. However, if you choose to shout, it will be futile because no one will hear you, and I'll make sure to torture all the evil out of you. Do you understand?"

Gemma nodded.

"And you promise not to scream?"

Gemma nodded again.

"Good girl."

Aaron ripped the tape off Gemma's mouth, and she suppressed her wail. "Why?" She sobbed uncontrollably. "Why did you kill her? And why are you trying to kill me?"

Aaron leaned over her vulnerable body, his head twisted and his expression full of rage. "You little brats rejected me. I was never as good as the ginger-haired Bailey twins. The Bailey twins were all my dad ever talked about, all anyone in this damn town cared about. And you spoiled little pieces of garbage already had all the attention in the world from your parents, and then the whole damn neighborhood became obsessed with you."

He wiped a tear from Gemma's cheek, and she turned away. He grabbed her face with both hands and forced her to look in his eyes. "Look at me. You did this to me. You made me a loser. Well, not anymore. I made something of myself, and once I rid the world of the ginger twins, I'll finally be able to be loved."

"We were just kids. We didn't know we hurt you." Gemma took a deep breath, knowing she was dealing with a level of crazy she'd never seen before. "We're so sorry."

Aaron stopped in his tracks. His expression fell blank. In his eyes, she thought she saw a reason for her to have hope. Maybe she would live after all. Then his expression turned darker than ever before.

"How dare you speak for the dead. What are you, a witch, too?" He came closer. "Georgia pushed me off of her that day, the day I first snapped and felt what it meant to be alive. I wanted her to be my girlfriend, but she rejected me." He laughed. "I figured, if I couldn't beat Georgia and Gemma Bailey, I might as well join them. But she wanted her sister. She screamed for you, 'Gemma, Gemma, Gemma' was all she said when I tried to kiss her. And it pissed me off. I hit her until she stopped screaming. But then she woke up. So I taped her mouth and buried her with her eyes wide open staring right back at me. I just laughed in her little, nasty, evil face."

"No, not my Georgia!" Gemma cried. "She was only a baby."

Aaron rolled his eyes. "Yea, well, you're not. And you would've just rejected me, too. But I wanted to reject you first. So I played the part, one you fell for with little effort. And those sentimental, meaningful roses every year on the anniversary of her murder were all part of it. I must admit I also stalked you, which was more fun—and the foreplay I needed for this moment. I learned your routine and embraced your lifestyle. Ah, hell, let's call it was it is. I spied on you, even at eight years old. I stole that picture and other things." He shook his head. "Not important. But what is important is that I won this game. And you lost. You're the loser now."

He got behind Gemma and began to roll her over until she reached the edge of the grave. "No, please. It doesn't have to end this way."

"Sure, it does. Your sister needs you."

Aaron pushed Gemma over the edge and she began to scream. As fireworks lit up the night sky, she plummeted in what seemed like slow motion six feet down toward her sister's skeleton.

About halfway down into the grave, she realized she was carrying a weight behind her. Her leg had hooked onto Aaron, and he came tumbling on top of her. They landed hard, and it took a few seconds of her to get her bearings. Aaron was untangling himself when Gemma used all of her energy to twist her body until she had her thighs around his neck. He grabbed her legs and pulled them apart, but a supernatural force took over her.

Maybe it was Georgia's spirit helping her one last time, or another form of divine intervention, but she had strength and flexibility that made no sense in the natural. Gemma squeezed her legs together as hard as she possibly could, using the strongest part of her runner's body. Within seconds, Aaron had passed out.

She wasn't sure when he'd wake up, so she pulled away from him and realized that from all the movement, her wrist ties were lost. She pulled with all her might and slipped out of one.

Once her hands were free, she untied her feet. She stood with barely any strength and tried to climb out, but it was no use. She was too short. She reached for her cell phone, thankfully in her pocket, and called 911.

Waiting for the angels in blue to save her, she said a silent prayer for her Georgia, the little girl who died because her sister couldn't save her. But today, on the thirtieth anniversary of her disappearance, she got the justice she so deserved.

When the police arrived minutes later, Aaron was still unconscious. They pulled Gemma out of the grave. She heard an EMT say that Aaron was still alive, but just barely. The ambulance took him away and she asked the universe for forgiveness as she silently wished he didn't make it.

Georgia hadn't, and for all intents and purposes, neither had their parents. Life had never been the same since Georgia's disappearance and although they'd find some comfort in knowing what happened to her, the grief would forever alter them.

Georgia's grave was a part of Tent City and her spirit would linger in Ocean Grove for all eternity.

# #

About the Author

Kristina Rienzi is a Jersey Shore suspense author who encourages others to embrace the unknown through her writing. When she's not writing, Kristina is sipping delicious wine, spoiling her pups, watching The Twilight Zone, listening to Yacht Rock, or rooting for the West Virginia Mountaineers. She believes in all things paranormal, a closet full of designer bags, manicures, the Law of Attraction, guardian angels, and the value of a graduate degree in psychology. Visit her at KristinaRienzi.com.

TRAITOR'S PURSE

Roberta Rogow

Peter Garretson considered his St. Nicholas Day party one of the best ever seen in the Colony of New Jersey.

He had spared no expense in entertaining all his neighbors in the small settlement called Slooterdam. He had laid on plenty of meat and drink; he had provided both savory and sweet cakes; he had even gone to the trouble of finding someone to play the part of Sinterklaas, the embodiment of St. Nicholas, who handed out tops to the five boys, wooden dolls to the six girls, and rare oranges to all the children. There had been much laughter, dancing, games...and now this!

"Gottes in Himmel!" Garretson swore as he stared at the body at his feet. "What happened here?"

"Someone killed Sinterklaas," Juba, the African servant who had played the part of Sinterklaas's assistant, Schwartz-piet, shook his head sadly. "I found him like this, Baas. It wasn't me killed the saint. Bad juju that is."

"Not the saint, but the man who played the part." Dr. Hendricks had followed his host, curious to see what was going on. He knelt to put a fat finger on the body. "Still warm, but cooling rapidly. It's getting chilly. Blood is coagulating. I would say this occurred not an hour ago."

"While we were all making merry within?" Garretson gasped in shock. "Who would do such a thing? And why?"

"That is for you to discover, Peter. You are the constable, after all. I am merely a physician." Hendricks heaved himself to his feet.

"I've been constable here for ten years, and I've never seen anything like this!"

Juba held the lantern while Garretson observed the dead man more closely.

"His skull is cracked clear through. This was done with great force, great anger. I hate to think that one of my good neighbors has such rage within him."

"Rage, indeed. And he must have been tall, at the very least as tall as this poor fellow. Who is he, Peter?"

Garretson shrugged. "I don't know his name. He was at Burnett's tavern yesterday when I went to fetch the cider and beer for today's party. He rode in on Hopper's wagon from Hackensack, a traveler looking for work, he said."

"He picked the wrong time of the year for it. Harvest is over, there won't be any farm work until spring," Hendricks commented.

"So I told him," Garretson agreed. "Then it came to me that he could play the part of Sinterklaas. He was tall and slender, and since the children didn't know him, the illusion would be better than if one of the men from hereabouts did it. I said I'd give him a shilling, a meal, and a bed for the night, for his trouble." He scanned the area near the privy. "Juba, hold that lantern higher."

Garretson walked slowly around the dead man.

"He must have come here directly from the party. He's still in the garb I gave him for his play-acting."

A tawdry costume, it was, too. The bishop's gown had once served as a lady's bed-rail, the red cloak was raggedly trimmed with squirrel tails in lieu of ermine, the bishop's miter was the stiff vellum used for legal documents, and strands of horsehair tied to a string made a straggling beard, but it was enough to convince the younger children that the good St. Nicholas had come in person to give them gifts.

"What's this I hear about a body here?" Oritani, the Peace Chief who spoke for the few Lenape who remained in the area, came into the circle of lamplight. "A man was beaten to death?"

"Here he is." Dr. Hendricks turned the body over so that Oritani could look at the face. "Do any of your people have a grudge against the English?"

"If by that do you mean did this man run afoul of any Lenape, I can only say that as far as I know, he did not. I have never seen him before this moment. If, as you say, he came from Hackensack, he would not pass one of our farms. They are upstream."

"There's something missing...." Garretson paced along the riverbank. "There it is! Caught in the reeds!"

"Sinterklaas's crozier," Dr. Hendricks exclaimed.

"Bloodied and broken," Garretson pointed to the hooked end of the staff. "The murderer tried to throw it into the river but fell short. Fetch it for me, Juba."

The servant stepped gingerly through the reeds to grab the staff and placed it carefully in front of his master.

"This must have been what killed him," Garretson stated. "See? The hook on the top is covered with blood and hair. And look at these marks on the shaft. This must be where the killer held the staff. What is this? Dirt? It's black."

Oritani peered at the crozier. "Not earth. More like burned wood or coal. The killer had dirty hands."

"What do we do with him?" Ever the practical one, Dr. Hendricks stopped all speculation.

"Take him to the barn," Garretson decreed. "Tomorrow morning, at first light, I will have to make inquiries." He sighed deeply. "Even if this was done by one of my good neighbors, as constable, it is my duty to uncover wrong-doing. Juba, you and Joseph take care of him."

As the two black men lifted the body, a small leather bag fell out of its hand, clanking loudly on the frozen ground.

"What's this?" Oritani picked up the bag and hefted it. "Something heavy and much of it." He handed the bag to Garretson.

"Coins?" Garretson peered into the bag. "Silver, by the look of them. Since these coins are still here, then this was no robbery. And if this fellow already had these coins, he'd have no need to ask for work."

"Inference? Someone gave him the coins," Hendricks said. "But why strike him down after giving them to him? And why leave them with him once he was dead?"

"A mystery indeed," Garretson said, as he followed the sad cavalcade back to the barn behind the house. "I told this fellow he could change his coat and boots in the barn, and once the children were gone he could come into the house, make himself comfortable in the kitchen, and have whatever was left over from the feast to refresh himself."

"Kind of you," Hendricks said.

"It's St. Nicholas Feast Day," Garretson reminded him. "No one should go hungry or cold on St. Nicholas's Day. The Good Saint wouldn't like it."

"Superstition!" the doctor scoffed. "And you a good Reformed Protestant!"

"As good as any Dutchman can be," Garretson retorted. "But Sinterklaas is for the children. I said as much to McBride yesterday at the tavern when he reproved the traveler for taking part in what he called 'Papist mummery'."

"McBride? Irish, isn't he?" Oritani oversaw the depositing of the body on the floor of the stable, well away from the horses, who stamped and shied at the smell of blood, and the cow who mooed loudly at the disturbance. "I thought they were all Catholics."

"McBride is Scottish, as he is all too willing to tell anyone passes by." Garretson eyed the dead man's meager belongings: a knapsack, with a roll of cloth strapped to it, a coat and hat, boots and small sword, all laid neatly in front of the water trough next to the door of the stable. He picked up the coat.

"Good fabric, well-made, but not lavish. No lace, but brass buttons on the sleeves. And the sword?" He examined the weapon. "Well-sharpened. Not a fop's toy, but a good blade. I don't know much about such things, but at a guess, French? Not Dutch, those have thicker blades, a more sturdy hilt."

Oritani checked the hat. "Brim is wide, not curled into a tricorn, like the one I saw last time I went to Hackensack. They say that's the new style in England. Feather stuck into the hatband, not one I know. Not eagle, not turkey."

Dr. Hendricks picked up one of the boots. "He's done some walking, to be sure. Heels are well-ground down, soles have been repaired."

Garretson shivered in the chilly air of the barn. "Let's take this knapsack into the house, and see if there's something in it to tell us more about this poor fellow."

He called out to the departing guests who were loading their families onto wagons for the ride back to their farmsteads.

"Halloo, friends, come here. Please take a look at our Sinterklaas, who has met with an...ah...accident. Do any of you recognize him? Did he stop at your farms?'

One by one the men looked the stranger over. Most gasped, some looked away at the dreadful sight, and all agreed.

Whoever he was, he had not stopped at any of the farms on the road from Hackensack to Slooterdam, nor on the path that skirted the Passaic River.

Garretson looked grimly after the last horse and wagon as it disappeared into the dusk. Then he and his friends returned to the warmth of the parlor, where Oritani's wife had gathered the children, ready to leave for their own house on the River Road.

"Dr. Hendricks, Oritani, stay a few minutes more. I'd like your advice on this matter."

Dr. Hendricks grunted his assent. "Nothing waiting for me but cold beef."

Oritani held a brief conference with his wife, who hustled into the kitchen with their children, to assist Anneke in the after-party chores, while her husband joined Garretson and the doctor in the parlor.

Garretson opened the knapsack and spread its meager contents onto the table that had been cleared of edibles.

"He traveled light," Oritani commented. "One shirt, a pair of stockings, an extra set of under-linens." He unrolled the cloth that had been strapped to the bottom of the knapsack. "A blanket."

A small wooden box tumbled out of the bed-roll.

Garretson opened it. "Razor, tin spoon, small knife. A needle, and a coil of thread. He came prepared for almost anything, He could repair his own clothes, shave himself, he had his own cutlery."

"He carried food," Dr. Hendricks observed, pulling a cloth bag out of the knapsack. "A round cheese, a hard bread roll."

"He must have got that from Burnett," Garretson said. "He got this leather jack of small beer there, too." He scrabbled at the bottom of the knapsack. "Aha! This is what I was looking for. Papers!"

He spread the packet of documents before him. "A letter, in English. And something with a seal on it. This isn't English or Dutch. Those I can read. Can you tell me what this is, Doctor? "Dr. Hendricks took the paper from his hand. "It's in French," he announced. "I translate: 'This is to state that the bearer, Guillaume Demarest, has been honorably discharged from the army of France. Sealed and signed, June 1717.' Guillaume...that is William in English, Willem in Dutch."

"A soldier," Oritani said. "That explains his sword and his fine coat with the brass buttons. But what is a French soldier doing here, in the New Jersey colony? We're not at war with France, are we?"

Garretson looked baffled. "Not that I know, but it takes time for news to get here from England. Besides there are all sorts of rascals who follow the drum, what with the wars in the Germanies over the years, English, Irish, Dutch, as well as French. Poor farmers cast off their lands, or younger sons with no inheritance, they leave home to seek their fortunes on the battlefield. This Demarest may be one of them. Now that the wars are over, he may have decided to try his luck here in the New World, since the old one has no more use for him."

There was still the small bag and its contents. Garretson spilled them onto the table. Silver coins glittered in the candlelight.

Hendricks pawed through the pile. "Interesting. This must be someone's life's savings. Here's an English shilling with King William's face and one with Queen Anne's. Not a French coin nor a German one in the lot."

"Not this man's savings, then. But whose?" A gleam of silver caught Garretson's eye. He picked up one coin and held it closer to the lantern to get a better look. "I know this coin! I gave it to Burnett only yesterday!"

"Are you sure?" Oritani asked. "All coins look alike to me."

"This one is fresh from the London mint. See, it has King George's face, and the date, 1719. It was given to me in my stipend last year when I went to Hackensack to be confirmed in my post as constable for another term. Now I wonder, how did this coin, which I gave to Burnett, get into a bag in a dead man's hand?"

Dr. Hendricks had sorted the coins into piles. "Interesting," he said. "I count thirty coins." He and Garretson exchanged meaningful looks.

"Thirty," Garretson said. "Thirty pieces of silver."

Oritani looked from one Dutchman to the other. "Does it matter that there are exactly thirty of these coins? And that they are silver and not common coppers?"

Garretson said slowly, "To a Christian, it matters. Thirty pieces of silver was the sum given to Judas Iscariot, the one who betrayed Our Lord."

"A traitor's purse?" Oritani thought it over. "If it was not his, then who gave it to him? And why?"

"Questions that must be answered tomorrow," Garretson declared. "Meanwhile, the body may remain in the barn. It's cold enough, it won't go bad. Tomorrow, we will look over the site of the murder. Perhaps in the daylight, we will get a better idea of what took place there. Good night, my friends. I wish there had been a better ending to our feast."

"It is not your fault that some villain decided to commit murder," Oritani assured him. "Dr. Hendricks, I can carry you to your house on the common, if you don't mind sharing the wagon with the children."

"Thank you, I'll walk. It clears the mind," Dr. Hendricks said.

As his last guests left, Peter Garretson stood alone by the parlor fire, packing his pipe with tobacco, mulling over the grisly end to the feast that had begun so joyously.

Anneke joined him. "A dreadful end to a good party," she said. "What will you do about it?

"I will do what I am sworn to do. I will keep the King's Peace in Slooterdam."

"Even if it means taking one of our own to the magistrates?"

Garretson nodded. "I hate to think that one of our good neighbors has such hate in him as to beat a man to death, but I can see no other solution. A passing bandit? A Lenape gone mad with bad ginever-water? Not very likely! No, Anneke, this must have been done by someone who knew this fellow would be at this house. Someone who knew who and what he was. What's more, it had to be someone who got the coin I gave Burnett yesterday. That bag with the coins, those were someone's savings, to be sure, and there are only two people in Slooterdam who insist on coin, not kind. And neither of them was present at our party."

"The tavern-keeper, Ned Burnett, and the blacksmith, Arthur McBride," Anneke said slowly. "Could one of them have done such a dreadful thing?"

Garretson drew on his pipe. "I would not like to think so, but as Dominie Cadmus reminds us, Satan lurks in unlikely places, waiting to trap us into sin. I will have to think carefully before I accuse anyone."

* * *

At daybreak, Oritani and Dr. Hendricks joined Garretson for a better look at the privy. Once they had examined the ground, they returned to the house, to sit at the kitchen table, where Anneke provided hot mulled ale and left-over olly-keks to sustain their mental efforts.

"The ground froze last night," Oritani observed. "Last night's footprints are well-preserved. "Many visitors to the privy, but they wore heavy boots or shoes with heels. There were moccasin-prints, which were mine and my children's. And there were other prints, a long, flat shoe. Who wore those?"

"Sinterklaas," Garretson said. "I gave him a pair of old shoes, the sort my grandfather kept from the Old Country, to play his part. He left his boots in the barn with his coat and hat."

"And his sword," Hendricks reminded them. "He didn't expect to be attacked."

"He knew his killer," Garretson stated. "He came directly from his play-acting to meet him."

Oritani closed his eyes, visualizing the scene. "Beside the reeds at the edge of the water, there were two sets of footprints. One, the long toes, one a heavy boot. They stood together, a pair of large shoes, a pair of smaller ones. The prints are deep in the mud. Then they went back to the privy, where the killer struck. The large boots went deep into the muck. Our killer is a large, strong man."

"He would be, to have struck such heavy blows," Dr. Hendricks agreed. "What else could you tell from the tracks?"

Oritani opened his eyes. "After he killed, he went back to the reeds and threw away the bloody club. Then he went to the path along the river, where he had a horse ready. I saw the dung."

Garretson said. "Now I am certain this was not done by any of my guests. None of them left the house between the time Sinterklaas left and Dominie Cadmus's blessing, and none of them is riding a horse. All their horses were hitched to wagons."

Oritani nodded agreement. "The prints of the boots and long-toed shoes are on top of all the others. I do not think any of our neighbors has the presence of mind to return to the house after having done such violence to another human being."

"It would take someone with great skill as a play-actor to hide such rage," Dr. Hendricks added. "And he must have been spattered with blood. You are quite right, Peter. Whoever did this was not at the party."

"That eliminates most of the good people of Slooterdam," Oritani said. "But not my people. I was the only Lenape invited to the party. A tribute to my high position as Peace Chief, I suppose?"

"And as my friend and deputy," Garretson assured him. "But you told me that none of your people knew this man and I believe you. This was an act of retribution. If a Lenape wanted revenge, he would use his tomahawk."

"And none of my people have as much as thirty silver coins," Oritani added. "And if they had they would know better than to throw them away by giving them to someone. Why? Revenge? To shame him?"

Dr. Hendricks took a swig of his ale. "Peter, you said you first saw this fellow at Burnett's tavern. Why come this far from Hackensack? If he was looking for work, he'd be more likely to find it there, not out here in the back-woods."

Garretson set his tankard down with a thump. "We need answers, not more questions. Let us begin at the most logical place. Gentlemen, we will visit Burnett's."

With that, Garretson donned his wig, placed his hat over it, and strode into the morning sunlight, southward down the path to the intersection of the broad road that led east to Hackensack and west across the rough bridge over the Passaic River.

Burnett's Tavern was the largest building in Slooterdam, an English-style cottage, with a thatched roof that hung over the Dutch-style double doors, standing on one leg of a roughly triangular patch of green on the north side of the road. Like most such establishments, it was the focal center of commerce in the tiny settlement, offering not only food and drink for the traveler but any other items that could not be made on the local farms. One wall of the large central room was given over to such goods as salt, molasses, woven cloth, and iron tools. Across the room from the general supplies, a long plank had been set up on trestles, and an assortment of kegs and bottles on the shelf behind it held alcoholic liquids of varying strengths, from relatively mild small beer to potent rum.

Ned Burnett stood outside his tavern, a tall, stout man in an English-style coat and breeches cut to the leg, his capacious midsection covered with a stained canvas apron. Beside him was a lanky youth, in a shabby coat and wide Dutch breeches, topped with the newly fashionable hat with three corners. Garretson recognized Joe Hopper, the wagoner, who brought goods from his father's warehouse in Hackensack to the outlying towns.

"Good morning, Burnett, Hopper." Garretson waved to them as the three men approached the tavern.

"Hallo, Constable, Doctor," Burnett greeted them. "What cheer, Oritani. Have you all recovered from your jollification? I trust my cider and beer was enjoyed by all."

"You may have heard that the jollification, as you call it, was called to a halt by a most sad discovery," Garretson told him. "A man was murdered last night."

Burnett's smile faded. "So said the folks who passed by on their way home. A terrible thing! Murdered, you say? And all the while you and your Dutch friends were eating and drinking, singing and dancing? Terrible! Who was it"

"The man who came to this tavern two days ago," Garretson said. "Tall, well-spoken, had an Irish cast to his voice, I'm thinking. He had a paper in his pack, said his name was William Demarest, that he was discharged from the French army."

"So he told me," Hopper admitted. "When we met–"

"When and where was this meeting?" Garretson interrupted sharply.

Hopper grimaced. "It was on the road, from Hackensack. The horse fetched up lame, just past the Saddle River. Treacherous footing there, the ice not quite solid and the ground slippery with it. This man, Demarest, was at the side of the road, had been a-foot. When the horse went lame, the wagon nearly tipped and one wheel caught on the stones. He helped me right the wagon, so I took him up, my orders be damned, begging your pardon, Doctor."

"Your father doesn't want you to take up travelers?" Dr. Hendricks said, with a knowing smile.

Hopper grinned back. "Afraid of robbers, but I saw no harm in this one. He didn't have the look of a highway robber. Besides, what would he steal from a wagon of goods? Flour? Cider? I was delivering, not receiving. I had no money on me, wouldn't have until I delivered the goods."

"He had a sword," Oritani pointed out.

"To be sure, he did, but it was sheathed all the way. No harm, I thought, in taking up an old soldier down on his luck. He made the hours pleasant with his tales of adventures." Hopper shuddered, "And now you tell me he's dead? His sword was no use to him, then."

"It was with his coat and boots in the barn when he was struck down," Garretson said grimly. "He'd been dressed for his play-acting as Sinterklaas. What was your impression of him, Burnett? I value your opinion, being that you've seen more than your share of passers-by. In your time."

"I can't tell you more about him than you already know, Constable. Young Joe had just pulled in with his wagon when you and your men came along, to take the supplies for your party. You paid me and I paid Joe."

"With the silver shilling, fresh from the London Mint."

Gerretsen nodded.

"The coin went from me to you, to Joe."

"That doesn't explain how it got into Demarest's hand," Dr. Hendricks said. He turned to the young wagoner. "You didn't play cards or dice with Demarest, did you?"

"Cards? Dice? I'm no gambler1 I took the wagon and horse to McBride, to shoe the horse and set the wagon-wheel on straight, and used the money Burnett gave me to pay him. My father won't like it, but there was no way around it. McBride only takes coin, tight-fisted Scotsman that he is. But if you want to know more, you can ask McBride yourself. Demarest went with me to the smithy and he and McBride had words there."

Dr. Hendricks frowned. "What does a man on foot need with a blacksmith?"

"Let's ask him," Garretson said, marching down the path to the smithy, the next largest building in Slooterdam. Like the tavern, it was half stone, half wood, a large barn-like structure with a slate roof, one side open to the weather. Hopper's wagon had been pulled alongside the open area, propped up on large barrels so that the wheel could be repaired. The horse that drew the wagon was tethered to one of the stanchions next to the smithy, happily munching on hay.

McBride, the blacksmith, was hard at work on his anvil, within the stone and wood structure, with his Negro assistants on hand to hold a wagon-wheel steady as he pounded it into shape. His well-muscled arms rose and fell rhythmically with each stroke; he grunted with the effort of lifting the heavy hammer.

"Hello!" Garretson shouted over the clanging.

McBride swung once more. "That should do it," he told his assistants. "Get that onto the wagon.

He took off the heavy leather apron that protected his chest from the sparks of the fire, hung it on a hook on the wall, and dipped his hands into the water-barrel that stood beside the door, ready to quench any stray spark that might instigate a general conflagration. Even so, his hands were still black with the residue from the forge when he turned and greeted his visitors.

"Good day to you, Constable, Doctor. Oritani, what cheer? What brings you out on a cold morning?"

"You may have heard there was a murder done last night," Garretson stated.

"So Farmer Brocker said last night, on his way back to his farm. What has this to do with me?"

"The dead man was one William Demarest, the wayfarer who came to Burnett's two days ago. Burnett says he came here, with Hopper and the wagon. What did he have to say?" Gerretsen asked.

McBride shrugged. "He heard my name, thought it sounded Irish, as he was. I put him right. My folk are no Papists, but honest Presbyterian Scots. We have no truck with such things as saints."

"Catholic, was he?" Dr. Hendricks remarked. "No wonder he didn't balk at playing the part of St. Nicholas."

Garretson smiled. "When I showed him the costume, he told me he'd played many parts in his time, but never a saint."

"A saint? Not he!" McBride snorted.

"Then you knew him?" Gerritsen pounced on the fact.

McBride frowned. "I knew a man called William. We were lads together."

"In Ireland," Dr. Hendricks hinted.

"In Ireland," McBride repeated. "But that was a very long time ago."

Garretson nodded. "A good deal can happen over the years. People change."

"Some do," McBride said. "Most don't. What one is as a boy, one is as a man. The William I knew was a liar and a coward." His mouth closed before he could say more.

"And a traitor?" Garretson watched McBride closely.

"I suppose that depends on which side you are on," Dr. Hendricks put in. "Sometimes it's hard to decide. Thirty years ago, our own Dutch Stadholder was called to England to be king. Now it's a German. And there's still the Stuart prince in France, who claims the English throne."

Garretson ignored the political summary. "McBride, did this Demarest tell you why he was in Slooterdam?"

"He asked me for work," McBride growled. "I told him I had none for him. I already have two good stout black men to help me. He was no smith, could not be of any use to me."

"And you did not give him any money?"

"I don't waste good silver on beggars." McBride glared at Oritani, who was standing beside the leather apron, still on its hook.

Garretson tried another approach. "Did you see anyone pass this way last night?"

"Those who were celebrating at your pagan feast, they passed by," McBride admitted. "Brocker, on his way to his farm. Vandercamp, Vanderbrook. Dominie Cadmus, I saw him come into his house. Fair muzzy with drink, too. A fine example to set! And yourself, Doctor. I saw you go to your house."

"No one else?" Dr. Hendricks continued to press for answers. "When did you go to bed?"

"I keep proper hours," McBride stated. "I don't waste candles on frivolous gaiety, much less Papist mummery. I had my evening meal at sundown, read my Bible, and was in my bed at moon-rise. Now, if that is all, I have my work to do."

He shoved Oritani out of the way, donned his leather apron and approached the cart-horse, who whinnied and stamped at his approach.

Garretson called after him. "McBride, what would you say if I told you that the dead man had thirty pieces of silver on him when he was found?"

Before McBride could answer, Joe Hopper came into the smithy.

"Isn't that wheel ready yet? I want to be on my way before noon. It's a long haul back to Hackensack, and I don't want to have to drive after dark. I've already overstayed my welcome. My father will be worried if I stay away another night."

McBride called from the forge. "My men will have the wheel on before the hour's up and you can be on your way. I can tell you no more, Constable. You will have to find your own way out."

"Hopper, a word with you." Garretson pulled the young wagoner aside. "You stayed the night at Burnett's?"

"Two nights, worse luck," Hopper groused. "My father's going to be right mad with anger that I broke the wheel and had to spend half what I got from Burnett to have it mended."

"Did you indeed," Garretson said. "You must have had some conversation with Demarest, seeing that the two of you were at Burnett's overnight, and there's but one bedroom he keeps for travelers."

"Nothing to that," Hopper said, hurriedly. "He had his own blanket."

"More to the point, what sort of tales was he telling?" Garretson asked.

"To hear him tell it, he had won every battle in the last thirty years single-handed, starting with something like Battle of Bones."

"The Boyne," Dr. Hendricks corrected him. "I was with Stadholder Willem's troops when he took charge in Ireland and beat the English King James and his rabble handily."

"I was only a lad then," Garretson added. "My father had settled at Newark and we heard about the fighting in Ireland long after everything was settled."

"Demarest was right hot in his politics," Hopper said. "He got to talking about the German king, said he was looking for men to go to France and put King James back on his throne."

"There's no King James," Garretson corrected him. "Only the son of the man the English would not have as their king. Too Catholic for their liking."

"Those English!" Dr. Hendricks scoffed. "They do not mind an adulterer, or a drunkard, or even one who prefers his soldiers to his wife, but they will not have a Catholic for their king!"

"And so, the English parliament found some cousin of old Queen Anne and put the crown on his head." Hopper laughed. "Not that it matters to us here in America. They send their royal governors and we go our own way and so I told Demarest. If he thought he'd find willing recruits for his schemes, he was wasting his breath. Anyone looking for adventure can just go over the mountains and find plenty of it there."

Garretson went on. "Did you hear what he and McBride had to say to each other when you were at the smithy?"

"I was more worried about the wagon and the horse," Hopper admitted. "Dobbin don't like to be shod, you see, so I had to hold him while the Negro did what had to be done. What with the noise of the hammer, and Dobbin fussing, I couldn't make out the words, only that McBride was more surly than usual. But when all was done, and we came back to the tavern for supper, Demarest had a smirk on him, what Mam calls 'the cat that got into the cream'. I reckoned that he got what he'd been looking for."

Garretson, Hendricks, and Oritani left Hopper at the smithy and made their way back to the tavern, where Burnett was waiting with tankards at the ready.

"Hot toddy, Constable? Doctor? I know you don't take spirits, Chief."

Garretson sat on the rough bench shoved along one wall. "I'll take the toddy, with thanks, Burnett. And have you recalled anything more about the traveler who came two days ago? His speech was Irish, you say? What was his manner? Was he surly, tired, angry?"

Burnett handed tankards to Garretson and Hendricks. "I would say, he was in good spirits, for one who had traveled far," he said. "He counted out some coppers when I served him, said he was looking for work. I told him most of the harvest hereabouts was done, that he'd do better in Hackensack, but he said he'd been there, and there was nothing for him."

"Not easy for a man whose only work has been killing to find someone to employ him," Dr. Hendricks said. "You say he went to the smithy?"

"He did and from what I saw McBride gave him the same answer I did."

"Did you hear what was said?" Garretson asked.

"Too far away and the wind in the wrong direction to blow the sound my way," Burnett admitted. "But when he came back here, this soldier–"

"Demarest was his name," Oritani put in.

"This Demarest, he had a sly look to him, as if he was the cat that caught the bird, as the saying goes."

"And that agrees with what young Hopper said," Oritani noted. "

"And if Hopper gave McBride the new shilling, then it must have been McBride gave it to Demarest," Garretson said slowly. He set down his tankard on the bench.

"McBride is a very large, heavy man," Oritani observed. "And I saw brown spots on his leather apron."

"And he lied when he said he went to bed at moonrise," Dr. Hendricks added. "I walked home by moonlight. If McBride saw me coming home, he must have been awake well after sunset."

"I think we must have another talk with Arthur McBride," Gerretsen said.

"You'll have to be quick about it," Burnett called out. "He's trying to mount young Hopper's horse!"

Oritani leaped forward and sprinted across the common to stop the escape, with Garretson and Hendricks pounding behind him.

"Stop, in the name of the King!" Garretson yelled.

Oritani wasted no time with words. With one last effort, the Lenape reached the smithy, where McBride had his hand on the horse's bridle, while he tried to push young Hopper aside.

"Dobbin don't like being rid!" Hopper called out, as the horse pulled away from the strange hand on his bridle.

Hopper and Oritani tried to grab the furious blacksmith, but he shook them off and made another attempt at mounting the cart-horse. Once more Oritani launched himself at the smith and managed to pull him away from the horse. Hopper's attention was for his steed; Oritani was left to subdue the smith by himself. They wrestled across the floor, just as Garretson arrived, breathless from his exertions.

It took him a moment to grasp what was happening. His eye fell on an ax-handle propped up against the wall. Without further thought, he picked it up and brought it down on the smith's head.

McBride's grip loosened so that Oritani could take another breath and break free. Burnett and Hendricks took over, grabbing McBride's arms, as the blacksmith's anger seemed to drain away.

Garretson straightened his wig, which had gone awry in the battle. "Arthur McBride," he intoned, "I arrest you on a charge of willful murder of William Demarest. We'll take you to Hackensack to the magistrate, to bring you to trial."

"There should be an inquest," Hendricks objected. "And that we can do here in Slooterdam."

"There will be," Garretson promised. "And I will produce evidence to show that this man, Arthur McBride, did willfully attack one William Demarest with a heavy stick, to wit, the bishop's crozier, used by Demarest when he portrayed Sinterklaas. What say you to this charge, McBride?"

McBride sagged against the smithy wall. "What can I say? I did what I had to do. I was an instrument of the Lord's wrath."

"But does not the Bible say, 'Vengeance is mine, saith the Lord?'" Dr. Hendricks reminded him.

"He should not have laughed," McBride said.

"You can tell us your side of this sorry tale elsewhere," Garretson said, looking about the smithy for somewhere to sit.

"My house is a step down the lane," Dr. Hendricks offered. "I think it would be better if we continued this business out of the public view."

Oritani and Hopper held tight to McBride as Dr. Hendricks led the group to one of the small cottages that filled the space between the main road and the church.

They crowded into the main room, which served as both living quarters and the doctor's examining-room, sparsely furnished with a table pushed against the wall, under the only window that let in the wintery light. A carved armchair, a relic of the doctor's days in Holland, and a stool next to the table along with a cabinet braced against the side wall that held the doctor's instruments and another shelf that held his few books.

Garretson plopped into the armchair, while the doctor himself made do with the small stool next to his writing-table. McBride stood sullenly in the middle of the room between Oritani and Hopper.

"Now then," Garretson said when he had adjusted his wig again. "Arthur McBride, what have you to say for yourself in defense of your actions last night? Dr. Hendricks, will you act as Recorder? The magistrate in Hackensack will want a written document."

Dr. Hendricks scrabbled among his papers for a clean sheet, prepared a quill, and looked at McBride, waiting for his confession.

McBride sighed deeply. "What is there to say?"

"You must have had a reason to throw thirty silver pieces at a man," Oritani said. "That is a good sum. More than a whole pound of English money."

"It takes a long time to save that much," Garretson agreed. "Thirty years is a long time. Almost a man's lifetime."

"Aye, it is," McBride said. "But I swore I would kill the man who showed the French soldiers the roads and the Lord led him to my hand. I have done what I promised."

"This Demarest, you knew him in Ireland," Garretson said.

"He was my mother's sister's son," McBride confessed. "And when the soldiers came to our village, he swore he would protect my mother and sisters from harm, but he did not. He let the French soldiers do what they would and he left with them, to go to France and fight there.

"I had gone with the Protestant troops, and when I came home it was to find my mother dead, my sister defiled, my father out of his wits.

"I prayed to the Lord for guidance," McBride went on. "I took indentures with a smith who was going to America, for I had no money of my own. I knew there would always be work for a blacksmith. Then, bit by bit, I saved what I could. I swore I would find William and repay him for what he had done. I knew the Lord would send him to my hand."

"And by purest chance, he came to Slooterdam?" Garretson asked.

"It was the Lord sent him to me," McBride insisted. "He did not even recognize me and when he did, he laughed and said we were well met. He asked for money, to find men to put the Papist bastard on the throne. Threatened to tell the new royal governor that I was on the side of the Irish thirty years ago at the Battle of the Boyne.

"Then you came along, offered to house and feed him if he'd take part in your Papist foolery. I told him to meet me once he'd finished his play-acting and I'd give him some money if he'd go away and stay away. I met him behind the privy, I threw the money at his feet. I thought to shame him, but he had no shame. He laughed! He laughed at me! He held the staff as he bent down to pick up the bag with the money and he laughed!

"And then it was as if all the rage of all those years came upon me, and the wrath of the Lord flowed through me, and I could not stop myself. I wrenched the staff from his hand. I beat him about the head until he stopped laughing!"

McBride stopped for breath. "And then, I rode back to the smithy. I scrubbed the blood off my leather apron and I sat and prayed to the Lord to forgive my anger. What I had done was just, as it is said, 'Eye for an eye, tooth for a tooth'."

"It's also written, 'Vengeance is mine, saith the Lord.'" Garretson corrected him. "Dr. Hendricks, have you written McBride's confession?"

"I have. All he has to do is sign it." Dr. Hendricks held the quill towards McBride, who scrawled his name on the paper.

"And what now?" Oritani asked.

Garretson said, "Arthur McBride, I must take you to the magistrate in Hackensack. Hopper, if you please, take McBride and me to my house, where we can load the body onto your wagon. I'll ride with you to the magistrate and make it up with your father for the extra night you had to spend here."

"And what's to be done with the thirty coins?" Dr. Hendricks asked.

"Rightly they belong to Demarest's heir, whoever that may be,"

Garretson replied.

McBride laughed, mirthlessly. "That is me! William and I were cousins, our mothers were sisters."

"So the coins go back to you?"

"Use them to free my Negroes. They can leave here, or stay, as they will. I was going to do it anyway, now is as good a time as any." McBride held his hands out. "You may put fetters on me or not. I will not try to run off. I have taken a life and I must accept my punishment."

"A sad ending to such a joyful holiday," Dr. Hendricks sighed, as he and Garretson walked back to the smithy, where young Hopper hitched Dobbin to the wagon. McBride scrambled into the wagon-bed without assistance. Garretson took his place beside Hopper.

"Drive to my house. I will have to pack a few things, and tell my wife I am going to Hackensack, to deliver a murderer to justice."

"What will you tell the magistrate?" Oritani asked.

"I will give him McBride's confession and plead for mercy," Garretson decided. "He was sorely provoked and he did not plan to kill Demarest."

"And his was the side that won!" Dr. Hendricks said with a sigh. "Those Irish! It will take ten times thirty years before they forgive each other for the Battle of the Boyne!"

# #

About the Author

Roberta Rogow writes historical mysteries, although she sometimes twists the history. After a 37-year career as a children's librarian in public libraries in New Jersey, she retired in 2008 to travel, attend mystery and science fiction conventions, and write novels, short stories, and book reviews. Her most recent series takes place in an Alternate Colonial New York, in a world where the Spanish Moors got to North America first (Last of the Mohegans meets Arabian Nights, with a Spanish Accent). Visit her on Facebook at Manatas Skyline.

JUSTICE FOR JAYNIE

Yvonne Ventresca

Rylie rushed to make the last train into Manhattan. The street remained quiet except for the click of her boot heels and a warm rustle of wind in the trees. No one else was around, but she felt safe in the small Jersey town of Haverfield, where only one friend even knew her real name.

She'd been reclusive ever since the scandal, when her career crashed and her boyfriend, Denny, asked her to move out of their DC apartment. She worked anonymously now, ghostwriting speeches and creating website content under a pseudonym. The months had passed as she bided her time, watching the gossip about her dwindle along with her savings. The apartment-sitting gig was about to end, and she needed a big story, something to redeem her reputation.

This lead could do the trick. The night shift custodian at a big New York hospital had finally agreed to discuss the Emergency Room doctor facing sexual assault charges from three of his patients. They were to meet in an hour at a coffee shop near the hospital.

She walked faster to make the 12:01 train, knowing this could be her lucky break. But when she arrived at the station, a temporary construction barrier blocked the entrance with a "Platform Closed" sign taped to it. Cursing under her breath, she checked New Jersey

Transit information on her phone; there was nothing listed about a closure for Monday night. The small building that housed the waiting area was locked and empty.

A guy and a girl emerged from the direction of the tracks, both in jeans and sweatshirts. They walked close together but not touching, their hoods up despite the warm April weather. A strand of red hair escaped the girl's hood, and she jerked her hand up to tuck it back underneath.

They both looked startled at the sight of Rylie. The girl stopped and stared, but the guy took her elbow and nudged her along as they walked between the building and the barricade.

Rylie froze for a moment at the sight of him. It was unnerving how much he resembled her ex, the black hair, dark eyes, thin face.

"The platform's closed," he said.

"How can it be closed?" Rylie asked.

He shrugged. "It doesn't say why."

The girl never spoke as they hurried away, but she looked over her shoulder nervously. The Denny look-alike and the anxious girl strode toward a dark SUV parked in the far corner of the lot. She glanced back again, and Rylie felt like she was somehow invading their privacy.

With a sigh, she turned her attention to checking her phone for the cost of an Uber. She desperately wanted the ER doctor story, but her tank was nearly empty and the nearest gas station would be closed. Should she splurge on a car service? Maybe just as far as Hoboken. She could get to the city on her own from there. She ordered a car and walked to the main entrance of the parking lot to wait.

As her Uber arrived, the SUV left from the opposite side of the lot. At 12:01, the train horn blasted, followed by a screech of brakes. The platform must not be closed after all. Annoyed, she hesitated at the open car door, but it was too late now. The Uber driver, a bald man with a gray beard and a scowl, did not seem like he'd understand if she ditched and ran for the train.

Minutes later, as they drove down Main Street toward the highway, she heard emergency sirens. Soon a police car raced by them, heading in the other direction, followed by another one. She hadn't heard sirens in Haverfield ever. Something big was going on and she was missing it.

"Turn around," she told the driver. "We need to go back to the train station. Please."

The driver did everything at one speed: slow. He refused to do an illegal U-turn. Then they got stuck at all three traffic lights, and by the time they arrived back at the train, both police cars were there. She jumped out of the car.

"Did I miss the 12:01?" she asked the young cop, feigning innocence.

"No more train service tonight, Miss. There's been an accident."

"What happened?"

"NJ Transit's in charge. I really can't say."

She gave him a please-tell-me smile. "I'm going to read about it tomorrow, right?"

He sighed. "The train struck something on the tracks."

An ambulance pulled up. It was more of a *someone* than a something.

"You'll have to make other travel arrangements. This station is closed until we finish our investigation." He hovered near the "Platform Closed" barricade, which had turned out to be eerily accurate.

Rylie pointed at the sign. "That was up before the train pulled in. I was here earlier."

The officer looked confused and left her to confer with another cop.

She surveyed the parking area as she returned to the waiting

Uber. Only one other car remained in the otherwise empty lot. Was there a story here? The feeling nagged at her, but the hospital custodian would be waiting. The police began photographing the platform closed sign as Rylie left the station.

* * *

In the morning, Rylie sipped her coffee and checked the news. Last night's train accident was an apparent suicide. According to the engineer, the male victim had lain motionless on the tracks as the train approached him, and the cameras on the front of the train confirmed that. The authorities would not release his identity to the press until they'd notified his family, and they were still awaiting the results of the toxicology reports. The victim's car had been found unlocked in the train parking lot.

That must have been the other car Rylie had noticed last night. She should have stayed at the station instead of schlepping into the city—a waste of time, it turned out, when the custodian didn't provide any substantial information. Had she followed the wrong lead? Made another professional mistake?

Staring out the window at the spring drizzle, she wondered what Denny was doing right now. Was he awake yet? Was the sun shining through their kitchen window?

She picked up her phone and hovered her finger over the button to call him. What could she say? That she was different now? Her previous apologies hadn't persuaded him. For all she knew, he had another girlfriend, someone unambitious and devoted.

She knew she had crossed the line, spending the night with the politician, gleaning whatever information she could. Corruption charges had been filed against him based on what she learned, but her relationship with Denny never recovered.

She couldn't call him. Not yet.

Instead, she busied herself by feeding the cat, texting the owner her daily picture of the beloved feline, then tidying the apartment. Her friend, Barb, had gotten her the apartment and pet-sitting job at a time when she needed to escape DC. With less than two weeks left in the arrangement, she started to feel desperation crawl across her skin like a spider. She kept mentally swooshing it away. Something would work out. Something always did.

She spent the morning on her writing assignments, researching productivity in the workplace, ten benefits of eating leafy greens, and corporate wellness initiatives. Finally, it was time for lunch. Maybe she would order something with kale.

She met Barb at the local luncheonette. It was more crowded than usual. While they sat near the entranceway waiting for a table, the TV news featured a story about another politician's affair. Rylie grimaced, trying to tune it out.

"Time does not heal all wounds?" Barb asked.

"Apparently not." She looked away.

"You know I'm not judging you. I just feel like . . . you're mourning. Your career, your relationship, whatever. And it's time to put away the self-pitying regret and move on."

"Ouch."

"You know I'm right."

Rylie stood, antsy from waiting. "I can't take being anonymous much longer."

"I thought you were cured of the spotlight-craving."

"I need to make a comeback," Rylie said. "I turn thirty in a matter of days. I always envisioned spending my thirtieth birthday with the man I love, celebrating my professional accomplishments, toasting to our future."

"You still miss Denny," Barb said.

Rylie gave her a look. "Miss" didn't feel like nearly a strong enough verb to describe the endless longing.

"One more table ahead of you," the hostess said.

"Thanks." Barb spoke quietly after the woman walked away. "Do you want news about him?"

Rylie felt dizzy, and she doubted it was from hunger. *Please don't let him be in love with someone else.* "I do," she said.

Barb nodded. Her husband was Denny's second cousin, but she had stayed neutral during the break-up.

"His mother passed away," Barb said. "Cancer."

"Oh." Rylie knew he would be devastated. "That's awful. I didn't know...." Of course, she didn't know. She'd been out of his life for months.

"The service will be in Spring Lake on Saturday. They're waiting for his sister to get home, too."

Rylie couldn't believe it. Denny was in New Jersey right now, not in DC. It seemed like she should know that, that the connection between them would somehow alert her to his presence. But she was being ridiculous. There was no connection there, not anymore. Not since her betrayal.

The news story changed to the local train accident just as the hostess came to seat them.

"What a tragedy," Barb said.

"Actually, it's a righteous death," the hostess said. "My brother works for NJ Transit. He told me they figured out who was killed." She paused by a booth. "This okay?"

"Yes," Barb said, sliding in.

"Who was it?" Rylie asked, transfixed.

The hostess answered in a stage whisper, "The Rape King."

"Sawyer Kingston?"

The student had allegedly drugged and assaulted several girls during his fraternity's parties at the local college, Archer University. Many of the rumored victims wouldn't come forward, but his last one did. Despite a seemingly airtight case against him, Kingston was acquitted of all thirty charges after a paperwork screw-up prevented several key witnesses from testifying.

"Yes," the hostess said. "They'll be announcing it any minute."

"You're sure?" Rylie slid in the seat across from Barb.

"As sure as he was guilty of those crimes," she said. "Your waitress will be over in a minute."

"Thanks," Barb said.

Rylie stared at the TV screen instead of the menu.

"What is it?"

"Reporters will be all over the campus when they announce this." Rylie didn't feel like mentioning that she had been at the train station last night, too. "It's an opportunity. . .."

Barb sighed. "Go. We'll get together another day."

"You're the best," Rylie said over her shoulder, rushing from the restaurant.

She sped to the university, fueled by the desire to know, to see firsthand what would happen on campus when the death of the Rape King was revealed. In front of the fraternity house, a group of reporters had already gathered along with a TV camera crew. She hovered at the edge of the crowd, itching to be in the fray.

"How do you feel, knowing your fraternity brother is dead?" one reporter called out to a group of guys approaching the house. A barrage of other questions followed.

The students looked shell-shocked. No one answered, and from the outskirts, she observed how some of them stared at the reporters blankly. One kid with clenched fists looked like he was holding back tears.

And then she saw him: the Denny look-alike, the guy who had been at the train last night. He walked toward the fraternity house, then skirted the crowd and went in a side entrance. No one seemed to notice. After someone from the university made an official statement about the tragedy and respecting the privacy of the students, the reporters dispersed, and Rylie found a nearby bench where she waited with a view of the doors. After an hour, her patience was rewarded.

The Denny-ish boy came out, wearing shorts and an Archer basketball sweatshirt.

"Brandon!" Someone from inside the house propped the door open and yelled after him.

She didn't catch the rest of it—something about dinner later—but at least now she knew his first name and his connection to the basketball team.

Staying far enough behind that she remained unnoticed, she followed him across campus on tree-lined walkways. She knew in DC the cherry blossoms would be in bloom, but she pushed thoughts of Denny out of her mind.

Near the library, a girl waited for Brandon, but not the nervous one from last night. Rylie recognized her right away from the news. It was Jaynie, the Rape King's outspoken victim, the one who hadn't gotten her victory in court. Brandon blocked Rylie's view as they spoke, so she couldn't judge any of the emotions behind the conversation.

Still, it was certainly an interesting development. Brandon had been at the train station right before the accident, and now he was meeting the person who would be the least sorry about Kingston's suicide.

Unless . . . maybe his death wasn't a suicide. Rylie shivered and moved off the path, out of their view. Could the Rape King have been murdered? The news hadn't made any reference to foul play, and the other reporters didn't seem to be exploring that line of questioning with the students.

With the combination of waiting for the train last night and seeing Brandon with Jaynie now, Rylie might be the only person who knew what actually happened.

For a moment, she fantasized about everything this could mean. A true crime book with her name in a huge font on the cover. A return to triumph, like the very first time she'd been right when she and her high school friends investigated their principal's false credentials and caused his resignation. A comeback for a disgraced journalist who had only ever wanted to report the truth and create justice.

She had to find out if her hunch was correct. Her heart raced as she followed them to a parking lot and spotted his familiar dark-colored SUV from the night before. On closer inspection, it was a navy Honda Pilot with Maryland plates. But disappointment set in as they pulled away; she had no way to continue the chase.

Still determined to learn more, she checked the Archer basketball roster online from her apartment. In under two minutes, she had his biography, complete with a photo. Brandon Hamilton was a junior, a sport and event management major who had attended high school in Maryland. That was half the puzzle. She wondered about the redheaded girl she had seen that night. Was she an Archer student as well? She scrolled through the women's sports photos on a lark but didn't find her.

The story stayed in the news the next day. Jaynie had been at a fundraiser to benefit sexual abuse victims at the time of his death. She released a statement, saying she was "relieved that fate intervened where the court system failed and that no one else would ever be victimized by that monster."

Regarding the suicide, one psychologist speculated that the acquittal didn't absolve Sawyer Kingston of his guilt and inner turmoil. But Sawyer's mother disagreed. "He was innocent," she claimed, despite the overwhelming proof against him. "There was nothing for him to regret."

Sawyer's parents even offered a substantial reward for anyone with information about the day of his death. Would Brandon and the girl come forward? Rylie needed that reward if she were being honest. She wanted the money. But the truth was, she wanted the story even more. This could be her break, her launch back into the limelight.

She spent Thursday and Friday on the Archer campus,

unobtrusively trailing Brandon in the hope that he would lead her to the redheaded girl. Instead, he spent most of his time in the library or the gym.

Then news broke about the toxicology report. Alcohol and Gamma-Hydroxybutyrate, the date rape drug, had been found in Kingston's system. There was speculation that he used GHB recreationally, as well as to allegedly drug his victims. But that was the single new development. Because the only crime Haverfield had ever experienced near the train was a stolen bicycle, no cameras existed at the station. There were no witnesses.

No *known* witnesses, anyway.

Rylie called her old boss in DC. He had seemed sad when he fired her. "You're determined and driven and smart," he had said before he went off about ethics and blah blah blah. Now she crossed her fingers that he would give her another chance.

"I have a lead on something interesting," she told him over the phone.

"I can't—"

"We can use a pen name. Run a special feature. I have a unique perspective on the Rape King's death. I need to do some more digging before I can say anything else."

"Call me when you have more information," he said. "I can't promise anything, but I'll think about it."

She hung up the phone. This story would take more investigation, but she could feel her life turning around, and just in time.

* * *

Saturday arrived, gray and dreary, and Rylie thought about Denny and the funeral. She wanted to see him, to be there for him at the church, even from a distance. She would try to stay in the background, but it would be impossible to remain unnoticed. Most of his family knew her well, and those that didn't would recognize her from the news. Still, she pulled her brown hair into a tight bun and put on her most solemn black dress. She could bear the cold stares if it meant supporting Denny.

After she arrived, she hovered in the back, scanning the room. She spotted Denny near the front and sucked in her breath. He was talking to a petite woman. A new girlfriend? No, she exhaled, realizing it was just his cousin. She stood transfixed, soaking in the sight of him, the way he tilted his head to listen, moved his hands to gesture. She loved those hands. How stupid she had been, risking their relationship to get the scoop on a story.

"Rylie?"

Forgetting she was supposed to be anonymous, she turned toward the voice.

"Aunt Wendy!" Wendy might be the one person besides Denny who Rylie was happy to see. Wendy wasn't a real aunt, but a close friend of Denny's father.

"How have you been?" she asked. "It's been a rough few months for you, I'd imagine."

"Yes," Rylie admitted, not even trying to lie.

Aunt Wendy patted her arm. "I'm happy you're here, regardless of what people think. Of course, everyone in the family sided with Denny during the . . . situation. Except for me. I'm the traitor in the family." She smiled.

"I'm glad there's at least one person who won't glare at me."

"I need to offer my condolences," Wendy said. "Come with me?"

She hesitated. "I think I'll keep a low profile."

Wendy nodded in agreement. "Take care of yourself."

Rylie was almost feeling good about her decision to come when Denny's older sister approached. From the beginning, she had said they were an ill-suited match, so she was no doubt gleeful about their break-up.

"I'm surprised you would intrude on this day of sorrow," his sister said. "Then again, maybe I'm not. You always did lack a certain sense of decorum. Has your presence even registered with my brother?"

Rylie looked over at him, and as if Denny had heard his sister from across the room, he finally saw her. She'd thought she was ready, that she was prepared for this moment, but it suddenly felt like too much. She gripped the back of the pew to steady herself.

"I came to pay my respects," Rylie said, not wanting to give her any satisfaction. But as soon as his sister moved on to speak to someone else, she practically ran out, not stopping until she reached her car.

Rylie cried on the way home, for Denny's loss of his mom, for her own loss of Denny. Then the sadness seemed to solidify into an angry stone in the pit of her stomach. Stupid older sister. She was a failed screenwriter who always used pretentious phrases like "this day of sorrow."

More importantly, what had Denny's expression meant, when he'd finally noticed her? He'd looked surprised, and something else, something that had made her heart quicken.

Never mind. She couldn't spiral into what-ifs now. She needed a distraction, like the death-by-train of Sawyer Kingston.

Back at the apartment, she changed into jeans and a plain black T-shirt. She unpinned her hair, put it in a ponytail, then drove to the campus. After stopping at the bookstore, she sported a new Archer baseball cap, hoping to look ten years younger. She found the same bench near the fraternity house and waited for some sign of Brandon. Finally, the door opened and she caught sight of him leaving with some fraternity brothers. At the parking lot, he split off from the others.

This time she had left her gassed-up car near his Honda, knowing if he drove someplace, she could pursue him. As she followed, her body tingled with the thrill of a possible discovery. It brought an adrenaline rush like no other.

Hoping he wasn't out on a lame errand, like a fraternity beer run, she trailed him several miles. Finally, he stopped at a diner and went in. Should she go inside, too? Wondering if he was meeting someone, she parked facing the doors and waited. They had passed at least two other diners on the way, so he had obviously picked this one on purpose. She drummed her hands on the steering wheel.

Then a redheaded girl appeared from the end of the parking lot and rushed into the diner. She had to be the one from the train, but there was only one way to be sure. Rylie needed to go in, too. It would be a risk, but if she could eavesdrop, it would be worth it. She pulled down the brim of the Archer cap and entered the glass door.

When the hostess moved to seat her in the room on the right, Rylie pointed to the left and slid into the booth directly in front of Brandon and the girl, with her back to them. Brandon sat in the connecting seat behind her. She would miss seeing their facial expressions, but this minimized the chance they would notice her.

While Rylie ordered chocolate chip pancakes and coffee, Brandon said something that she didn't catch. After the waitress left, she leaned into the seat back, straining to listen.

"I can't really sleep," the girl said.

"It will all fade. In a year, no one will even be talking about it."

"I guess." Ice tinkled in a glass. "Have you talked to her?"

"I saw her on campus," Brandon said. "She's doing better already. Like a weight was lifted."

"But she can't know," the girl said.

"No one will ever know, Chloe."

"What about the reward?" she whispered. "What if that woman from the train comes forward?"

Rylie was motionless.

"I doubt she would remember what we even looked like," Brandon said.

Oh, you have no idea, Rylie thought.

Chloe spoke so quietly, Rylie barely made out the words. "I'd remember her," she said.

"Me, too," Brandon said. "Anyway, they still think it's a suicide. We'll be safe."

"He deserved it." Chloe's whisper had grown fierce.

If only I could legally record this.

They stopped speaking for a few minutes. Brandon shuffled in the seat behind her. The waitress delivered Rylie's food, and she looked up to thank her just as Brandon walked by the table. He turned to glance back at Chloe and his gaze passed over Rylie.

She ducked her head too late. A glimmer of recognition flashed in Brandon's eyes. He about-faced, returning to Chloe.

"We need to leave," he told her.

"What's wrong?"

"Shh! We just need to go."

Rylie pretended to search through her bag to avoid looking at them as they quickly paid the cashier, then left the diner.

That hadn't gone perfectly, but it wasn't a disaster. They realized she overheard them, which complicated things, and they might wonder why she followed them. She knew Brandon's name and where to find him, which was way more than they knew about her. Still, it would be risky to show up at Archer again. Brandon might be on the lookout for her.

She'd need to focus on the mysterious Chloe.

When she arrived home, she decided to research the photos taken at Kingston's trial after his acquittal was announced. She focused on the many photos of the victim, checking the friends and family surrounding her. Jaynie had three sisters, but none of them was Chloe. She zoomed in on any female under twenty-five that stood near her. Nothing.

Frustrated, she went to sleep. Sunday morning, she fed the cat and listened to the morning train.

Her phone buzzed with a text. It was Denny, thanking her for stopping by the church service.

She hadn't heard from him in so long. *It's the least I could do*, she typed quickly. *So sorry.*

With the phone in her hand, she waited, hoping he would reply and keep the conversation going. She realized too late that she should have asked a question, something he could respond to.

Had it only been yesterday that she saw him? She mentally ran through her short time at the church. Seeing Denny, and his sister, and Aunt Wendy, the traitor. Wendy's flip-flopped loyalties made her smile.

And then it hit her: Loyalties.

Maybe she had Chloe all wrong. She had been looking for Jaynie's connections, but maybe Chloe was a traitor. She went back to the photos, this time focusing on Sawyer and his family. And there she was, identified in the caption as Sawyer's cousin, looking nervous even then.

"Yes!" she shouted, causing the cat to scurry away.

This was an even better story than she'd hoped. Everyone knew Sawyer would have been behind bars if it wasn't for the administrative mistake. Then a secret act of revenge was carried out, not by relatives of the victim, but by two people on the other side, a fraternity brother who may have known more than was ever revealed in court and a relative of the rapist.

Forget a true crime novel. This could be a blockbuster movie.

Brandon and Chloe had pulled it off. Rylie closed her eyes and imagined Sawyer's last night. Chloe drugs his drink and gets him to the train, maybe under the pretense that they were going out for a night in the city. Maybe they even sit in the parking lot and drink while they wait. She gives Sawyer enough to sedate him. Then Brandon meets them there, helps her move his unconscious body to the tracks. They put up a barrier to keep away interfering bystanders, then they drive away knowing justice has been done.

Justice. There had been a hashtag throughout the trial: *#JusticeforJaynie*.

Rylie thought of her next steps, the additional facts she would gather. She'd need Chloe's last name and information about their family dynamics. She'd want to know more about Brandon and Sawyer's relationship, the fraternity brother who was less than loyal. As she made a list of interviews she wanted to conduct, she had the buzz that always came when a story heated up. This would enable her to renew her career, even under a pseudonym. Eventually, if she could gather enough information, Brandon and Chloe would be arrested for murder.

* * *

On Monday night, Rylie met Barb for a drink at a bar near her apartment. Still in a celebratory mood, she decided to splurge on a chocolate martini. Barb ordered her usual Chardonnay.

"How did your story turn out that you left me in the lurch for?" Barb asked. "The big reveal of Sawyer Kingston's identity?"

Rylie flushed, feeling guilty about skipping out on their lunch. "Great. I have more work to do, but it's promising."

"I'm glad he's dead," Barb said. "And I don't say that lightly. The whole situation, him roaming free, celebrating and victimizing how many other girls? If it had been my daughter . . . well, never mind. A lot of Archer mothers will sleep better with him gone."

Rylie sipped her martini, but it made her queasy. The drink was too sweet or too strong or maybe both. She switched to water and steered the conversation to Barb's job and her family and the garden that needed planting in her backyard.

"What should we do to celebrate your birthday?" Barb asked. "The big three-oh. Do you want to come over for a barbecue on Saturday?"

Rylie sighed. She was lucky to have Barb as a friend, but that was not how she envisioned celebrating her landmark birthday.

"I'm not sure," she said. "The apartment sitting is almost up, and—"

"You can stay with us!" Barb's usual enthusiasm was magnified by the wine.

"I might . . . I might move back to DC," Rylie said, realizing even as she spoke the words that she had to make it happen. "I miss living there. And I need to try one last time to make things right with Denny. Even if our relationship doesn't work out, it's where I belong."

"I have a friend in DC. I was waiting to tell you," Barb said. "He's looking for someone to write advertising copy. It wouldn't be exactly like your old job, but I can make the introductions if you want."

"Thanks. Let me think it over, okay? I haven't made any concrete plans yet."

"Of course."

Their conversation wound down, and Barb called a car service while Rylie walked the two blocks home. It was nearly midnight she realized, then she detoured to the train station instead.

Exactly one week later, the parking lot was empty and no sign warned of a fake closure. She wondered if the police had fingerprinted the barricade. Brandon and Chloe had probably wiped it clean, in which case the lack of any fingerprints might be a red flag. If Sawyer had put it there, he wouldn't have bothered to remove his own prints. Had the police checked?

The 12:01 was due any minute. She walked by the locked waiting area and stood near the track until she felt someone come up behind her.

Brandon.

"I thought you might be here," he said, as casually as if they had bumped into each other in the campus cafeteria. "Do you live nearby?"

She raised her eyebrows at the presumption that she'd tell a murderer where she lived. "I didn't see your car," she said.

"I parked on the other side this time."

She nodded, surveying the deserted platform where she stood alone with him. A tremor of fear rose inside and she took a step back from the track.

"You figured it all out, didn't you?" he said.

"I don't have any proof." The train sounded in the distance. Her heart beat so hard she could feel the pulse in her ears. She took another step away.

He noticed her movement and laughed. "Oh, you have nothing to worry about. Justice for Jaynie was one thing. Hurting an innocent stranger is another."

"I'm a reporter," she said.

He exhaled loudly. "Wow. That's certainly bad luck for us. We knew the risk when we planned this. I mean, when I planned it. Do me a favor. Leave Chloe out of it, okay? It could just have been me here that night. Me and Sawyer."

The train approached the station.

"Sawyer deserved it," Brandon said. "Whatever you decide to do next, please know the truth." Then he turned and walked away. He was gone by the time the train screeched to a stop in front of her.

* * *

Rylie didn't sleep well that night. The truth. She had always been after the truth. When she slept with that politician, when she trailed Brandon on campus, when she'd done other things she wasn't necessarily proud of, truth and justice remained sacrosanct.

Now Sawyer Kingston was dead. Maybe he deserved it. Maybe people also deserved to know what really happened that night, even if it landed Brandon and Chloe in jail.

Tuesday morning, she called Barb. "Are you friends with anyone in the Haverfield police department? Or New Jersey Transit? I need to speak to someone about the Sawyer Kingston suicide."

"The police chief is an old friend."

Rylie laughed. "Of course he is Barb. You're friends with everyone. Can you set something up for today?"

A few hours later Rylie was in the police station, pretending that she was researching a special report on train suicides. But he didn't have much information that she hadn't already gleaned from the local news.

"What about the barricade sign?" she asked.

"That was key," he said.

She leaned forward. "It was?"

"Yes, it showed his planning and intent to die. He didn't just fall onto the track in a drugged stupor. He made sure no one else would come by and stop him."

The police chief closed his folder as if the matter of Kingston's death was firmly settled in his mind.

"Thanks for your time," Rylie said.

She drove back to the train and sat in her car for a long time, considering. Should Brandon and Chloe be held responsible for what they'd done? Who was she to decide? If she hadn't been at the station that night, would the world be any worse off, not knowing about Brandon and Chloe's actions? Truth and justice had always been entwined in her mind. But maybe in this situation, they weren't the same thing. Maybe this time, the truth should remain hidden.

She drove to campus and found Brandon's parked SUV. After writing him a note, she left it on his windshield.

#JusticeforJaynie

Then she returned to the apartment and packed for home.

#

About the Author

Yvonne Ventresca is the author of two young adult novels. BLACK FLOWERS, WHITE LIES (Sky Pony Press, 2016) won an

YVONNE VENTRESCA

IPPY Gold Medal for young adult fiction. Her debut novel, PANDEMIC (Sky Pony Press, 2014), won a Crystal Kite Award from the Society of Children's Book Writers and Illustrators. Yvonne's other works include the short story "The Art of Remaining Bitter," selected for the MYSTERIES OF DEATH AND LIFE anthology. Visit YvonneVentresca.com *for more information.*

GOLDEN ADVENTURES

Joann Zajack

Life is lived by our accomplishments. We work toward the day we can enjoy retirement adventures with our little white poodle Lucky, joining us in our golden years. Today we've reached a milestone in our marriage of thirty years.

My husband, Dave, and I always enjoyed sailing, snorkeling, and many other water sports. So, it seemed without a doubt that our retirement would be spent doing what we loved. Dave and I decided to buy a forty-foot sailboat.

"Ruth, what shall we name our sailboat?" Dave asked.

"Miss Sunshine, because we plan to always be out sailing in sunny Florida."

"Great name! Miss Sunshine, it is," Dave said with a grin.

We decided to sail the Treasure Coast of Florida, settling down with a condo in sleepy Stuart, looking out at the Atlantic Ocean every day.

The waterfront marina was ten minutes from our condo on the Intracoastal waterway where boats lined up in rows of proud beauty. Each day we met others who were doing exactly what we were: enjoying the beautiful waters of Florida. We fell in love with the Treasure Coast almost at first sight.

Dave was talking to a few boaters at the marina when the conversation dove into the sunken ships with treasures of gold. An older experienced mariner approached him.

"Will this be your first sailing here on the Treasure Coast?

"Yes, my wife and I are taking our maiden voyage."

The older mariner sat and proceeded to speak. "Did you know in 1715, they called the ships the *Spanish Treasure Fleet*. It seems they hit a hurricane. All the ships were destroyed along the coral reefs here on the Treasure Coast scattering treasure from Sebastian to Stuart."

* * *

Dave sat and listened to the old timer for several hours. When he got home to the condo, I could tell he was more excited than usual.

"You look like you had a great afternoon," I said as he headed for the shower.

"I did," he called over his shoulder. "Tell you about it over dinner."

At sunset, we ate dinner at Shucker's Restaurant on Hutchinson Island, sitting out on the patio overlooking the Atlantic Ocean. I doubted there was a prettier place anywhere in the universe.

"This is the best crunchy grouper fish sandwich ever," Dave said. "How about tomorrow we head out early and look for some sunken treasure?"

I almost spit out my wine. "Are you kidding?" I laughed.

He shook his head. "No, we can pack a lunch. I'll get the charts, and put the depth finder on to look into the waters below. Then we can try our luck. It could be fun."

"But Dave, do you know what to look for?"

"Sure, how difficult can it be? Dave tapped my hand. "We wanted an adventure, right? Well, here it is."

* * *

Early the next day, we set out with plenty of water, sandwiches of peanut butter and jelly on rye, chips, apples, and chocolate chip cookies, Dave's favorite, the perfect lunch for a retirement adventure. We laughed and carried on like teenagers as we finally set sail on Miss Sunshine.

Though it was still early, the sun was hot as we sailed along. I relaxed as Dave tended to his charts and depth finder. Further and further we went and I felt my eyes grow heavy. I was as content as a cat on a cushion in a bookstore.

When I woke, I looked around. Uh oh–

"Dave, where is land?" I asked nervously.

"Don't worry Ruth, I have it covered," he said with a wave of his hand.

Easy for him to say. I took a deep breath and sat up taller on the seat. "All right, whatever you say Captain! Let's have some lunch." I took my hat off and fanned myself. "It sure is hot."

Dave laughed. "That's life in the tropics, my love. Now you were talking about some lunch?"

We enjoyed our lunch as we sailed the beautiful blue waters. The day seemed to drift by until I looked toward the horizon and realized the sun was pretty low in the sky.

"Dave, it's getting late. I think we should turn back."

He shook his head and pointed at the chart on the screen. "No, not yet! We're getting very close."

We sailed for a while longer, though I couldn't ignore my growing concern. We'd never get back to the marina before dark.

Just as I was about to insist that we abandon our treasure hunting adventure, our precious sailboat began to pitch and spin. Then there was a crash!

The boat swayed violently to one side, then to the other. I slid off the aft cushion, and the wheel started to turn faster and faster as Dave struggled to keep control of it. The water seemed to take us in a full swirl. We and everything on the boat got tossed about like the toys of an angry child. I remember reaching for Dave as he flew in my direction.

* * *

When I regained consciousness, I was lying on the deck in pain. I couldn't move my arm.

"Dave, Dave, where are you?" I shouted in the deep twilight. I struggled to my knees.

I saw him sprawled across the bow. When I crawled to him, I could see him breathing, but he had a large gash on his head. I grabbed a bottle of water that rolled against my foot and poured it on his face. He shook his head slowly, focused on me, then opened his eyes wide.

"Ruth, are you alright?" he cried, reaching for my hand.

"I'm fine. Well, except for my arm. What happened?"

"I'm not sure," he said as he moved to sit upright. "The boat just spun and spun."

We were able to stand up after a few minutes. By that time, the sun was setting. Dave tried to re-start Miss Sunshine.

"Nothing. She won't start, Ruth. Let's just light the lanterns from the cabin and wait. I'll get the flashlight, too," Dave said quietly.

"Bring up the first aid kit and I'll see what I can do about that gash on your head," I called to his retreating back.

When Dave returned from below deck with his hands full, his face drained of color.

"Everything below is upside down. The ship-to-shore radio isn't working. I found two bottles of water and some cookies. Let's just drop the anchor. When daylight returns, I'll be able to check the radio," he said softly.

I cleaned the blood from his forehead and knew that, without ice, come morning he would look horrible as the bruising took over. The bleeding had slowed to a trickle, so with Dave's help to hold one side,

I used my working hand to apply all the adhesive bandages in the kit to close the cut.

"Thank you, Florence Nightingale," he said with a bow. Then he held out his arms. "May I interest you in the meal du jour?"

We shared our meager ration of cookies and bottled water, keeping one cookie and one water for the following morning. It was quite clear we'd be there come morning.

As the dark blanket of night surrounded us, Dave shot off a flare in hopes that someone, somewhere might see it. And that exhausted our options, except to try and sleep.

"How's that arm?" Dave asked as he pulled the blanket up around us where we cuddled on the cushioned bench at the stern.

I glanced up at the beautiful starlit sky and sighed. "Hurts like blazes, but I don't feel any bones sticking out, so it will be all right."

* * *

I woke to the sound of Dave's voice. "May Day! May Day!"

After a few minutes, he returned top deck with an apple, a cookie, and water. We nibbled and discussed what to do.

"Dave, I'm scared out here. We could be here a long time before someone finds us. Can we put up the sails and go back?"

He shook his head. "I'm more worried of sailing off in the wrong direction, especially without any supplies. I'm not sure of our location. I've gotten all turned around."

He smiled at me, but I could read the worry in his eyes. Thirty years together does that. I smiled back.

"I can keep trying the radio. I'll check the connections. I'm sorry Ruth. I don't know what happened." He glanced at my left arm which was swollen and discolored. "How is the pain?" he asked with tears in his eyes.

"Not too bad if I don't breathe," I moaned.

He shook out three of the last five aspirin and gave them to me with the water. "It's all we have, but it may help a little."

I took them, passed the water back to him and got as comfortable as I could. I slept for a bit, I'm sure.

A few hours passed with no response to our mayday, nor sighting of a bird, a boat or anything else. Dave still tried the ship to shore radio every few minutes.

"May Day! May Day! Miss Sunshine," Dave shouted over and over again.

The sun was higher in the sky and it was too hot to be comfortable. Gingerly I got up and stretched from time to time, adjusting my wide-brimmed hat to try and keep the reflection off the water out of my eyes.

I ducked my head below deck and got Dave's attention. "Why not go diving? Maybe you can see what's below us, get a clue about where we are? Just don't forget to put your depth gauge on your wrist."

He looked at me as he thought it over. "What about your arm? What if you need something while I'm down there?"

"I'll stay right here by the radio, just in case we get a reply. If I don't move too much, the pain isn't too bad. You go into the water. Cool off, see if you can match up something from the chart to the sea bottom."

He gave me a gentle hug, kissed my cheek and gathered up his gear. I made my way to the deck and sat on the aft cushion again. He adjusted his tank and facemask, then smiled my way. I noted his depth gauge and relaxed.

With a wave, he flipped off the side of the boat and splashed into the beautiful blue water.

Carefully I moved back toward the console so I could reach the radio if someone answered our calls. I too called the mayday sign about every ten minutes until I heard splashing.

* * *

I went to the back of the boat and saw Dave, his breather out of his mouth, but his mask still in place. He was grinning like a boy on Christmas morning.

He lifted a small, gold-colored chest that was going to be lovely when cleaned up.

He tossed his mask onto the deck, then rested the chest on the gunnel. I reached my right hand out to steady it for him while he climbed back on the deck.

"I was down about thirty-five feet, according to the depth gauge," he shouted. "We're on some sort of reef, I think. Lots of stuff down there in the grasses and plants." He pointed at the box.

"I hit this with my fin and when I turned back this was jutting out of the seaweed below. I pulled it out. What do you think of it?"

"It's beautiful. Looks like it has been in the water a long time," I replied. "Great find, Captain," I drawled. "But reefs have sharks, right? Glad you are out of the water. Can you match up the water depth with the chart, maybe?"

Dave shrugged out of his tanks and dropped them on the deck. "I can try. Let me get some shorts on and I'll give it a go."

His shoulders had just cleared the cabin door when I heard the radio.

"Calling Miss Sunshine, come in, come in. Over."

I said a prayer of thanks and heard a clatter, then Dave cursed. In his excitement, he'd probably dropped the mic.

"Come in, come in, Miss Sunshine here. Over."

"Miss Sunshine," the voice started, "what is your location and situation? Over."

"No power, location unknown. Over."

"Miss Sunshine, are you anchored? Any injuries?"

"Yes, and yes," Dave replied. "Wife has a possible broken arm."

"Marina reported you left yesterday morning at 0700. Is that accurate, Miss Sunshine?"

Dave confirmed their information. "We were looking for the Lady of the Stars wreck. It's on the chart, but we got all turned around. No idea where we are now."

In a few seconds, the voice came back. "Miss Sunshine, stay calm. We know approximately where you are. We'll get Sea Tow out for the boat and a helicopter will come for you and your wife."

* * *

The helicopter ride and the visit to the hospital on top of our long night and injuries left us totally exhausted by the time we walked through our front door.

What a sight we were; Dave with his bandaged head wound and me with my badly sprained arm in a sling. But our condition meant nothing to Lucky. He was jumping happily like a small kangaroo, upon our arrival home.

All I wanted was a shower, but instead, I collapsed on the sofa. Dave set the little golden chest on the coffee table. He had already cleaned it and the shine was unbelievable.

"What are you going to do with that bag of seaweed you brought back?" I asked, nodding in the direction of the foyer.

"Oh, I almost forgot about it," he said with a laugh.

We heard a loud crash from the front door area.

"No Lucky, no!" Dave shouted as he jumped to his feet. "He's probably so hungry he'll eat anything!"

Dave returned to the living room holding something, while Lucky jumped up and down.

"What is that and where did it come from?" I asked.

Dave, looking startled, said, "It's part of a human skull. It was in the bag of seaweed I brought home. I had no idea it was there. I was focused on the box that was so tangled in the weed. When I freed the box, I never went back into the bag. Lucky must have smelled something and started to dig it out."

"Dave, you offered me a day of excitement, but this was far above all you promised. Love the golden chest, but not so happy about a human skull," I said, holding my slinged arm.

"But Ruth, we found a treasure!" Dave laughed pointing to the golden chest. Then he looked at the skull fragment in his hand and his smile faded. "We need to let someone know about this fellow, though...."

"It *all* belongs to the history of the Treasure Coast here in Stuart. So, what do we do with it, honey?" I asked.

"It could be part of history, maybe from the boats from the Spanish Treasure Fleet departed from Havana that I read about."

"Let's take the golden chest to the Elliott Museum on Ocean Boulevard in Stuart. See what they have to say. I remember when we were there, they had a lot of memorabilia from Hutchison Island and Stuart history," I suggested. "Maybe we'd best call the police about the skull, though."

"Great! This could be our contribution to Stuart's history," he said with a pirate's grin.

I shivered. "I wish the contribution didn't include body parts. I just wonder who it is...."

* * *

I sat on the verandah sipping my morning coffee, thinking of the last few days. My arm was painful, but I still enjoyed the view of the sun dancing on the blue water of the Atlantic Ocean. Dave joined me with his coffee. Lucky joined us also, carrying his favorite toy, a squeaky palm tree that wouldn't be squeaking much longer by the looks of it.

"It was interesting when the Curator stated that the golden chest could be a missing link to the history of the boats that sank off the Treasure Coast," Dave said. "And, maybe they'll get some information on that skull, too."

"I know he'll call us when it's been identified," I replied. "You know, maybe we can just enjoy our retirement on the Treasure Coast. Already in a short time, we have golden memories and many more to come. But I don't like finding human remains at all." I winked at him. "Did you remember that today is our thirtieth wedding anniversary?"

Dave turned with a boyish look. "How could I forget the best day of my life? We'll plan a special celebration."

The phone rang and Dave scurried into the condo to answer it. He returned two minutes later almost breathless.

"That was the Elliott Museum," he said. He reached out a hand to me. "Come on! They want to see us."

"Today? What now, Dave?" I asked sarcastically.

* * *

When we arrived at the Elliott Museum, the Curator showed us into a very impressive conference room with a long mahogany table, lined on both sides by high back chairs–three crystal chandeliers lined the ceiling above. People sat around the table.

After introductions, the man sitting at the head of the table, Mr. Campbell, proceeded to describe the little golden box and what had been discovered.

We sat and paid close attention to Mr. Campbell as he spoke.

"The Spanish Treasure Fleet sunk in a hurricane off the coast of Florida. Seven days after leaving the port of Havana, almost all of the ships and massive treasures sunk on July 30, 1715. Some of the treasure has been recovered since, but occasionally people continue to discover artifacts that wash up.

"There were about one-thousand Spanish survivors who managed to escape in lifeboats and relayed the message to the crown. The Spanish Empire sent a team to try and salvage the massive amount of wealth lost, however they were about to be interrupted by the earliest members of the Flying Gang who decided to plunder the salvage camp of the Spanish in one of the greatest pirate heists of all time."

Then Mr. Campbell introduced Mrs. Costello, who began to speak.

"Since the ancient times, there were particular periods in which piracy was a constant threat throughout many seas and oceans. However, it was in the early 18th century, when the pirates were the most overwhelming and influential in the history of the world. It was a time in which almost all-important sea-trade routes were constantly impacted by enormous numbers of notorious sea-robbers. That period is idealistically called the Golden Age of Piracy.

"The Golden Age of Piracy began in the mid-1680's, just as the last buccaneers disappeared from the Caribbean. It was a result of many circumstances like the end of many wars and lack of decent naval employment. Many sailors and privateer type of pirates found themselves without jobs. Therefore, they naturally chose piracy as their trade, knowing it was the best opportunity for them. What encouraged them most was a lack of a strong government in the Caribbean islands and in other American colonies which allowed pirates to sail free and pillage ships without any potential punishment.

"The Golden Age pirates plundered ships in the Caribbean mostly, but the Atlantic Coast, west coast of Africa, Indian Ocean and the South China Sea were also constantly terrorized. It was also a time of most famous names among pirates. Legends like Blackbeard and Bartholomew Roberts plundered many ships and killed countless victims in the early 1700's. They have been giving inspiration to many writers for over three-hundred years and are well known today.

"People like Woodes Rogers were famous privateers; the governor of Bahamas was the most responsible for suppressing piracy. He and his followers brought order, not only to the Bahamas but to the entire Caribbean Sea. Many pirates were hanged, many retired and a few tried to find their luck in the Atlantic Ocean. However, one thing was certain; the Golden Age of Piracy was coming to an end. Around 1730, increased military presence and international anti-piracy laws banished almost every single pirate and finally put an end to their reign."

He pulled the black cloth off an object on the table that was in a clear glass box. There was the fragment of skull that Dave had found in the seaweed. "The police turned this over to us when they realized how old it was. It was discovered, with many years of research, that the Captain of the Contessa Louise had a mutiny aboard the ship which was loaded with golden treasures from the pirates killing and stealing. The crew wanted their share, but the Captain was a greedy man and always drunk. He refused which caused a mutiny. They hung the Captain shortly after the takeover. The Contessa Louise was destroyed by a hurricane off the Treasure Coast of Florida."

"We have to believe the Golden Box you discovered came from the Contessa Louise. Engraved inside was the ship's name. We took great care in prying open the box. Thank you for not trying to open it and bringing it directly to us. Inside was a key with Contessa Louise engraved on it. It was common in those times to put a treasure box key into another ship of the fleet. If there was a problem, the treasure could be claimed, but in this case, all was destroyed." He pointed at the box. "Lodged in the bone was a round lead ball."

"During what is commonly referred to as the Golden Age of Piracy, the early 18th century, or "the pirates of the Caribbean time," pirates were often armed. This is not surprising as they were criminals who took things by force. It may be, in fact, silly to think of them without weapons, as their weapons have become a part of their costume. Clearly, weapons such as hammers, marlinspikes, whips, flails, and garrotes could, and I'm sure did, come into play. Yet, those were not the common weapons of pirates, but rather the weapons of convenience. Knives, swords, axes, and guns were the common weapons of the time.

"The most common weapon was the knife because it was also a tool of both hunters and sailors, which is where Buccaneers came from. Knives were also commonly used because they're small and easy to carry concealed between your teeth while climbing up the side of a ship that you're about to attack. Quick and quiet, knives made the best weapons for taking a ship in the dead of the night. Versatile, as they can be thrown, used to puncture or slash, plus lightweight and easy to carry. It is easy to see how the knife was clearly a pirate favorite.

"Pirates also used swords. The most common type of sword was the cutlass. Their short, heavy blades sharpened only on one edge made excellent machetes and shipboard tools, as well as weapons. The reason for that design was the use of the weapon; dual-edge swords can cut on both the forward swing and the backswing. There is much less control on the backswing and an accident could mean damage to the sails and sheets of the ship. It was true that some sailors and pirates used rapiers. This was rare, however, because the rapier is primarily a thrusting weapon and it takes great skill to master. The rapier is the weapon of a duelist, not a murderous thug.

"From the Fifteenth century and the arrival of the Spanish in the Caribbean, pistols became the premier personal weapon. They were highly prized by pirates. In some ship's articles, it was agreed upon by the entire crew that the lookout that spotted a ship that ended up as a prize got the choice of the pistols found aboard. Unfortunately, despite their incredible popularity both in history and in fiction, pistols of this time period are neither accurate nor reliable. This is especially the case when mixed with the humidity of the Caribbean region. Simply put, black powder weapons absolutely require dry powder to fire properly and it is incredibly difficult to keep the powder dry in a place where the air is saturated with water.

"Flintlock muskets were the mainstay between 1660 and 1840. A musket was a muzzle-loading smoothbore long gun that was loaded with a round lead ball. The weapon was loaded with ball, or a mixture of the ball with several large shots called buck and ball and had an effective range of about 75 to 100 meters. The operator loads the gun, usually from the muzzle end, with black powder from a powder flask, followed by lead shot, a round lead ball, all rammed down with a ramrod that is usually stored on the underside of the barrel.

"The bone with the lead ball could belong to the Captain, who may have been shot during the mutiny. We have in our possession pieces of a musket from that era. We believe it came from the Contessa Louise. It washed up on the beach a few years ago after Hurricanes Jeannie and Francis hit the U.S. here on the Treasure coast of Florida. Divers are always bringing us items from the same area where you found the golden box and bone.

"We are under the assumption the bone could be from the Contessa Louise and got caught up in the seaweed located near the golden box. The last big storm is probably what dislodged it, leaving it for you to discover. Then, when you scooped up the box, the bone clung to the seaweed which, in turn, clung to the Golden Box. With your discovery, now a piece of history will be complete."

* * *

Dave poured us a glass of wine and with Lucky following, we went out to the veranda. Another breathtaking sunset on the beautiful blue Atlantic Ocean awaited us. We had to be the luckiest people in the world.

He raised his glass. "Here's to a memorable and happy thirtieth wedding anniversary and to maybe someday finding another treasure in our golden years."

We clinked glasses.

"I'm not sure I'm quite ready to tackle the seven seas just yet," I said with a laugh, waving my navy-blue sling in his direction.

"We'll put this in our book of memories as a Golden Adventure," Dave sang as he kissed my hand.

##

• • •
246

About the Author

Joann Zajack, recently retired, resides in both Florida (The Treasure Coast) and New Jersey with her husband, Ted. She is a member of Sisters in Crime–Central Jersey and is published in Crime Scene: New Jersey 3, Snowbird Christmas, Vol. I and Snowbird Christmas, Vol. III. Writing has always been a hobby and with encouragement, it has become a newfound adventure.

IF YOU FOUND A NEW AUTHOR WITHIN THESE COVERS, LOOK FOR OTHER BOOKS BY THEM!

Several have stories in the SNOWBIRD CHRISTMAS short story series (Vol 1-3) available in print and eBook formats, others have novels and non-fiction books available.

Thank you for coming along on this journey with us! We wish you good health and good books in your future!

Comments about this book? Please write the publisher!

Email: OnTargetWords@Gmail.com

Made in the USA
Lexington, KY
30 October 2018